Bloody Twine #6
Twisted Tales with Twisted Endings
Matthew L. Marlott

This book is a work of fiction. Any resemblance to actual persons, living or dead, is purely coincidental, and it was never the intent of the author to include any such person within this work of literature.

ISBN: 978-1-964407-06-7

This book is for all who just wish to sit back, relax, and enjoy some twisted tales with twisted endings. This book is dedicated to fans of traditional horror.
If you like this book, give it a good review and tell me what your favorite story was in this collection.

Table of Contents

Preface

These stories were originally published on my own personal site, bloodytwine.com. It's a little site that has received an equal amount of little attention, but it's mine, and I'm proud of it. I use this site to perfect my stories, and thanks to it, you have these bundles of fine short horror tales you can now peruse and enjoy at your leisure.

Imagine walking into an abandoned storage room filled with old newspapers and magazines, all articles stacked in bundles neatly tied with twine, but then you discover other bundles, bundles not so neatly tied, ragged bundles of yellowed and partially-charred paper tied in bloodstained twine.

You see, some stories are meant to educate, and some stories are meant to entertain, but some stories…some stories are simply looking for a victim.

Enjoy.

Bloody Twine #6

Houdini had his secrets.
The cabinet in question was little more than a small, square, black box with gold filigree along the edges. Sadly, it did not look "antique" so much as it looked "plain." If it weren't for the filigree and the small gold latch and turnkey on the right side of it, Annie would have passed it by altogether. In fact, it was barely more than a square foot in size…
Average Read Time: 41m 22s

Just forget about it.
Next to that wall was a rusty metal chute jutting from the floor like an Industrial-Revolution-era machine pillar. Someone had spray painted a large orange #13 across the front of it, and that should have given the chute a sense of normalcy, but this did not ease the feeling of dread that seeped into him. He could sense a heat from the old chute, but that heat made him feel cold after a few seconds, a chill that went right down to the marrow of his bones…

Total Average Read Time: 13m 8s

The future is plastics!
The first sign was all white with the figure of "Fancy Joe" on the left side of it.
Fancy Joe was a cartoon man in a dapper black tux and red bowtie, his short-cut blond hair slicked up and back in that iconic '50s style, his dress shoes a gleaming

black in the late-day sun. The words "Do you know Joe?" were doled out in a curvy red font right next to him…
Average Read Time: 52m 28s

A promotion doesn't necessarily mean "easier."
"Subject 13" was a young, skinny, Caucasian girl with long, straight, brown hair, a wafer of a girl with slender arms and legs. She was dressed in a private-school uniform, that uniform complete with a white dress shirt, a dark-blue vest jacket, and a dark-blue skirt. She wore white ankle socks with small black dress shoes, and she was sitting in a simple wooden chair in the middle of the room, another agent staring down at her in solemn silence…

Total Average Read Time: 16m 3s

It's all about perspective.
There was an eye drawn in white ink upon the countertop, probably with some kind of marker, but where one could get a white marker was a mystery in itself. The eye was drawn in the most basic style, just a circle within lids, lines like lashes extending out from it, something even a child could do in terms of artistic quality…

Total Average Read Time: 16m

"In what distant deeps or skies, burnt the fire of thine eyes?"—From "The Tyger," by William Blake.
Moving through the trees was a lithe but massive shape, a beast that vaguely resembled a tiger, but one twelve-meters-tall and twenty-five-meters-long, a

gargantuan shape with flames rippling across whatever it had that passed for skin…

Total Average Read Time: 14m 34s

When that weird little girl is not so much "weird" as she is "deadly."
This little blonde thing had pale peach skin, skin painted over with a light brush of peach upon alabaster, and she possessed ruby red lips that held a light sheen in what little light there was. She had striking green eyes, an eye color that was rare in combination for a natural blonde. Her adorable face was settled within a circlet of blonde ringlets, a face that was both cute yet disturbing in its…well…*adorableness*, and combined with her antiquated clothing, her very presence unsettled Lorena, if only because the girl looked like a walking and talking porcelain doll made flesh…

Total Average Read Time: 34m 22s

When the obsessive fanboy is the least of your problems.
Ahead of them was an old-fashioned carriage parked out in the street, four very real horses hooked up to it, four horses of jet-black hue, those horses chomping at the bit and ready to go. The carriage was all black with a rather pale, morose-looking driver at the lead, the tall man dressed in an all-black suit with a black top hat upon his bald head…

Average Read Time: 52m 27s

When everything comes together to form a perfect picture of nothing you actually wanted.

A small screen, much like a regular flatscreen TV, appeared upon the door before them. Within it was the stark form of Mr. Clemm, Lenore's carriage driver, the pale man wearing a black suit accented by a black top hat. The man was standing in the soft glow of his own lantern, a lantern which he held aloft in his left, black-gloved hand, as it was most definitely the middle of the night outside…

Average Read Time: 52m 3s

Some buttons are hard to swallow.

It was beyond delicious…He had never tasted anything like it before. This "candy" was nothing like the white food blocks everyone ate. This "candy" button tasted so good that Asher couldn't wait to eat the rest of them. In fact, he could not even describe the taste that melted across his tongue. All he knew was that it was wonderful…

Total Average Read Time: 17m 49s

Finding what you're looking for isn't always fun.

It looked like something out of an elementary-school book, maybe something conceived by a bored fourth grader, and it had clearly been made on an art program, but poorly; the houses and trees were of different models, as were the roads, and the road lines didn't even match up, but…it was good enough…

Total Average Read Time: 19m

#1…THERE'S NOTHING LIKE THE CLASSICS

Houdini had his secrets.

"What have you got for me, Annie?" asked Mr. Pascuzzi.

Annie carefully handed the teapot to the old man, who gingerly took the ceramic piece of history in order to inspect it.

"Ah, yes," said the old shopkeep. "This is from the late '20s. There are some things that have tipped me off on its age, but for the layperson, you can tell by the art deco design. It's in very good condition. Where did you get it?"

"I…I told you, Mr. P.," stammered Annie. "My brother bids for storage units. I get to keep some things for helping him out."

"Well, I suppose there are worse ways to come across antiques," said the old man. "It's not as valuable as I would like, but I'll take it. I'll just put it in the back until I have time to thoroughly inspect it."

"Oh," said Annie in disappointment.

She could not help but feel the burn on this one. She had been hoping the teapot would net her some more comics, but it was swiftly looking like she was only going to get a small amount of cash for it.

Mr. Pascuzzi, however, picked up on her crestfallen demeanor right away. Annie could tell as much by the sympathetic look drawn all over his weathered face.

"Oh, come now," he snorted. "Don't droop like a sad sack. I know what you want, and I have it right here."

"You do?" asked Annie in surprise.

He turned, shuffled past a number of shelves filled with old antiques of this and that, and picked up a small stack of three comics from his wooden purchase counter, the articles carefully placed within their protective plastic sheathes.

He shuffled back to her and handed her the valuable magazines.

"There you are," he said happily. "Those should keep you satisfied."

She looked through the three issues and practically drooled over them. All three of them were from the '60s, right after the great comic purge of the '50s. It was a time when horror comics were just starting to be rereleased, so these were valuable through sentiment alone, let alone what they were actually worth in a monetary sense.

"I...I can't afford these," said Annie unhappily.

"Consider them an even exchange for the pot," smiled Mr. Pascuzzi.

Her heart leapt in her chest, a leaping of unbridled joy over such a boon.

"Are you sure!" she gasped.

"Those are meant to be read and enjoyed," nodded the old shopkeep. "I've yet to meet another youngin' that likes these, especially an older teen girl like yourself, not one that collects the classics like you do.

Most older teen girls come in looking for vintage dolls or teapots like this one."

Annie stared down with starry eyes at the picture of the werewolf fighting a vampire on the cover of the top magazine. She'd already read this one online at the library, but to hold an actual copy of it in her hands…?

"There's nothing like the classics," sighed Mr. Pascuzzi. "These vintage rags stayed true to the old ways of horror, and they've endured the test of time. I loved watching Lugosi, Chaney, and Karloff, and these old comics were built off them…Who's your favorite, huh? Which old actor do you—"

"Chaney," spurted out Annie. "I've seen *The Wolf Man* fourteen times. There's something about the transformation scenes I love."

"Ah, Lon Chaney Jr.," said the old man. "Did you know he had to sit for hours for those makeup effects? That kind of meticulous detail was revolutionary back in the '40s."

"Yeah," grinned Annie. "I love those practical effects. Everything today is always CGI. It looks so fake."

"Practical effects?" snorted Mr. Pascuzzi. "We just called them 'effects' back in my day…but I do agree with you. All of this new technology has sucked the soul right out of the movies…But you didn't come here to listen to an old man jabber on. You want to go home and read your comics, right?"

"Yeah," said Annie as she continued to stare down at her latest catch.

"You let me know if you come across anything else you want to trade," smiled the old man.

"Oh…about that," frowned Annie.

She couldn't help but feel her spirits sink quite low, because due to extenuating circumstances, she doubted she would be coming back here again.

"My brother and I move around a lot," she said unhappily. "This may be the last time I'm in here. I think we may be leaving by the end of the month."

"Well, that is a shame," said the old shopkeep with an unhappiness to rival her own. "You have an old soul, Annie…You have an old soul with a vintage name…Have you ever read the *Little Orphan Annie* strips?"

"Y…Yeah," said Annie nervously. "I have brown hair, though, not red. It's short and straight and cut like a boy's, not all poofed out and curly. Besides, I think my mom named me after Annie Oakley, if you really want to know."

"There's nothing wrong with that," nodded the old man. "You're still an old soul. Only old souls appreciate the classics. It happens all throughout history. Why, if it weren't for old souls, the classics would have died out altogether. You're doing a good thing by keeping them alive."

"I guess," said Annie nervously.

This was getting awkward. It was probably time to say her goodbyes.

"Well, I should get go—" she started to say.

"Now, hold your horses there, young lady," said Mr. Pascuzzi. "Since you've been such a good customer, I want to show you something."

"Oh?" asked Annie.

"Right this way," said the old shopkeep. "I'll show you the prize of my collection. No one else has gotten to see it, but I'm getting too old to even get around in here, so there's no sense in me keeping it all to myself anymore."

He shuffled to the back of the shop, shuffling past yet more antiques of this and that, shuffling along until he reached a locked door just beyond the stairs to the second floor.

"In this room is where I keep my most valuable acquisitions," he said in an eager tone. "You'll be the first person to see my most prized possession since my wife passed away. She'll always be my number one love, but this is my number two."

He unlocked the door via a brass key he pulled up from a keyring on his belt, opened the door, and waved both hands in a gesture to usher her in.

"You know, I'd better go in first to show you the way," said Mr. Pascuzzi. "I know it's rude to enter before a lady, but it's safer this way. I can't afford any accidents in here. These antiques are too valuable."

Annie had never really thought of herself as a lady—she wasn't exactly refined—but the old shopkeep was from a different generation, cut from a different cloth, so she didn't correct him.

She followed him in after that, but not without a moment's hesitation…It occurred to her that the old man could be dangerous, but she decided rather quickly that her hesitation was silly…It wasn't like he was a psycho or anything. She seriously doubted he could defend himself, even if someone as little as her attacked him.

The small room they walked through had a collection of porcelain dolls, old clocks, metal crosses, antique dinner plates, a couple of very old firearms, some swords, etc.…It was a little much to take in.

"Here we are," said Mr. Pascuzzi as he waved both hands toward a small wooden cabinet. "I am pleased to show you the one…the only…Mercutio's Cabinet."

The cabinet in question was little more than a small, square, black box with gold filigree along the edges. Sadly, it did not look "antique" so much as it looked "plain." If it weren't for the filigree and the small gold latch and turnkey on the right side of it, Annie would have passed it by altogether. In fact, it was barely more than a square foot in size.

"What's Mercutio's Cabinet?" she asked.

"This belonged to Harry Houdini," said Mr. Pascuzzi with an eager nod. "Now, Houdini is probably the most famous stage magician who's ever lived, but there were rumors that his magic was real, and I believe it. I know, because this cabinet was one of his creations, and it works."

"Oh?" asked Annie. "What's it do?"

"I was hoping you'd ask that," said the old man.

He looked around for a brief second before picking up a pair of scissors he'd left next to some plain brown wrapping paper.

"I just need a small lock of your hair…" he said as he reached up for her hair.

Annie decided to humor him, but in her own way. He was a sweet old man, but she knew better than to let anyone else mess with her hair outside of a salon. She had her dark-brown hair in a pixie cut, short on top and buzzed around the bottom, just as she preferred it. Messing with that was…whuff…not good.

With her blue jeans, retro jean-jacket, and the plain white T-shirts she always wore, she looked like a boy most of the time, but that was also the way she preferred it. Greg liked it that way anyway, and she didn't want to make him mad again by changing it.

"I'll…take that," she said as she gently pried the scissors from Mr. Pascuzzi's trembling fingers.

She took a tiny snip of her hair from the top of her head and handed both the scissors and her hair snipping to the old man.

He set the scissors down and stared at the tiny bit of hair she had given him.

"This should do," he said, his tone one of audible happiness.

He opened the small cabinet via the latch and turnkey, but the interior was just as plain as the outside. Inside the box was nothing more than empty space…It was just a small empty cabinet.

"Now, I just place your hair in here…" he said.

He gingerly set the tiny cutting of her hair in the cabinet and then fished around in the right pocket of his grey tweed pants for something. He pulled forth a penny a second later, held up the zinc and copper coin, and then placed it inside the cabinet. He then shut the cabinet door, locked it with the latch and turnkey, turned his old head to stare directly at Annie, and gave her a wide grin.

"You see, I don't even think Houdini knew what he was doing when he made this one," smiled Mr. Pascuzzi. "Yes, yes, Houdini made a serious effort to debunk spiritualists and psychics, but I believe this was a cover to convince people that magic and the afterlife weren't real. I think he did this to hide his own knowledge of the occult.

"He made several magical artifacts, most of which are lost to time, but this one is not. You see, I came across this piece of wonder back when I was barely out of my teens. I was given this cabinet from an old woman whom I helped a long time ago. Inside it were instructions to its use, those instructions written by Houdini himself.

"I'm successful today because of this cabinet. You see, the old woman—whose name escapes me— didn't know about the properties of this cabinet, and she's long since passed away, so no one but me has known about Mercutio's Cabinet all this time…Now that I've shown it to you, you know about it, too."

Annie's curiosity was definitely piqued, but the old shopkeep had yet to fill her in on the details.

"You still haven't told me what it does, Mr. P.," she said.

The old man raised one wrinkly finger, his right index finger, and nodded a couple of times for emphasis.

"It's different for any object you put in it," said Mr. Pascuzzi. "The effects can be harmless or beneficial, or they can even be profitable; it depends. I don't use this cabinet on a regular basis because the outcome can be really dangerous, but I'm only using a penny for this demonstration, because I already know the effects of that."

"Uh, huh," said Annie in slight confusion. "So, are you saying this is real magic?"

"Without a doubt," nodded the old man. "Now, the person who wants to use the cabinet has to put in a piece of themselves…a lock of hair, a fingernail clipping…something like that, and then they put in the object they wish to connect to…or vice versa…that part doesn't really matter…Wait?…Where was I?…Oh, yes…

"You see, Houdini believed that all objects were connected in spirit and could thus be connected to the human spirit, or the human soul could be tied to the object, you see. When tied together, the object lends its power to the human soul."

"Uh, huh," said Annie in growing doubt. "If that's true, then what will a penny do for me?"

"You'll see," winked the old man.

"It's not going to kill me or anything, will it?" frowned Annie.

"No, no," snorted Mr. Pascuzzi. "Just think of it as a little gift from me to you. A…A going away present, as it were. Besides, I'll take out the lock of hair and the penny in a few hours. That should give you more than enough time to see how the magic works.

"Houdini believed the cabinet used two things to make the magic work. He had the focus and the fetter. The focus is the object you want to bind to. The fetter is the piece of yourself the magic seeks out. The magic of the cabinet is the glue that holds them together.

"The penny/hair combination is a really harmless example, because like I said, using this cabinet is dangerous. If the cabinet were to have something sinister in it as a focus, or if you used a more powerful fetter, such as blood, then trust me when I say…you don't want that. That's why we're just using a penny and some hair, and

I'll be taking them out tonight anyway. I'll leave them in just long enough for you to see how the cabinet works."

None of this sounded legit, because everyone knew magic wasn't real, but Annie decided to humor the old man. There was no harm in that.

"Whatever you say, Mr. P.," she shrugged. "I think the cabinet is really neat, but I've got to go. My brother is waiting for me back home."

"You shoo then," said the old man. "If you're ever back in town, you stop by here, okay?"

"Absolutely," nodded Annie. "It'll be my first stop."

"Now, you get on home and enjoy those comics," urged the old shopkeep.

"Will do," smiled Annie.

She took her leave after that. She left the old man in his private collection room and departed the shop, the prize of her collectable horror comics still gently clutched within her eager hands.

She was definitely happy about the exchange, but the truth was, she needed to hide this from Greg. He was probably not going to be happy with her anyway, because he was never happy with her about anything. She had enough bruises to prove that.

*****

Annie made her way up the wooden steps to Greg's apartment. She cringed every time she had to return, because there was no telling what mood he was going to be in. Considering his old white van was parked outside, she already knew he was here, but how long he had been here, she did not know.

Greg was barely taller than her and average in the face, but he had good muscle tone from lifting furniture for a lot of years, so he was attractive in his own way. Nevertheless, he had a mean streak the size of Kansas, so ticking him off was not on the schedule.

She unlocked the door to the apartment and walked in. The place was a mess, of course, but that was due to the clutter, the clutter of various items Greg had "liberated" from different storage units, "liberated" being used in the most liberal way possible.

Annie walked around a small dresser and narrowly avoided knocking over old lamps stacked on cardboard boxes filled with dated magazines. She wanted to get her comics to her room in this little two bedroom before she ran into Greg.

She had just reached her room and had turned the doorknob when Greg's voice cut into her from behind.

"Where in the hell have you been!" he barked.

She winced at that tone. It was always the same with him. He never let her do anything.

"I was just out awhile," said Annie.

"Oh, really?" asked Greg. "Then what's that you've got there?...Have you been stealing from me again!"

His accusation was nothing new. Because he was a thief, he automatically accused her of being one every time. It was a psychological thing. She *had* taken the teapot, of course, but considering he controlled any money that came their way, she had no other way of getting anything for herself.

Right now, though, she needed to lie, because Greg was not the forgiving type.

"It's j…just some comics I picked up," she stammered. "I traded some of my old things for them…You won't let me have anything…I don't even have a phone…You never give me any money…"

"So you can waste it on this crap?" snorted Greg. "And you don't need a phone. You don't have any friends anyway…Put that trash away and come help me with this haul."

She did as he commanded, but not because she wanted to. She simply wanted him to simmer down.

She walked into her room and stuffed her comics in her dresser drawer. There would be time to read them later.

Greg was waiting for her when she walked out, but he did not look happy. Of course, he never looked happy, so this was no surprise.

"Where did you get those comics?" he asked.

"I…I traded some of my stuff for them at this antique shop," said Annie. "It's that one a few blocks away."

"Haven't been there," frowned Greg. "They let you trade for stuff there?…Wait…What did you say? Did you say something stupid? You'd better not have told them anything."

"No," said Annie. "No, I didn't say anything. I lied and told him I had to get back to my brother, just like you told me to. I lied like you said."

"You told who?" asked Greg.

"The old man that runs the place," said Annie. "He's a nice old man."

"Hmmph," snorted Greg. "Don't hide things from me. From now on, you tell me when you're going out and where you're going. I don't want the police coming down on us."

"The police aren't going to—" she started.

"Don't argue with me!" yelled Greg as he raised the back of his right hand up to her face.

Annie flinched in natural response. She did not want to get hit again. Greg did not know his own strength, and she'd been seriously hurt by him before…She did not want that to happen again. It had taken months for her ribs to heal the last time.

"You're lucky I don't throw you back out on the street where I found you!" hissed Greg. "You're lazy and worthless most of the time…You're also lucky you're such a good lay, or I'd just find myself another girl."

"Don't say that…" whined Annie.

She couldn't help but whine. He reminded her quite often how worthless she was.

"Who else are you going to find that can pick locks without a bump key?" she asked.

Sometimes, she needed to do some reminding of her own. Picking locks the traditional way was a talent she had picked up before she'd run away from home, and it was the talent (other than her skill in bed) that Greg prized her for.

"Yeah, yeah," he scowled. "Get your head out of your little butt and start searching through this crap. I can already tell most of it's junk. Even so, we might find something valuable. We need some serious cash before we ditch this burg. I want to put some miles behind us before anyone catches on."

He grabbed her by her left arm with his right hand, but his grip hurt, and she had to protest his manhandling.

"Ow! OW!" she cried. "That hurts!"

"Stop whining and get started on that dresser!" he growled. "I didn't haul it up here by myself so you could be lazy! You wanted to keep that piece of crap, so it's your responsibility to clean out any dead bugs or mouse turds…Don't look at me like an idiot! It's your frickin' dresser, so it's your responsibility! Get moving!…I should have thrown out that piece of trash."

She wondered if the trash in question was her or the dresser, but that thought was irrelevant, because it was cut short by the sudden pain that followed.

He let her go, and "SMACK!" went his hand to her bottom. It was a windup strike, a pulling back of the hand for maximum damage. The sound of his palm striking her butt echoed around the small apartment, causing her to jump and shriek at the same time.

She had to take a moment to rub her stinging butt cheek…That was going to leave a mark.

She wiped a tear from her right eye as she knelt down to inspect the small children's dresser Greg had lugged up here for her. She had indeed wanted it for some reason that escaped her at the moment, but picking through it was going to be a nightmare, because a lot of the storage units they raided were owned by old people who stored things for years, and some of those units had some horrors in them…She'd once found a dead cat in a cardboard box. The thing was so old, it had mummified.

She was afraid that one day she was going to open some furniture or a box and find a dead baby, a body part, or something like that, but Greg did not seem to share her fears. No, he was only in it for the money.

Their routine was simple. They'd scout out a unit, Annie would pick the lock, usually a basic padlock, and then they'd raid the unit. Yeah, there were cameras in some places, and there were security guards, but if you just wore a hoodie and acted like you owned the place, you could rob them blind. You raided the unit and locked it back up. It really was that simple. The owners never seemed to check their units often enough anyway.

Aside from that, she was still wary about opening anything.

She peeled off the masking tape that was keeping the drawers shut. Annie then opened the bottom drawer of the dresser and pulled out its only occupant, a large plastic freezer bag full of pennies. She held up the bag and shook it a bit, and considering how many pennies were in it, it was quite heavy.

"Huh," she said to herself as she sniffed and wiped at her eyes one more time.

She opened up the next drawer and pulled out two more plastic freezer bags full of pennies. Both of them were just as heavy and as stuffed as the first, and their discovery left her wondering.

There were four drawers in all within this children's dresser, and she was going bottom up, so she opened the third drawer and discovered three more bags of pennies in that one.

"What the hell?" she asked herself.

She stood, opened up the top drawer, and discovered four small plastic lunch bags full of pennies. She pulled those out and set them next to the other six larger bags.

"Greg!" she called out. "Greg!"

"What!" he called back in a hostile tone.

He stomped over to her, his face a burning glare of irritation.

She ignored that look and waved toward the pile of pennies.

"Look what I found in the dresser!" she said happily.

"What the hell?" he said uncertainly as he stared down at the bags of coins.

"That's what I said!" she replied in excitement.

"This is good," he said as he nodded his head. "Take those bags aside and start sorting those pennies by date. There might be some valuable ones in them. All of the worthless ones I'll take to a bank and convert to bills. I doubt there's actually a lot of money there, but money's money, so I'll take it."

"There's not a lot here?" asked Annie.

"Eh," shrugged Greg. "They're pennies, Ann. You have to have thousands of them to make any real cash, but…eh, whatever. We might get ten, twenty bucks off that."

"Can we order out?" asked Annie hopefully.

'Yeah, I guess," shrugged Greg.

"I want pizza!" grinned Annie.

"Yeah, why not," sighed Greg.

"Yay!" she squealed as she jumped up and down.

She hugged him around the waist, and he returned the gesture by squeezing her bruised bottom. It hurt a little, but she was willing to ignore that pain. It was better than the alternative, because the alternative was Mean Greg, and she did not want to deal with Mean Greg.

As it stood, this day was turning out better than she had anticipated. She was going to eat a decent meal, take a hot shower, and then read her comics. Those pennies still had to be sorted and counted, but that was nothing she couldn't handle.

*****

Annie pulled open the front door to Mr. Pascuzzi's shop, her new trade offer clutched within her eager hands.

She had an old, slender, and fine-looking knife in her possession, a needle-pointed thing that had to have some value. She was hoping to get some kind of trade for it. Honestly, it looked like an old letter opener with some fake gems on it, so it wasn't like Greg was going to miss it.

Her thoughts wandered over the night before, and that night had been a good one, last night's good time leaving her with a good-time high, hence why she wanted to trade in one last thing before leaving this town.

Last night had been a banger, literally. They had ordered a couple of pizzas, and then Greg had taken her to his room and had his way with her, but she hadn't minded that. That was a celebration of sorts.

It had started because Greg had been wrong about the pennies. There had been way more than twenty bucks in pennies in those bags; there had also been nickels, dimes, quarters, and dollar coins buried here and there within each bag. The total of all those coins was actually about a hundred-and-ten dollars, so that was more money for Greg, money Annie was never going to see, but that was why she was trading in something anyway. What Greg didn't know only benefitted her, but she had to be careful about what she took, or he would certainly beat the crap out of her…again.

Even so, Greg had "rewarded" her with pizza, the crust stuffed with cheese, and then he'd rewarded her with…well…a stuffing of another sort, but she'd take what she could get. It was better than Mean Greg. It was a night that stood out because it had been good, and that's all that mattered in the end.

She let those thoughts slide as she was greeted by Mr. Pascuzzi.

"Come in! Come in!" called out Mr. Pascuzzi. "We have…Oh, it's you, Annie!…I thought you were leaving town. Do you have something for me?"

"I do," smiled Annie. "My brother and I won a big auction, so here's what I have."

She gingerly handed him the knife, and Mr. Pascuzzi received it, but he stared at it with wide eyes before saying anything at all. She could tell something was wrong, but what that something was, she had no idea.

"Oh, Annie, where did you get this?" he asked quietly.

"I…I told you," she stammered. "It was in a storage unit. We won it in an auction."

That was a lie, of course, but she had been lying to him from day one anyway. Everything Greg had was stolen, and she definitely wasn't Greg's sister, but Mr. Pascuzzi didn't need to know any of that. Handing over this stuff was a boon for the old man…At least, that's what she kept telling herself.

In truth, Annie didn't want to steal, but she didn't have a choice. Greg wouldn't let her work, and he wasn't giving her any money, so what else was she supposed to do?…She didn't even have a phone.

Besides, the stuff she took was stuff he'd stolen anyway. It wasn't like he was going to miss any of it. She'd said that before, but she had to repeat it in her own mind for her own mental wellbeing. Greg could—and would—seriously injure her if he found out she had taken anything.

Right now, though, she needed to figure out what was going on with Mr. Pascuzzi. The old shopkeep looked a little out of sorts, and she needed to know why.

"What's wrong, Mr. Pascuzzi?" she asked.

She used his name on purpose. Greg had taught her that. When in doubt about someone's intentions, good or bad, it made her look more legit and less like a lying thief.

She didn't want to get in trouble. As bad as life could be with Greg, she did not want to end up in jail or prison. The thought of that scared her on a deep level.

"Well, this was my late brother's," said Mr. Pascuzzi.

There was a hint of sadness in his voice, but more importantly, what he'd just said spiked Annie's adrenaline and nearly caused her to panic.

However, she did not panic. Greg had taught her to act concerned in moments like this in order to deflect blame. She couldn't sweat or act nervous, because those were tells. She had to go with it in order to come up with a plausible lie, or she was screwed.

"It is?" she asked. "What do you mean?"

"This was stolen from my brother nearly thirty years ago," sighed the old man. "We'd never thought we'd see it again. Who would have thought it would have been squirreled away in someone's storage unit right under our noses? I can't believe it's returned to me.

"I think my brother can rest easy now…over this anyway. He had a good life, so it's not like this was a major loose end, but I am grateful you've brought it to me, Annie, and if my brother were here with us today, he'd be grateful, too. It would have meant a lot to him. It means a lot to me; I know that."

Annie felt her thoroughly-wired muscles melt back into her body. The danger of being caught was averted for now, and that was a good thing, though she was still on edge. Nevertheless, this was a boon for her as much as it was for Mr. Pascuzzi, because if the knife had sentimental value, the old man might reward her with some of the good stuff.

"I didn't know this was so special," she said honestly.

That she didn't have to lie about.

"This is a genuine, early-sixteenth-century, Italian bejeweled stiletto, Annie," replied the old man.

There was a softness to his voice as he studied the piece in his hands, his weathered lips turning upwards in a gentle smile.

"You can see the rubies along the hilt," he continued. "Those are real rubies, by the way. This knife is actually worth a lot of money, and it belongs to my family. Guiseppe inherited this from our father, but he never did tell me how he'd lost it. He'd always said it was stolen, but I suspect he'd lost it gambling. He had a bad habit with that…I am glad it's returned, though…I take it that whoever owned the storage unit passed away?"

"Yeah," said Annie. "Huh…Well, if it belongs to your family, I guess that means it's all yours, Mr. P."

She thought about this, but the conclusion was a dry one. Now that she was thinking about it, this "stiletto" was already his property, so it didn't look like she was going to score anything today. That was okay, though. She kind of felt like Robin Hood for stealing the thing back for him. It made her feel warm inside.

"I guess I'm out of luck today," she shrugged. "This is yours anyway."

"Nonsense, nonsense!" grinned the old man. "You deserve something, Annie!"

"I do?" asked Annie in surprise.

She was kind of taken aback. She had not expected to get anything after Mr. Pascuzzi's heartfelt story.

The old man lifted his right index finger and shook it up and down a couple of times.

"I know just the thing!" he said excitedly.

He motioned toward the back of the shop, and then he trundled in that direction, his old legs moving as fast as they could without the help of a cane.

"Follow me!" he said eagerly. "I'm taking this back to the valuables room. You remember the valuables room, right? There's something in there I want you to have."

Her heart jumped for a split second…Something from the valuables room?

She followed the old man back to the "valuables" room.

Mr. Pascuzzi unlocked the door with a brass key, opened the door, and then ushered her inside. He shut the door and nodded toward the back of the room. His gaze landed upon the small, black, wooden cabinet that he'd shown her just the day before.

"Mercutio's Cabinet," grinned the old man. "I want you to have it."

Not exactly ideal. Annie would have preferred more comics…What was she going to do with a dusty old cabinet?

"Oh, that's okay, Mr. P.," she said nervously. "You don't have to do—"

"Didn't it work?" he asked in a hushed voice. "I put the penny and your hair in it yesterday. Tell me it didn't work, Annie. Tell me it didn't work, and I'll let it go."

Annie felt like a thunderbolt had struck her right through the brain, lighting up all of her neurons at once. It was her own shortsighted stupidity that had played against her on this one, because she had completely forgotten about the penny and the hair, but all of that weird supernatural "magic" stuff Mr. Pascuzzi had told her about the cabinet suddenly came flooding back…She'd found all those pennies…

She turned pale as she thought about this.

"I…I think it did work," she said in a shaky voice. "I found all these bags of pennies in an old dresser last night. My brother and I counted them out. There was over a hundred dollars in pennies and…and other coins in those bags…I was so excited with the find that I…I forgot all about the penny and the hair."

"Ah, ha!" exclaimed Mr. Pascuzzi in visible excitement. "I told you!…Now, I'm getting too old to keep something like this around, so I want you to have it…Here's the thing, though, Annie. You have to keep it secret…This is real magic we're talking about here, and if it fell into the wrong hands…"

"Real magic…" trailed off Annie.

The possibilities were endless. Heck, with this thing, she could make money hand over fist…She didn't even need Greg anymore…Not that he'd let her go, but that was beside the point. She could hide the cabinet's magic from him. He certainly didn't need to know about that.

"Annie, are you listening?" asked Mr. Pascuzzi.

The old shopkeep waved his hands in front of her face.

"Oh, sorry, Mr. P.," replied Annie. "I just got excited there for a moment."

"Well, don't get too excited and lose your head," said the old man. "Remember what I said about real magic? It's dangerous. You need to keep your wits about you when you use this thing.

"Mercutio's Cabinet is made from real magic, and real magic comes from an outside source, a…a divine source or an infernal one, like an angel or a demon. Considering the rumors swirling about some of Houdini's artifacts, I'd say this thing was made by a dark force. I'd be careful using it."

A demon? She didn't believe in de…Of course, the cabinet had actually worked, so…No, no, she could risk it. She wasn't stupid. She could make it work without getting fried…

It was worth a shot for financial independence. She could make money on the side with it, and Greg never needed to find out. He could pay all the bills and stuff, and she could live comfortably with the money she made off the cabinet…She could even get a phone…It was a win-win.

Of course, it could all just be coincidence…The old man could just be eccentric about this piece of Houdini history.

"I don't know, Mr. P.," said Annie. "I'd just be happy with some comics."

"You see, that's what I love about you, Annie!" grinned the old shopkeep. "You have a real love for the classics! Why don't I give you some comics for your trouble, and you can take the cabinet, too. It's my thanks for what you've done."

Win-win…Cha ching!

"Sounds good to me," smiled Annie. "I can't turn that down."

She could test out the cabinet tonight, and Greg would never know about it.

"Now, remember," said Mr. Pascuzzi. "This is dangerous, so only use safe items like that penny, and don't use anything of yourself but a lock of hair or a fingernail clipping. This is real magic, and I don't even think Houdini understood how it worked...

"There's no telling what might happen if you break those rules. I don't want to see a fine young lady such as yourself get hurt…or worse…

"Remember what I told you about the focus and the fetter? Don't put in anything nasty as a focus, or it could warp you, possess you…and don't use anything but some hair or a fingernail clipping. The fetter is kind of like a sacrifice, so the more of you you put in the cabinet, the more powerful the effect will be, and you don't want that. There's no telling what could happen if you spilled blood in it…"

He shuddered and shook his head as if to chase off some gruesome thought.

"You just promise me you won't do anything rash, okay?" said the old man.

"You got it, Mr. P.," said Annie. "I'll be careful."

If what he was saying was true, then it would be prudent to follow his directions. Maybe finding the pennies was a coincidence or maybe it wasn't, but she wasn't going to screw around and find out the hard way.

"Okay," said the old shopkeep. "You take that cabinet, and I'll give you some comics, too."

"Sure thing," grinned Annie.

Real magic or not, life was looking pretty good right now.

*****

Annie walked into the apartment and set down her new cabinet. She opened the cabinet, took out her stack of newly obtained vintage comics, shut the cabinet, and then turned to go put them away in her room. Unfortunately, she never made it there.

Greg appeared out of nowhere. He grabbed her by her right wrist with his own left hand and yanked her forward.

She dropped her comics as she shrieked in both pain and surprise. His grip was like a vise, and it hurt her to the point where she thought the slender bones within that grip were going to break.

"Where is it!" he yelled.

"What are you talk—" she started to say.

His fist buried itself within her solar plexus, and she immediately felt the air leave her lungs. She doubled over from that vicious blow, her eyes wide, her mouth agape in shock and surprise.

His rough hands wrapped around her waist, her vision whirled in a crazy dance as the room spun, and then she was on her back, slammed to the floor without mercy. Her comics were now beneath her, scattered about the one empty space of flooring within this cluttered two-bedroom apartment.

Annie tried to cry out as a bruising pain erupted around her bladder, the cause of that pain a swift kick from the pointed toe of Greg's right boot. She had no breath in her to scream, so all she could do was squeeze her eyes shut, the tears flowing, her mouth wide with nothing but silence.

If Greg was anything, he was an expert on leaving bruises where no one else could see.

"You lying little thief!" screeched Greg. "I know you've been stealing from me, but I've let it slide because you only took the cheap stuff!...But this time, Ann...this time, you...are...done! Do you hear me! You took the one valuable item we had! That was our paycheck, you little skank!"

Annie curled up into a fetal position and desperately sucked in some breath. She cried out in a pathetic whimper, and she wanted to break down and bawl, but she couldn't even do that.

"Look at this cheap crap you traded it for!" yelled Greg. "What is this garbage!...A black box? Some cheap comic rags? What the hell is wrong with you!"

"The box...is magic..." wheezed Annie. "It's...real magic...It's real..."

She had no idea why she'd said that. Greg was going to have a field day with that one.

And he did.

He choked out a sarcastic laugh as he ground his right boot into her inner right thigh. She knew he was aiming for her crotch, but thankfully, he was off a bit. Still, it hurt to the point where she cried out from that brutal, twisting pain.

Greg lifted his boot and stamped it down upon the floor.

"Magic!" he exclaimed. "Magic!...This isn't a fairytale, you moron!...I swear, Annie, you have two frickin' braincells, and one of them is permanently switched off! No one smarter than a bottle of aspirin would fall for that *Jack and the Beanstalk* crap!...There's no such thing as magic, you idiot!

"That knife you took had real rubies in it! It was a genuine antique worth a small fortune!...That was a verified bejeweled renaissance stiletto, you brainless meat sack!...Did you think I wouldn't notice it was gone? I had a buyer already tagged for it!"

Annie curled in on herself and squeezed her eyes shut even harder. She was genuinely scared now, because she didn't want Greg to hit her anymore, but he was furious, so she knew more pain was coming, and he was not going to hold back, not this time.

Still, there was always begging.

"I'm sorry!" she choked out. "I'm sorry! You never give me any mon—"

"Shut up!" he yelled.

She listened to the sound of his boots stomp off toward her bedroom. She heard him fling open her bedroom door, stomp in, and then stomp out a few seconds later. She did nothing during this time but weep and fold in on herself, but that was all she could do. She felt helpless and broken, and that's all there was to it.

"I should have done this a long time ago," he said in a deathly-quiet tone. "You've had this coming, because it's clear to me you're not going to learn…Get up!"

She screeched again as he yanked her up by her right arm. She opened her blurry, tearful eyes and tried not to sob in front him. She wanted to, but she was afraid to, because Greg wasn't the merciful type, and seeing her break down was only going to enrage him further.

"Look at me, Annie," said Greg. "Look what I have."

His voice was menacing, commanding. She was really in for it now.

He held up one of her seven-inch, plastic, movie-monster figures she loved so much. He must have taken it off her shelf above her bed.

She wiped her eyes so she could see more clearly…The figure he was holding was her classic werewolf figure. The classic horror movies were her favorite films, that figure was her most prized possession, and Greg knew both of those things.

"You like this crappy old movie, huh?" he asked. "You love this stupid thing, don't you?"

He was going to break it. She just knew he was going to break it.

"Please, don't!" she choked out. "Please, give it back to me!"

"You've brought this on yourself, Ann," scowled Greg.

He picked up Mercutio's Cabinet and thrust it at her. She took the priceless artifact and held it closely to her as he opened up the cabinet's door and tossed in her werewolf figure. He shut the cabinet door and turned the gold latch to keep the door from swinging open.

"You've brought this on yourself, Ann," he said again. "Get your butt down to the van."

Annie wiped at her eyes and cheeks and tried to stop the inane sounds of weeping coming out of her mouth. She really didn't like crying, but she was scared, so ending her weeping was taking up most of her concentration.

"Where are we going?" she choked out.

"Get moving!" yelled Greg.

Annie jumped as he shoved her toward the apartment door. It appeared they were taking a trip.

She tried to set down her cabinet, but Greg stopped her.

"No, you don't!" he barked. "You're taking that with us!"

"Greg!" she whined.

He was going to do something terrible to her stuff. She'd just gotten this cabinet, and if it really was magic, Greg was just going to smash it…or burn it, or whatever…not to mention her werewolf figure. That figure was the first thing she'd bought after she'd escaped her parents. It was her comfort, her anchor to a better life, and now Greg was going to destroy that, too…

He was no better than her parents. If she had known that, she would have never hooked up with him in the first place.

She knew there was nothing she could say to make him believe her, so this time she really did sob. She cried out in loud wails as her tears started flowing all over again.

"Shut up!" yelled Greg. "Shut that crap down before one of the neighbors hears us!...Do you hear me! You brought this on yourself, so quit your bawling!"

He pushed her forward as she clutched her most prized possessions to her chest, and they left the apartment. They walked down the stairs and out to Greg's van, and during that time, Annie did her best to stifle her weeping, but it was difficult.

Annie reluctantly strapped herself into the front passenger's seat of Greg's old white junker, Greg strapped himself into the driver's seat, and they were off.

They drove west out toward the city limits, and during that time, Greg said nothing. Annie took that opportunity to compose herself, but it was difficult. She mostly wiped at her eyes and clutched her cabinet to herself for some small comfort, but that was really all she could do.

They drove out of town, and they drove for what seemed like an eternity, but to where, Annie did not know. The sun went down on the horizon, darkness fell, and the light of the full moon shone down upon them.

Annie didn't dare say anything during the drive. She was not stupid.

It wasn't until they had driven several miles upon a lonely stretch of gravel road surrounded by thick woods did Greg pull over and shut off the engine.

"Get out," he said gruffly.

"Greg…" she whined.

"Get out!" he barked.

Annie undid her seatbelt and quickly exited the vehicle. Whatever was going on was not going to be good, but she didn't want to get hit again, so she complied.

She stepped out into soft and pale moonlight.

The road they were on showed no visible signs of human habitation. There were only the thick, leafless trees of late winter/early spring surrounding them, the calls of various insects waking from winter slumber chirping in the distance.

Greg exited the van, walked around to the back, opened up the double doors to the back of the van, and pulled out a shovel and flashlight. He flipped on the flashlight, slammed the doors shut, walked up to Annie, temporarily put the flashlight in the crook of his left arm while holding the shovel with his left hand, and grabbed her by her right arm, only to shove her forward.

"Get moving," he ordered.

"Greg, I'm sorry…" whined Annie.

"I don't care," said Greg coldly. "Get moving before I break one of your bones…I mean it, Annie…Move!"

She stumbled forward into the warm glow of the flashlight as she was forced through the trees.

"We're going to bury that box, Ann," he growled. "We're going to bury that box where no one will ever frickin' find it."

She felt her tears flow again. She couldn't help it.

"Greg, I'm sorry," she choked out. "Please, don't do this! These things mean everything to me; you know that!"

"Yeah, well, you should have thought about that before you stole from me," said Greg in a cold tone. "Losing that stiletto has set me back a fortune."

"Greg…" whined Annie.

"Move!" yelled Greg.

They walked a little farther until they came to a small empty patch of dirt and leaves surrounded by trees.

"Stop," commanded Greg. "This is good. There's some soft ground here where I don't have to worry about roots…I'd have you dig, but that would take us all night, so it looks like I'm going to have to do it…You just set that box right there."

Annie sobbed as she set the box down into the leaves and dirt of the small, open copse they had stopped in.

"It's a full moon tonight," huffed Greg. "That's frickin' ironic, considering what's in that box…Fitting is what it is."

Annie sobbed into her hands for a few seconds before wiping at her eyes. She did not know where they were, so there was no chance she was ever going to find this place to dig up the cabinet. It was like looking for one particular needle in a haystack made of needles.

"Stop crying, Ann," said Greg. "You've had this coming for a while now. Honestly, I should have done this a long time ago, but one thing or another made me hesitate…No more. Tonight's the night to take out the trash."

"Greg, please, I'll never do it ag—" she began.

She looked up as she was speaking, and she saw the bright muzzle flash as the ringing "BANG!" went off in a deafening thunder. She jerked backwards as a tremendous blow struck her in the stomach. She was on her back a second later, plunging into soft dirt and twigs and leaves, but her first instinct after realizing she was on the ground was to touch where she had been struck, though she felt no pain.

Her hands were covered in a sticky wetness, but she had fallen, so she must have landed in something. She brought her hands up to her face to inspect what she had fallen in, the ring of Greg's light fell upon her, and her eyes widened in horror as she stared at the scarlet liquid that was smeared all over the slender fingers of both her hands.

She felt a searing, lancing pain after that, a pain so terrible that all she could do was open her mouth and let forth a weak moan of shock and despair.

"You love this stupid crap, don't you?" came Greg's voice, though it sounded distant, muddled. "Well, I'm not heartless, you know. You may think I am, but I'm not. That's why I'm going to bury you with your 'magic box' and that stupid werewolf figure. If you love this crap so much…well…wherever you're going, you can take it with you."

Betrayal…Horror…Realization…Terror…These things flooded Annie's mind as she struggled against the savage pain that was quickly and brutally killing her. It had honestly never occurred to her that Greg would do something like this. He had always been abusive, true, and he had always been a paranoid thief, true, but a killer?...She had never even considered that a possibility.

She was going to die. What had happened had finally registered, and she was going to die. Where Greg had gotten a gun, or how he'd hidden it from her, she did not know, but one thing was clear…She was going to die.

Everything she'd ever done up to this moment had been for nothing. Enduring the failure and bullying of school had been for nothing. Escaping her draconian parents had been for nothing. Suffering out on the street had been for nothing. Suffering through Greg had been for nothing. None of it had mattered, not one bit of it.

Greg was right in some respect. She had brought this upon herself, but only because she had hooked up with him. That's where she had gone wrong. She hadn't done anything to deserve this…not this…

If only there was some real magic in the world, she'd make him pay. She'd make him pay, and then she'd be free…

But there was real magic in the world, wasn't there? At least, that's what Mr. Pascuzzi had told her.

A thought occurred to her, one last gasp to go out on. She was dying, fading out and in severe pain, but if there was a chance…

Annie choked out blood-soaked spittle as she turned and reached for Mercutio's Cabinet. The pain was so terrible that she nearly passed out right then, but something inside her, some will that she dredged up from deep within her soul, bubbled to the surface and allowed her to turn the latch-key on the cabinet.

"You don't steal from me, Ann," she heard Greg's distant, fading voice. "Nobody steals from me. I decide what belongs to me…When you have a pet that bites your hand and craps all over the carpet, you take that pet out back and put it down. I should have done this a while back."

Annie opened the cabinet door, reached inside, and smeared her life's blood across the interior cabinet bottom. Her fingers briefly touched her prized werewolf figure, a comforting moment, but she retracted those fingers and closed the cabinet door. It took everything she had left to reach up and turn the latch-key, but she managed it.

She could hear the sounds of Greg's digging. The scumbag hadn't even waited for her to die.

"Yeah, you were a good lay, but I can find another woman," he said. "What's between your legs ain't special…Still, you could pick locks without a bump key. I guess I'll just have to figure out how to pick locks myself from now on. I'm not putting up with another disobedient pet…Nobody steals from me, Ann. You're damn straight I'll make sure that never happens again."

Annie closed her eyes and breathed in the dank air of the forest. She slowly exhaled as she felt the soft light of the full moon upon her skin, a strange blanket of pale warmth that tingled and touched her in forbidden places.

It started as a heat at first, a whisper of wilderness at the back of her mind, and then it came flooding in, a rage, a concentration of animosity that boiled up from out of the abyss of her own psyche.

Annie sat up and then slowly stood upon two unsteady legs. She was angry now, truly angry, angry for once in her life and *not* afraid, and that made all of the difference in the world.

She could feel it coming, the rush, but it wasn't quite there yet. What she could *not* feel anymore was pain, and that was a good thing.

"What the fu…?" trailed Greg in momentary surprise. "You're actually still alive?...Oh, well. I was hoping to save on ammo, but whatever."

There were three bright muzzle flares, three flares in the moonlit darkness accompanied by three loud "BANGS!," and Annie, slender and small as she was, jerked back three times but did not fall.

Annie felt the bullets spit from the bloody wounds in her chest and abdomen. The metal slugs ejected from her body to fall to the dirt and leaves below.

"Th…That's impossible!" stammered Greg.

There was real fear in his voice now, and that fear, that audible tremble, was the onset for the rush in Annie's blood.

Greg was a bully, an abusive sleazebag with no real guts, and he only picked on those who could not defend themselves, so it was no surprise he would fold at this moment, a moment that was beyond his abusive control.

"Why aren't you dead!" cried Greg. "No one can survive that! Why aren't you dead!"

He fired twice more, the bullets slammed into Annie, and then he pulled the trigger over and over as the gun clicked again and again, the chambers empty.

The fresh bullet wounds in Annie's chest spit forth their metal slugs as the wounds themselves healed within seconds, healing as if there had never been any wounds at all.

The rush ran through her like an orgasmic venom, enraging her further, exciting her to new heights, giving her a toxic ecstasy like no other.

"Why aren't I dead?" asked Annie. "It's pretty simple, Greg."

Her voice lowered an octave as the moon shone its pale light down upon her.

"It's a full moon," she growled. "It's a full moon, Greg, and those bullets aren't silver."

She let the change overtake her, the rage and the fury, and she reveled in that sensation.

She grinned as her teeth turned into fangs, and she shook and trembled in strange ecstasy as thick brown fur sprouted from her skin. On some level, this was what she had always wanted, to live out her favorite movie, and now she was getting to do just that.

Mr. Pascuzzi had been right. There was real magic in the world.

There was no pain, only rage. There was only rage and hunger, and she let those primal urges complete her. She could hear everything now, see everything now, and most of all, smell everything now…Her new snouted, dog-like nose could smell Greg's fear, and that delectable scent was all it took to rush him.

He trilled out a rather unmanly high-pitched scream as her new fangs tore into his throat, the hot blood spraying, the taste of salt and chunks of carotid in her mouth.

#2…FILE 13

Just forget about it.

Kordell walked past four aisles of busy cubicles to the boss's office. Mr. Barrington was not really someone he wanted to deal with, but in Kordell's hand was an outdated invoice, a faded and stained white-paper invoice from 1973. It had been discovered behind some loose plaster down in Accounts Management, but since Kordell was the new guy, it was his job to take it to Mr. Barrington.

The old invoice was for a small shipment of the long-discontinued Jerryman Percolator, a safety hazard that had set ablaze kitchens across the country, a safety hazard that had nearly ruined the company back then.

The boss's eyes widened into dark saucers as he stared down at the old invoice. With trembling hands, the old man gave the crumbling piece of paper back to Kordell, who gingerly received it with great care.

"This is the old McAllister bill!" gasped Mr. Barrington. "The McAllister mansion burned to the ground while entertaining a number of foreign dignitaries…We managed to avoid that lawsuit due to a lack of evidence...Oh, this requires a…a burial of sorts…No one can remember this, not even me…Oh, it had to come to this…"

He ushered Kordell out of his office and onto the main floor.

"File Thirteen it," ordered the old man.

The cubicles upon the main floor went silent as if on command. Kordell looked about in both confusion and slight fear as all of the other employees poked their heads from out of their workstations and stared directly at him. Kordell had no idea what was going on, but whatever this was, it was enough to get the attention of everyone, and it was more than enough to rile the boss.

Mr. Barrington tapped him on the shoulder to get his attention.

"Focus, young man!" hissed the boss. "This is important!...Ahem…Now, listen carefully…Kordell, is it?...Take the service elevator down to the basement storage. In the back of storage, there's a rusty door that's off limits…You'll open that with a key I'll give you, and you'll return that key once you're finished. In that room is the…the back storage…I…I hate to do this to you, but…I'd take it myself, but I can't be allowed to remember this. I can't afford to."

"O…kay…" said Kordell nervously.

"The back storage is a…a confusing place," continued Mr. Barrington. "It's technically a small room, but you can get lost in there…Don't get lost!...It's not safe. Just get in there and get to the back. In the back is an old rusty chute, the chute that we use for anything that's File Thirteened. We drop anything down there we want to forget about…forever.

"Now this is very important, so listen carefully. *Do not*…put anything down that chute but this bill. Understand? No trash, no scraps of paper…*nothing*…but this bill. *Nothing…at…all*…Understand?"

"*Okaaaay*…" said Kordell uncertainly.
"Whatever you say, Mr. Barrington."

"One more thing," said Mr. Barrington. "When you're in there…there is…is uhhh…Just…Just dump the bill and get out of there as fast as you can. Understand? Don't linger; it's not safe…I'll give you the rest of the day off after this. Just go ahead and leave after you return the keys to me. Consider it hazard pay with a bonus."

Mr. Barrington gave Kordell an encouraging swat on the arm, and Kordell grinned in return. All of this was weird, but what the heck, right? A free day off with pay sounded good to him.

Mr. Barrington handed Kordell the keys for the service elevator and the rusty door. The service-elevator key was just a normal key on a ring, but the rusty-door key was…odd. It was a big, rusty, metal thing with a skull on the handle of it, the handle as long as Kordell's hand, and this kind of creeped him out. Nevertheless, he took the big key and nodded once to the old man.

"Good," nodded Mr. Barrington in return. "Just remember, young man…everything dies…even time…even reality. Everything dies…and this keeps Death very busy. But Death has a way of…of getting what she wants. She's a terrible little thing…a lonely, jealous little thing…Just keep that in mind."

"*Ooookay*," replied Kordell. "I'll uhhh…I'll keep that in mind, Mr. Barrington."

Kordell walked off to do his job, well aware of the keen eyes of everyone else upon his moving figure. He shook his head at all of this but took to the service elevator anyway. He used the service key and headed down to the warehouse-sized area that was the company-building's basement.

He wandered through a mess of shelves stacked with old files and equipment until he reached the back wall, and embedded in that wall was a tall, rusty, iron door. Kordell took the strange old key and jammed it into the door's huge lock, and even he, fit and muscular as he was, had trouble turning the thing, this strange rusty key with a skull on the end of it.

The odd key turned over with a loud clunk, and Kordell pushed open the heavy iron door. He walked into the flickering light of overhead bulbs hanging from the concrete ceiling, but he left the door open…He was not stupid.

Inside this room was yet another mess of shelves stacked with old files and equipment, but this room was somewhat smaller than the warehouse that was the company basement. He could see the mortar of the back wall in the distance, so he headed in that direction, though it was not a straight shot.

He wandered toward the back wall within a maze of shelves, but his skin crawled as the hairs on the back of his neck raised…He did not like this place at all. There was something about this room that scared him, and he was not one to be easily pushed.

Nevertheless, he made it to the back wall after a few minutes of nervous wandering.

Next to that wall was a rusty metal chute jutting from the floor like an Industrial-Revolution-era machine pillar. Someone had spray painted a large orange #13 across the front of it, and that should have given the chute a sense of normalcy, but this did not ease the feeling of dread that seeped into him. He could sense a heat from the old chute, but that heat made him feel cold after a few seconds, a chill that went right down to the marrow of his bones.

"Let's just get this done," said Kordell in a nervous tone, but his voice sounded thunderous within the pure silence of this place.

He reached for the rusty chute's metal lid, and he tried to pull back the heavy swinging cover, but the old lid was rusted tight, and it took him to straining all of his muscles to open it. He managed to pull down the lid to where it came down with a terrible screech, rusty metal grinding against rusty metal, but at least he managed it.

The odor that wafted up from the black pit that was the opening of this chute was like nothing Kordell had ever suffered before. It was dust mixed with rot mixed with disease mixed with…It made him sick to the point where he had to cover his mouth with his right hand.

He tossed the old McAllister bill through the yawning opening, and it vanished into that pitch dark.

"Kordell…" came the whisper of a child's voice from behind him.

Kordell jumped as his left hand caught the open lid of the chute. The lid popped up with a terrible screech, and his wedding ring came loose from his finger, only to clatter along the lid and pitch into the yawning hole that was the chute. The lid slammed shut, Kordell let out a little shriek, and then he ran, thoroughly freaked out by everything now.

He tried to run his way back toward the open door on the far side of the room, but it was not that easy. A large metal shelf of files and old products tipped forward in front of him, and he jumped backwards just in time to avoid being crushed beneath all of that junk.

He heard the giggle of childish laughter around him as the lights flickered overhead. Panicked, he made his way through several aisles of shelves, but various boxes and outdated products flew from the shelves at him, flying out as if on their own accord, and he was bruised and battered as he shrieked in pure fear.

"Kordell…Kordell…Kordell…" taunted a child's voice.

Kordell screeched and ran in a mad panic from one aisle to the next. He could see the front wall above the shelves in the distance, but he couldn't seem to reach it. He turned past two shelves to reach another aisle, but this time he skidded to a halt.

Before him, in the flickering light, there was a child, a little girl by the looks of her dark-blue Sunday school vest and skirt, African American by the color of her bare legs, the dark curls of her hair done up in pigtails, her back turned toward him.

By her size, she couldn't have been older than six, but she simply stood in the aisle within the flickering fluorescence, her shiny little black shoes in stark contrast to the grey concrete floor beneath them. Her head was lowered to stare at the floor, and though she should have been small and nonthreatening, her sudden presence, her very existence down here in this hellhole, set Kordell's teeth on edge.

"H…Hello?" he stammered.

"Kordell?" came the child's voice. "Won't you play with me?"

The little girl turned around, and as she did, Kordell saw her face, or rather, her lack of one. Where her face should have been was a clean white skull, the grinning, ivory-white skull of a child, and this was too much for him.

He screamed and ran once more. This time he bolted at near the speed of sound, and three aisle turns later, one left, one right, and one more left, he saw the open doorway and ran toward it. The shelves surrounding him pitched over as he passed them, but he did not look back, even as everything crashed behind him.

"Come back, Kordell," came the little girl's voice. "Come play with me…"

He ran through the doorway and quickly slammed shut the heavy metal door. He jammed the boss's key back into the lock and twisted the key with all his might. The lock clunked over, and Kordell breathed out a long sigh of relief.

He took the service elevator back to the main floor, and everyone stopped working in order to stare at him as he crossed the room to the boss's office. He was beat up, scratched in places, and his work clothes torn in some spots, but at this point, he didn't care if everyone else decided to gawp at him or not. He just wanted to go home.

He made a beeline for Mr. Barrington's office, opened the door, and let himself in, closing the door behind him. After what he had just been through, "worker protocol" was the last thing on his mind.

This bold maneuver, however, did not bother the old man in the least.

"Great job, my boy!" said Mr. Barrington as he clapped Kordell on the arm. "You'll get a big bonus for this! I don't know why you had to go down there, but I don't send anybody down there unless it is *extremely* important."

"What?" asked Kordell in rife confusion. "Do…Do you even know what's down there? You sent me down into that…that *hell,* and you can't even remember why?"

Mr. Barrington held up the rusty door key and gave Kordell a pert frown.

"Listen, young man," he said in a grave tone, "you need to take the rest of the day off. Take tomorrow off, too…Believe it or not, I've been down in back storage. I know *exactly* what goes on down there."

"Y…You do?" stammered Kordell. "And you sent me down there? Willingly?"

"I knew you'd be all right," frowned the old man. "You see, the more times you go down there…the worse it gets. You don't have to go down there again. Once is enough for a lifetime."

"You think!" cried Kordell. "Why do you even have a place like that!"

Mr. Barrington sat down on his desk and raised his left hand, palm out.

"It's always been there," he said calmly. "You see, some places in the world are very close to

Death…Death can go anywhere, mind you, but some places…some places are places where…where she has a…*special* grip, a death hold, if you will. The backroom storage is one of those places. We send things to the backroom storage that we want to die…It's a very clean way of getting rid of something.

"If there's a product that we want to discontinue that is somehow a fad, we send a working model down there, and 'poof,' the fad ends for one reason or another, and we can move on to something better. You go down there, open the door, find a shelf to put the thing on, and leave. It's not that bad…as long as you don't wander. I can tell by the way you're beat up that you did some exploring. Not a good idea down there."

"Wander?" asked Kordell in rightful indignation. "I didn't wander! You sent me down there to throw that invoice down that old chute in the back!"

Mr. Barrington popped up off his desk and gave Kordell a look of wide-eyed alarm.

"What did you say?" asked the old man in a panic.

"You told me to throw that old invoice down that chute," repeated Kordell.

"Oh…Oh, no…" said Mr. Barrington.

"What?" asked Kordell. "You said you send stuff down there to die…"

"No…no, no…" said Mr. Barrington with a shake of his head. "No, the chute is different. If I sent you down there for that, that means whatever 'invoice' I gave you was File Thirteened."

"Yeah," nodded Kordell. "That's what you wanted. That's what you called it."

"That chute is…is oblivion," replied Mr. Barrington.

"Oblivion?" asked Kordell.

"In the thirty years I've worked here," said Mr. Barrington, "I've only had to use it twice. This will make a third time."

"Uh, huh," frowned Kordell. "That doesn't tell me anything. What's the chute for? Why is it different?"

"That chute is oblivion," explained Mr. Barrington. "It's where both time and reality go to die. When we throw something down that, it's not for it to just die. Death is, at least, something. Whatever gets thrown down there is *erased*…It's gone as if it had never existed at all.

"Only the person who threw the item away will ever remember it, because the reality of throwing the object away must still exist for it to occur in the first place, but…whatever you threw down there for me, young man…you'll find that no one *anywhere* will remember anything about it. It's gone…It never happened in the first place."

Kordell's shoulders sank as he nearly had a heart attack. He held up his left hand and felt horror grip him as he stared at the dark, bare skin of his now barren ring finger.

#2a…BONUS STORY: RUBBER DUCKIE

His mother set him down in the bathtub and turned off the water. Joey had just turned three, and though he liked to play in the water, there was something that he did not like at all. It was one of his toys, the one he did not like, and he did not like it one bit.

The phone rang in the living room, and his mother stared down at him and frowned. The young woman pulled away her pretty red dress to keep Joey's splashing from getting the fabric wet, and her lips crinkled as the phone continued to ring.

"I have to get the phone, Baby," she said, a clear note of unhappiness in her voice. "Your father is working on this year's ad campaign for the new 1957 model that's coming out soon. You just sit tight and play. Here…I'll give you one of your toys."

She pulled a toy out of the little wooden bin under the sink and dropped it in the tub with Joey. The little toy hit the water with a splash, but Joey did not like this, not one little bit.

"I'll be right back," she said as she hustled off to answer the phone.

She left the bathroom, and Joey stared in fear at the red rubber duckie floating in the water of the ivory porcelain tub they both shared.

This thing had a huge grin on its beak, with white, human-like teeth in that sinister bill. It possessed little feathers on the sides of its small head that looked like horns, and its black and soulless pupils were mere pinpoints in large ovals of white, those deranged eyes staring at him as it bobbed up and down, up and down in the clear liquid surrounding it.

He didn't even have time to cry before it attacked; no tears were shed because of a dire need for survival.

The water rippled forth from the front to the back as it pushed Joey against the back lip of the tub.

The first wave roiled over him as the malevolent little bath toy bobbed forward upon that evil tide. Joey tried to cry out as water entered his open mouth, and he was sputtering and flailing as the second wave of water washed over him.

His bare feet, bottom, and hands slid down along the smooth finish of the porcelain beneath him, and water entered his nose. It was all he could do to push up from the bottom of the tub, only to choke out more of the suffocating liquid as a third wave rocked him.

He was pushed down again, and looking up through the water revealed the bottom surface of the floating red rubber duckie.

He pushed up against an invisible force in a desperate attempt to right himself. The clear water was like pushing through mud, but he found the strength to push up, to push up and against the malevolent force trying to drown him.

Joey pushed up with both hands until they felt a rubber surface. His little hands burned as if he had touched a hot stove, but he would not give in. He could not.

The evil little toy flew from the bathtub to bounce across the white tiles of the bathroom floor, and he sat up above the waterline and took in some deep breaths.

Today was a victory, but Joey knew that tomorrow…tomorrow would bring a whole new struggle for survival.

#3…ROAD-SIGN JOE

The future is plastics!

Miguel took his bag of chips and his energy drink to the counter. He needed some sustenance in order to continue on with his journey, that journey being the three-hour drive to his little sister's house. Isabella's wedding was swiftly approaching, and he needed to reach the family with enough time to prepare for his role in the ceremony.

He had stopped at this little out-of-the-way gas station on his way to the highway, originally stopping here to ask for directions. He was as poor as a church mouse, so he had no GPS, no smartphone with internet, and no up-to-date map. Maps were behind the counter here, so he would purchase one along with his necessary provisions.

He set his energy drink and his bag of chips down upon the counter and nodded once at the old man who worked here.

The overweight elderly man in a white tank top and brown suspenders nodded once back at him and made his way to Miguel from behind that counter, briefly taking a moment to turn down the volume on an old-fashioned radio.

Miguel had no idea why an old man would be working at such a place at such an age, or why, even, the old man worked at all. Miguel figured old age was for retirement and enjoying the rest of your life, not for working through it.

"This it?" asked the elderly man. "You want anything else?"

"I need one of those road maps," said Miguel.

"Where you trying to get to, son?" asked the man.

"I'm just heading north to the interstate," said Miguel. "I know where I'm going, but I was hoping to find a shortcut to shave off some time."

"You in a hurry?" asked the old man.

"My sister is getting married," replied Miguel.

"How far we talkin'?" asked the man.

"It's three hours from here," said Miguel. "Up in Engles."

"Ah," said the old man. "Well, why don't we just have a looksee, then. Ain't no point in buying a map if you don't need one."

The old man walked over to a rack, pulled forth a map, unfolded it, and laid it out on the counter.

Miguel looked around in a nervous hush for other customers. He did not want to hold up the line, but he was the only one in here at the moment, so he shrugged off that anxiety and peered down at the map alongside the old man.

The overweight elderly man ran one fat wrinkled finger along a trail of lines upon the map as Miguel's eyes followed that leading digit.

"It's a straight shot to the highway, son," said the old man. "You just head on up to it, then it loops 'round here, connects to the interstate, and you're home free. Just follow the signs…Ain't no shortcut, though."

Miguel studied the map with keen interest. There was, actually, a road leading between the highway and the interstate, one that cut between the loop between the two. That short road would save him at least forty-five minutes plus the headache of a longer driving time through the dangers of the interstate.

He could not understand, however, why there was such a huge loop around that road, a loop that was so wide, it was wasteful. It was as if the highway authority were deliberately avoiding that entire area, all but ensuring people had to drive much longer than they needed to.

Nevertheless, a shortcut was a shortcut.

"What's this road, then?" he asked.

"No, no," said the old man with a vehement shake of his head. "No, you don't want to take that road, son. No, you stick to the highway."

"Why?" asked Miguel. "Is the road closed?"

"That's Jepson Road," said the old gas-station attendant. "It's supposed to be closed, but there's always some cockamamie fool that gets it in his head to go up it…No, you don't want to go that way."

"Why not?" asked Miguel. "This is the shortcut I was looking for."

"Now, listen, son," said the man, and Miguel could hear the frustration in the old attendant's voice. "You don't wanna go up there. Ain't nobody goes up Jepson Road. It ain't safe, and it ain't been safe since the accident."

"Accident?" asked Miguel. "What accident?"

The old man leaned over the counter, rested his elbows upon the map, and shook his head twice.

"Now, you listen here, son," said the old attendant in a near whisper. "I'm trying to he'p ya. Ain't nobody goes up Jepson Road. That's where the old Fancy-Joe-Jepson plastics factory used to be. Place been closed down since the late '50s."

"And?" asked Miguel. "Why doesn't anyone go up it?"

"I was ten years old when that factory shut down for good," said the old man. "There used to be road signs from here as far as the eye could see advertising this here and that, but it was the Fancy-Joe-Jepson signs that always caught our eye. So many signs with the Fancy Joe mascot that folks 'round here used to call ol' Joe, 'Road-Sign Joe.'"

"That doesn't…That's not even…" said Miguel with a shake of his head. "What does that have to do with anything?"

"There ain't no signs of Joe no more," frowned the old attendant. "Do you know why, son?"

"Uhhh…because…it's been like…since the '50s?" asked Miguel.

"All them signs got torn right on down by 1961," said the old man. "They got torn down because someone, somewhere, wanted people to forget, forget about ol' Joe and the plastics factory."

Miguel could smell a conspiracy theory here, but that was fine. Some old people liked to talk, so he would listen for the moment, if only to humor the old man…He was still in a hurry, though.

"What did they want to forget?" he asked.

"Whatever it was they was doing out there," said the old man. "Somethin' happened that day of the accident back in 1958. I remember it well…

"My grandpappy was driving me and my brothers 'round here in town when we all saw a bright green light, a green light coming up from the plastics factory out yonder, a green light just come a shooting up like one of them 'mushroom clouds' you see from an atom bomb, only not an explosion, but like a…a shape almost, just a big ol' shape like a mushroom or a broccoli stalk, but made a light."

This was really beginning to sound like science fiction, but the old man seemed convinced of his own fantasy, and that self-conviction was its own strange proof, so Miguel continued to listen, though he really was short on time. He needed to get going.

Still, he wanted to hear the rest of this story.

"What happened next?" asked Miguel.

"Army come out here and shut down the roads," said the old man. "We had the National Guard out here for a whole week. Cordoned off the whole area 'round the factory. Claimed the place was 'toxic.' Now, I don't know 'bout no 'toxic,' but I do know some higher-ups made damned sure nobody go sniffing 'round that place. Erased every bit of the old factory from the papers and books and whatnot."

"If that's true, then why is the road still on the maps?" asked Miguel.

"Road weren't on the old maps," said the old attendant. "Govn'ment wiped the road clean off 'em. These new maps, however, are made with that fancy 'satellite imaging' and stuff. That's why we keep getting folks up here still asking 'bout the old Jepson Road in the first place."

"So is the place radioactive?" asked Miguel. "What's the deal with it?"

This was a legitimate concern. He did not want to develop cancer just by being in close proximity to the place.

"Ain't no radiation," said the old man. "Naw…but the place is like a bad penny. Gives off a bad feelin', which is why folks avoid it. Something tells you at the back a yo'r mind to 'stay away.' Govn'ment ain't had to do much to keep people out a there, but there's always some damn fool who goes on a bet or a dare or somethin' like that, and then they ain't never heard from again."

"Uh…huh…" said Miguel. "How could a plastics factory do all that? What kind of accident would even do that?"

"From what I heard over the years, the place was a front," said the old man.

"A front?" asked Miguel.

"Yeah," replied the old attendant. "Govn'ment was doin' experiments out there. Messing 'round with stuff they shouldn'a been. That's why everything was hush-hush. That's how these things happen."

"*Riiiight*," grinned Miguel as he nodded twice. "Government experiments with a plastics factory…Sure."

This was definitely a local-yokel story…He should have known.

"Now, I'm not joshing with you, son," frowned the old man. "You just keep a clear of Jepson Road. Don't go anywhere near that old plastics factory. Too many people have vanished out there over the years. Govn'ment keeps it quiet, hushed up.

"Last one askin' 'bout Jepson Road was some little lady that does them interwebs vi'jeos. Her and her friends come askin' 'bout the old plant. They all went up to the plant, and they come back 'round not too much later, but she wasn't with 'em. They said they wasn't goin' in. They all got that bad feelin' at the entrance to the road, turned right around, and come back here, but she went in anyway…

"Yep, she went right on in alone…That was years ago. Ain't never heard a her since. She ain't even on the interwebs no more. Vanished…just like all the others. Friends never came back 'round for her, either. I'm thinking the govn'ment paid 'em off to keep it all hushed up."

Miguel shrugged. He didn't believe a word of this, but at this point, he'd say anything to end this conversation. He really had to get going.

"Okay," he said. "If it's that dangerous, I'll just take the highway, then."

"That'd be the smart thing to do, son," nodded the old man.

Of course, Miguel had no intention of doing that. There was no reason not to take a clear shortcut when he had one. If that old road saved him a good chunk of time and some of the nightmares of the interstate, then he was all for it.

✳✳✳✳✳

Miguel pulled onto the out-of-the way dirt road that led toward the old Jepson Road. There wasn't much out here but scrub grass and dirt—no houses to be seen—so this little detour was proving to be…problematic.

He had not realized there would be one turn off after the next, so taking this ill-advised route was beginning to look…ill-advised, if only for the sheer waste of time it was going to be.

He had the option to turn around, to turn around his old and beat-up light-green truck, but he'd already come this far, so he was sticking to his guns.

"Can't lose any more time," whispered Miguel to himself.

He drove up to the so-called "entrance" to Jepson Road.

The road, itself, was cracked and broken asphalt, that entrance marked by two falling-down wooden booths on each side of the road, those booths clearly having once been guard checkpoints. There was a rusted and broken guard gate, the turn pole off its hub, that gate collapsed to one side, the left side from his point of view.

Aside from that, someone had clearly been out here recently, but they hadn't stayed long.

There was a rusted metal plate that may have been part of the right booth, that plate propped up against what was left of the booth, and someone had quickly affixed what looked like new chain-link fencing around it, only to hang up an old and rusty "KEEP OUT" sign to that new fencing.

It was as if someone had used a keep-out sign that had already been here, slapped the chain-link fencing up as fast as possible, affixed the sign, and then ran, and Miguel had no illusions as to why.

He could sense the black aura about this place, a deviation of mood that sank into him like a dark cloud, a dark cloud laced with nails, and he did not like it one bit. It was a presence almost, a stifling sensation of being smothered by…something, though he did not know what.

Still, he'd lost too much time already.

"I can't go back," he whispered to himself. "Isabella is counting on me to be there."

There was nothing more important in his life than family, and even though he had been away for some time, he was still connected to them through the heart, so he was not going to turn tail and run, not now.

"It's just some old man's tall tale," he said to himself.

Even so, he said a silent prayer in Spanish, made the sign of the cross, closed his eyes, and took in a deep breath. He released that breath, opened his eyes, and nodded once to himself.

"Let's do this," he said firmly.

He put his old truck in drive, wheeled forward, and carefully went around the collapsed guard gate. His tires rolled onto broken asphalt, and then he was on his way.

He drove for about three minutes before he spotted the first of the road signs. The cracked and broken asphalt of this abandoned road gave way to fresh asphalt, a new blacktop untouched by time, and the road signs in the distance looked new as well, unmolested by whatever fish story the old man at the gas station had fed him.

He felt like a fool for even remotely believing in anything that crazy old codger had spouted.

"I should have known he was playing me," frowned Miguel.

He drove on this clearly restored road toward whatever was ahead, passing the first of the road signs, that road sign on his immediate right.

The first sign was all white with the figure of "Fancy Joe" on the left side of it.

Fancy Joe was a cartoon man in a dapper black tux and red bowtie, his short-cut blond hair slicked up and back in that iconic '50s style, his dress shoes a gleaming black in the late-day sun. The words "Do you know Joe?" were doled out in a curvy red font right next to him.

"No, I don't know Joe," smirked Miguel.

He didn't need to know Joe to know Joe had way too much money and time on his hands, two very important things Miguel had never had.

"I don't want to know Joe, either," he finished.

The next road sign came up a minute later, this time on the left side of the road. This sign was nearly identical to the first one but with some minor differences. Fancy Joe had both hands out with both index fingers pointing down toward the road, and the sign read, "Joe knows you."

"Joe doesn't know me," smirked Miguel. "Even I don't know me."

A third road sign popped up into view on his right, but this one was a little…odd.

The third road sign had a black background, not white, and it portrayed the full face of Fancy Joe, a weird grin plastered all over the mascot's clean-cut, cartoon face. The lettering on the sign was in bold, white, block caps to stand out against the black background, that ivory lettering centered beneath Joe's oddly-grinning face, and it read, "JOE WATCHES. JOE WAITS."

Miguel had nothing to say about this one. The sign was too weird from him to comment upon, even if he was only commenting to himself. Nevertheless, the strangeness of it, the sheer oddness of nonconformity in picture and word, made him shiver right down to his tan work boots.

He shrugged off that superstitious nonsense, chalking the whole thing up to a terrible marketing campaign. The '50s were a different time, so who knew what those people were thinking back then.

Besides, someone had clearly come out here and was in the process of restoring the road and the signs, so it was a good bet they were restoring the factory as well. Perhaps some private company had come out here and bought the land…Miguel had no idea, but things seemed safe enough, so there was no reason not to take this shortcut.

Still, he could feel an oppressiveness, a sensation as if slowly being covered in glue, and this did not sit well with him. Nevertheless, he chalked this up to even more superstition, so he quieted his own mind, a stillness that acted as a wall against primal fear.

He saw her walking on the right side of the road after that brief interlude of stifling silence for himself, and the act of simply seeing another human being, no matter how mundane such an action was, perked him up by an infinite measure.

The young lady walking along the dirt and scrub grass on the right side of the road was walking toward the direction he had come from, but what she was doing out here on this supposedly abandoned road, or better yet, what she was doing out here alone, he did not know.

He slowed down to check her out. Normally, he wouldn't give a stranger the time of day while on the road—it was simply too dangerous—but she seemed harmless enough.

The young white woman in question had short-cut hair, that hair clearly dyed to a raven black, with streaks of dark crimson in her bangs. That look stood out because it was edgy without the edge…Most girls he knew like that had fully-dyed hair with a nose ring between their nostrils. Facial piercings were popular anymore, but this young lady had none that he could see from this distance.

She wore a black T-shirt that held some jagged white lettering and a picture of some death-metal band, and this look was accented by her black cargo jeans, the kind with the extra pockets along the legs and bottom.

She also wore a pair of black boots much like his own tan ones, black outdoorsman boots meant for hiking or perhaps work, so her feet probably weren't suffering in this terrain like they would have from ordinary sneakers.

Once again, he normally wouldn't have stopped for anyone, and he was going to keep on driving—he had only slowed down to take a closer look—but she waved her hands at him in what appeared to be an effort to get him to stop.

He really needed to keep driving, because the clock was ticking on reaching his family before Isabella's wedding, but if his family had taught him anything, it was to help those in need if he could.

Besides…she was built like an hourglass with fairly big boobs underneath that T-shirt, and she was cute in the face.

He felt a momentary twinge of guilt for thinking those last thoughts, but he was also human, so he slowly drove to a halt as he pulled up next to her.

The young woman walked around to the driver's-side window, and Miguel rolled down his window to talk to her. The weather was fairly nice out here for mid-to-late spring, but he'd had the windows up anyway, if only for his own privacy.

"Hi!" smiled the young lady.

"Hello," said Miguel in awkward reply.

He was not particularly good with girls, but he wanted to be.

"Ummm…I'm trying to get to the plant up ahead, but my ride ditched me," said the young woman. "Could you give me a ride? The factory's just up ahead."

This young lady had to be around his own age, in her early twenties, and she was friendly, so Miguel had no issues with giving her an equally-friendly lift. He probably wouldn't have done this for—oh—a man, but he pushed down those selfish thoughts and did not dwell on them.

"Sure," smiled Miguel.

He realized he was grinning like a fool, and he tried to suppress that stupid grin, but "chasing tail" was not something he was accomplished in. The thought of anything occurring between him and this young woman was incredibly stupid and unrealistic, but it was still there, and he could not ignore it. Besides…Isabella would understand if he were a little late. He had a little bit of time he could waste.

"Hop in," said Miguel. "I'm heading in that direction myself."

It occurred to him that she had been walking in the opposite direction of the plastics plant, but she probably had her reasons for that. He wasn't going to question her decision to go back the way she had come from.

The young woman walked back around the front of Miguel's truck, opened the passenger door, and stepped up to take a seat. She buckled in, looked over at him, and smiled a broad smile.

"I'm Kelly," she said.

"M…Miguel," said Miguel nervously.

This young white girl had flawless skin, shiny almost. He could see the curves of her breasts beneath her black T-shirt, and the shapes of her large nipples were quite obvious as well. It was clear she was not wearing a bra.

Madre de Dios, she was definitely out of his league. He found his features to be a combination of rugged and awkward, though he did not consider himself ugly. Even so, there was still a chance…They were around the same age, right?

Of course, he had never dated anyone before, and this was a white girl, so even if he did somehow and by some miracle manage to hook up with her, his family would…

These thoughts were stupid. He needed to focus.

"Uhhh…you said the plant is just up ahead?" he asked. "I'm actually heading to the interstate."

"Oh, that's okay," smiled this "Kelly." "You can just drop me off at the plant."

"Oh…" replied Miguel, but he could not fully hide the disappointment in his voice.

Well, so much for any stupid thoughts of hooking up with some random hitcher…Oh, well. Still, he could make conversation with her. That was always nice.

He thought no more on it.

He put the truck in drive, pushed in on the clutch, and they were off.

His new passenger wasted no time in starting conversation, so there was no awkward silence, and Miguel had absolutely no problem with that. He didn't mind the conversation anyway. It was better than not talking at all.

"Yeah, my friends and I were going to investigate the old Jepson plant," said Kelly. "We have our own channel, *Witches and Ghosts*. The others bailed out at the last second, though. They got a 'bad feeling' and bolted. They never went past the south entrance. What a bunch of cowards."

"Uhhh…yeah," he said, unsure of how to answer that.

"I decided to go it alone just to check the place out," said Kelly in a confident tone. "I've tried to call them I don't know how many times, but my phone isn't getting any reception out here…This must be a dead zone."

She fumbled around in the front right pocket of her black cargo pants and pulled out a small red flip phone. The thing was a veritable dinosaur anymore with the advent of smartphones, but Miguel couldn't even afford a flip phone, so at least she had some kind of phone. That was a step above him.

In fact, he had to use a friend's phone for family calls, but that was okay. He'd have money once his career was up and running, and that meant finishing his trade school in mechanics. His family sent him just enough money to survive on every month, and he was grateful for that, because it was a lot for them to send…He wasn't really a complainer anyway. Oh, he had his moments, but he was just grateful for what he already had.

Kelly flipped open her dinosaur of a phone but shook her head in disappointment.

"Still no service," she said unhappily. "I guess connection just sucks out here, you Joe?"

"Yeah," said Miguel, but honestly, he had no phone anyway, so it didn't really matter.

He could see a building complex in the distance. Apparently, they were arriving at Kelly's destination far faster than Miguel had anticipated.

"That's it," nodded Kelly. "That's the old Jepson plant. They say it's been hidden here since the '50s, but we couldn't find any records on it. We filmed my interview with an old man at a gas station, and he had a few colorful things to say, so I knew investigating here was the right call. That old guy was spooked about the possibility of us Joeing up here, though. Let me tell you, he was a strange one, you Joe?"

"Yeah…" said Miguel, but then he thought better about it. "Wait…What?"

"If I had known those losers were going to ditch me," continued Kelly, "there's Joe way I would have trusted them with this. I should have Joewn. Anyway, here we are."

Miguel shook his head a couple of times. He was not sure if she was playing him or if he was just tired. He could have sworn she had replaced some words with "Joe," but that didn't make any sense…

He was probably just tired.

He drove down the main drag of this complex, but the buildings here did not look "abandoned." They looked normal, untouched by time, though he could not see any people in the immediate vicinity.

Yeah, it was clear now that someone had bought this land and had restored the factory.

They drove for a bit past large factory buildings coupled with smaller buildings of unknown purpose, but Kelly had him stop before one particularly huge building with giant, off-white, concrete, cylindrical stacks protruding from the center of it, like what you would see at a power plant. Of course, Miguel had no idea what a power plant looked like, but he had an image in his head of their likeness, so that was good enough.

"Yep, right here," smiled Kelly.

Miguel put the truck in park and gave her a nervous smile in return.

"Aww, you're such a good Samaritan, Miguel," said Kelly. "I think you deserve a reward."

"I do?" asked Miguel.

He had no idea what this was about.

"Yep," nodded the young woman. "We can park here for a bit. You don't have to run the engine…We can talk a little."

"Oh…" said Miguel in slight surprise.

This was interesting. He did not know what she wanted, but…he was willing to give her some time.

He turned off the engine, put the key in his left jeans pocket, sat back, and gave her his full attention.

"Roll down your window," nodded Kelly. "Let's get some fresh air in here. Let's enjoy each other's company for a few minutes."

Miguel felt his heart flutter as he rolled down his window. This was definitely getting interesting.

He once again turned his full attention back upon her, because this was kind of exciting.

Kelly stuffed her flip phone back into her top cargo pocket and shone him a devilish grin. That grin surprised him a bit, mainly because he did not know the meaning behind it.

"Okay," he said nervously. "What do you want to talk about?"

"You seem like a good little Christian boy, Miguel," grinned Kelly. "Are you a good little Christian boy?...Don't answer that, because I already Joe the answer. I can tell you're a good little Christian boy."

He did not know how to respond to that.

"I…uhhh…" he trailed.

"Personally, I'm as naughty as they get," continued the young woman. "I don't see anything wrong with being expressive in my sexuality…and…I can tell that's what you really want, Miguel. It's written all over your face…I can tell, you Joe."

He gave an anxious laugh and shrugged. He really didn't know what to do with this kind of conversation.

"Does little Miguel want a treat for helping out naughty, naughty Kelly?" asked the young woman in a condescending tone, her lips puckering for added effect.

"Uhhh…" said Miguel nervously.

He really had no idea where this was going, but whatever this was, he was definitely intrigued.

"I…I guess," said Miguel. "What…kind of…treat…are we talking about?"

He'd drawled out those words, because he had an electric excitement running through him now. His hands were shaking, because he was truly hoping this was leading to something more.

"You're too moral, too sexually ethical," said Kelly. "You're a good little boy, aren't you? I can tell, so…you can touch my boobs, Miguel. You can feel me up…That's what you want, isn't it? I Joe it's what you need."

"Excuse me?" asked Miguel.

He felt his cheeks burn with an inner fire. This was…unexpected. He had hoped it would be something like this, but that hope was your average guy's unrealistic, inane fantasy, not reality. He'd never dealt with anything like this before…It stumped him into frozen silence.

"Come on, don't be shy," said Kelly. "I've got pretty big boobs, and I Joe you want to touch them…I knew that the moment you looked at me…

"You need to get hard, Miguel. You need to get nice and stiff in order to loosen up those nasty morals that are holding you back…Just reach over and feel them, Miguel. I'm not wearing a bra…You can run your fingers over my nipples. They're nice and perky right now. You can pull them, feel what they're like…Besides, I like it when my nipples are pulled…Come on, touch my boobs, Christian boy, and I'll give you an even better treat."

Miguel had no idea what to do or what to say. Perhaps this was how white girls flirted, or perhaps this was just Kelly's way of starting something more, something Miguel had only briefly fantasized about. Nevertheless, he was no fool. He was not passing up this opportunity.

"I…uhhh…I…Okay…" he stammered.

He awkwardly unbuckled his seatbelt as Kelly unbuckled hers.

She turned to face him and puffed out her chest in expectation.

He had never done this before, but she clearly wanted it, so who was he to judge? This was like a rite of passage for him anyway…Oh, he was definitely telling the guys at school about this.

He slowly reached over and gently cupped both hands beneath her ample, braless breasts.

It only took him a few seconds to realize that, not only was something wrong, something was very, *very* wrong.

Her rather large breasts felt hard and smooth, like hanging gourds, and her nipples, though erect, were as hard and as firm as the flesh of the breasts he was cupping. It was as if her breasts were entirely fake, because he was pretty sure they were supposed to be soft and pliant.

"What the fu…" began Miguel, but that expletive died in his throat as he looked up at her face.

"Don't you Joe all perverts go to Hell, Miguel?" asked the young woman.

She was grinning at him, a huge smile filled with perfect teeth, but her face was shiny and smooth as if coated in plastic, as if *she* were plastic, all of her, that plastic vibrantly colored with a semblance of life that was uncanny, a shock and disturbance of sanity that froze Miguel in place.

Even her perfect teeth looked like little alabaster plastic pegs lined up beneath her crimson plastic lips, but it was her dark, shiny, plastic eyes that disturbed him the most. Those plastic orbs really terrified him, because they were soulless, empty, like doll's eyes.

He was too stunned to even cry out.

Kelly reached up with her mannequin-like right hand and gripped Miguel's left wrist with a vise-like force that immediately caused him to wince in pain.

"Do you know Joe, Miguel?" she asked. "Joe knows you. Joe waits for little perverts like you. He's always watching, you Joe."

He stared down at the black T-shirt she was wearing. The death-metal logo on it had been replaced by the grinning, eerie face of Fancy Joe, the lettering beneath that cartoon face stating in bold, white, block, capital letters, "JOE KNOWS."

There were no thoughts in his head as Miguel flung open the driver's-side door and launched himself from his own truck. He ripped his left wrist out of her firm grip, for even though she was unnaturally strong, the slick plastic of her "skin" afforded him some escape route, if only due to her surprise from his quick reaction.

He took off toward some buildings across the street, but he didn't make it very far before he heard Kelly's shouting.

"HE'S HERE!" screamed the young woman. "HE'S OVER HERE!"

One person after the next came walking out of the buildings across the street. They were a varied lot, the men dressed in suits and ties, the women in business dresses, some of the men in guard uniforms, a couple in army uniforms, all that clothing dated, their hairstyles dated, all of them white people, all of them plastic in skin and rigid in their walking form.

Miguel turned and ran the opposite direction. The only escape route was toward the large building with the stacks, so he headed for that.

"Where are you Joeing, Miguel!" yelled Kelly. "There's nowhere for perverts like you to Joe! Joe waits, Miguel! Joe watches!"

"Do you know Joe!" came the voices of many people in the distance. "Joe knows you!"

Miguel did not look back as that line of plastic horrors marched in plastic time to their own plastic beat.

He practically slammed into a singular metal door embedded in the brick wall of the large factory building he was escaping to.

By some miracle of fate, the door was not locked, though this was not necessarily a good thing. It occurred to him that he needed to find a way to bar that door as he stepped into the darkness of this old building, so he swiveled on his tan leather work boots and flipped the turn lock on the door the moment he slammed that entrance shut.

He took a moment to stare through the wire-crossed, reinforced glass of a small rectangular window, that window centered at the top of the door. The crowd outside had stopped moving; they had stopped advancing, but they all stood in a perfect stillness, each with shiny plastic skin, each with those weird plastic grins and dead, soulless eyes.

He could see them chanting in unity, the crowd chanting something over and over again, and though he could not read lips, he was certain of what they kept repeating, a certainty born out of a swift and unnatural understanding, that repeated chant ushered forth by so many plastic lips:

"Joe watches. Joe waits. Joe watches. Joe waits. Joe watches. Joe waits…"

His fear of this insanity was not helping. He needed to get his bearings.

Miguel turned to inspect his surroundings.

This place was dark compared to the outside, but there was dim electric lighting shining down from various rectangular lamps mounted on the high ceiling, that ceiling two stories up, those overhead lamps large enough to give light this far down, but how this place even received power or electricity anymore, he had no idea.

There was a brick wall to his left with a set of staggered metal stairs leading up, and to his right were a number of offices with wooden doors and frosted glass across them. He could see lighting in those rooms as well.

He was in some kind of administration area. He had noticed double doors to the left of the door he had entered, three pairs of double doors, but he had chosen the singular door, and…he was probably trapped.

It occurred to him there might be weapons in the offices, maybe even a gun, but he was not sure how much damage he could do to these plastic people…Those walking mannequins looked tough, not to mention the sheer strength Kelly had possessed while grabbing him.

The situation looked bleak.

Of course, there was always the stairs up…

"Who are you?" came a small voice from off to his right.

Miguel let out a startled shriek of surprise, but then he came to his senses upon viewing the source of that voice, or rather, the child that had spoken it.

A boy of eleven or twelve stood before Miguel, but where this kid had come from, Miguel had no idea.

This little towheaded white boy with blue eyes was dressed in a nice brown dress jacket and brown slacks with black dress shoes on his feet. He had a little black bowtie on his white, button-up dress shirt, and this formal style of dress, coupled with the boy's sudden appearance, caused Miguel to take a step back.

"Where did you come from!" gasped Miguel.

"I'm stuck here, just like you," frowned the boy.

"Who are you?" asked Miguel.

He was feeling a little braver now, because there was an aura about this boy, a sort of light that did not give off the oppressive feeling of impending doom Miguel had felt outside of this building. In fact, the mere presence of this boy calmed Miguel somewhat, though he did not know why.

"I'm Peter," said the boy. "My dad is the lead scientist here…or at least, he was. He…died."

"Oh…" said Miguel.

Honestly, he did not know how to reply to that.

"Now…who are you?" asked the boy. "I asked you first anyway."

"I'm Miguel," said Miguel. "Do you know what's going on out there, Peter? These people are…I don't know what they are, but they're dangerous! You have to get out of here!"

"I've tried," shrugged Peter. "I can't go out there, or they'll get me, so I'm stuck in here. They won't come in here…This is where my dad worked…upstairs. The plastic people don't come in here for some reason."

"Upstairs?" asked Miguel. "What's upstairs?"

"That's the overlook," said Peter. "That's where my dad and the other scientists watched over the experiments. My dad called it a 'control room.' There's a big window up there that looks down on the experiment room. There's some kind of machinery down there, but I don't know what any of it does."

"So this building isn't for plastics?" asked Miguel.

"Uh, uh," said Peter as he shook his head no. "Not this half. This building is really big, because one side is for plastics and the other is for the experiments, but like I said, I don't know what the experiments were for. I just know that…something went wrong, and everybody died."

"Wait…You're telling me that old man was right?" asked Miguel.

"What old man?" asked Peter.

"Never mind," frowned Miguel. "It doesn't matter…We have to find a way out of here, Peter."

He could sense this kid wasn't a threat, and if this boy wasn't a threat, then Miguel needed to get him out of here. Miguel was not the kind of person who would leave anyone behind, especially a child. That simply didn't sit right with him.

"I've tried," frowned Peter. "I've snuck around out there, but the plastic people are everywhere. The ones who didn't die during the experiment became the plastic people.

"Anybody that comes here? The plastic people grab them and take them to the plastics vats. They dip them in the molten plastic, and then those people become like them, like plastic…I know; I've seen it happen."

"So that girl out there?" asked Miguel. "The one I picked up? She said her name was Kelly…Was she—"

"I know her," said Peter. "I followed them when they grabbed her off the road. They took off all her clothes and threw her in a vat…She screamed as she went in, and her skin melted, and…and…her face…I ran…I…don't want to talk about it."

"But she wasn't like that when I first met her," said Miguel in confusion. "She looked like a normal person."

"That's how they get you," frowned Peter. "They can disguise themselves as normal people…but they don't come in here. That's how I knew you weren't one of them."

"Wait…" said Miguel as he shook his head in even more confusion. "Kelly…She said she was shooting a video, that she had her own channel. She said she filmed that old man at the gas station…"

Something burned its way into Miguel's forebrain, something the old man had said that screamed at him with an illogical sense of chronology.

"Wait a minute…" he breathed. "That old man at the gas station said something about a missing girl who did internet videos, but he said she went missing years ago…That doesn't make any sense…unless…No, wait…The old man said the accident happened in the 19…No, that can't be right..."

This was thoroughly confounding him. He had a theory as to what was going on, and that theory was pure science fiction, but if he was right and that theory turned out to be true, then everything had just gotten so much worse. Nevertheless, he had to know.

"Peter, what year is it?" he asked.

"Why would you ask me that?" asked the boy in visible confusion. "It's 1958."

Miguel felt the blood drain from his face. Apparently, his theory was not so much a theory as it was reality…Time stood still here. It certainly explained the way the road and the buildings looked…No one was rebuilding out here, no. No, nothing had actually aged.

"What's wrong?" asked Peter. "You look funny."

Miguel shook his head and steeled his resolve. He needed to get both himself and Peter out of here, and right away. His truck was right outside, and he had the keys on him, so all he needed was a way to get to his truck…or fight his way to it.

"Do you know if there are any weapons in here, Peter?" asked Miguel. "My truck is right outside. If I can get us to it, we can drive out of here."

This caught Peter's attention. The boy immediately perked up at the slim chance of escape.

"The army had some soldiers here before the accident," nodded Peter. "They were here along with the security guards. There's a room upstairs with some rifles in it…My dad told me I couldn't mess with them, so I never did, but…but they're still up there!"

A rifle would do. A rifle could possibly have enough punch to kill some of those things.

Miguel bent down and grabbed both of Peter's shoulders.

"That's good!" said Miguel in excitement. "Let's go get a rifle!...I hope there's ammunition we can use."

"There is," smiled Peter. "The rifles are already loaded. My dad called them M14s. They're army rifles."

"Great!" grinned Miguel. "Let's get one and get out of here!"

Peter grinned in return and then led Miguel up the staggered metal stairs to the "overlook." A heavy metal door barred their way, but it proved to be unlocked, which was good, because a rifle was pretty much the only plan Miguel had at the moment.

They walked into the control room, and Miguel took a moment to look around.

It was the bodies that gave him pause.

There were desiccated, mummified bodies scattered around the room, all lying in various positions on the grey-tiled floor, save one, that singular corpse slumped over a large desk with various, very-dated electronic equipment built across it. There was a large window spanning the north wall, and Miguel could look out that window to see the lab room below.

The bodies around the room were still wearing suits and white lab coats, though there was no dust or signs of damage due to time upon their clothes. Miguel did not know what had happened to them during this "accident," but whatever had happened, it had not been good.

He had been to funerals before, so he had seen dead bodies, but he had never seen dead bodies like this…definitely not this many, either.

"Peter…what happened in here?" he asked.

"I don't know," shrugged the boy. "The alarms went off, and then my dad shoved me in the back room over there. That room is where the guns are. My dad shoved me in there and then locked the door. That's the only thing I can remember about the accident."

"Uh, huh," said Miguel. "Well…let's get that rifle and get out of here."

Peter nodded toward another metal door, this one across the control room at the east wall.

"It's that room over there," said Peter. "I can't go in there, though…I just can't go in there again. I don't want to."

"It's okay," said Miguel. "I'll go in and get the rifle. I can understand if you don't want to go in there."

"There's something bad in there, Miguel," warned Peter in a near whisper. "I can feel it. That's why I never go in there, so…be careful."

"Bad?" asked Miguel. "Oh, boy. It's always something, isn't it?"

He closed his eyes, shook his head once, and steeled himself again. He opened his eyes a moment later and gave Peter a serious stare.

"I've got to get that gun," he said firmly. "Bad or not, we need that rifle, so…I'm going in."

Even so, Peter's warning stuck with Miguel as he maneuvered around dead bodies to get to the east door, but he had to ignore that warning…He didn't have a choice.

He pushed down the handle of the door, but the singular metal door was thoroughly locked.

"Peter, this door is locked," said Miguel. "Did you lock it when you left it?"

The boy shrugged and gave Miguel a clueless look.

"I think my dad has the keys to it," said Peter. "He's over there…at the console."

Miguel looked over toward the singular, mummified body that lay slumped over the control-room console desk.

"*Ooooh*, great," he breathed. "Time to get the keys…Okay…I can do this…"

He stepped around bodies again as he walked over to the console desk. He gingerly pulled back the corpse's lab coat, but then he felt the weight of something in the deceased man's left coat pocket.

"Sorry, Peter's Dad," he murmured.

He pulled forth a ring of keys, breathed out a sigh of relief at their welcomed sight, and then walked back to the east door. It took him a bit of fumbling to find the right key, but one of them turned over the lock, and that was all he needed.

Miguel paused and took in a deep breath. He needed to be careful opening this door. If there really was something bad in this room, he needed to be prepared to immediately slam the door shut and lock it.

He released his held breath and turned the door handle.

"I'm going to open the door now," he said firmly. "Peter, stay back."

"You don't have to tell me twice," said the boy.

Miguel opened the door and quickly scanned the room, but honestly, he wished he hadn't.

This room was actually a small armory, with working electric lighting displaying the room's contents, so there was no issue of finding or turning on a light. There were racks of rifles along the south and west sides of the room and metal lockers and lockboxes along the north and east walls, so there were definitely guns in here, but that was not the issue.

"Don't look, Peter," he said gently. "I'll be right back."

"Be careful," said the boy once more.

Miguel stepped into the room and closed the door behind him. He did not want Peter to see what was inside.

Miguel walked forward and inspected the small body lying on its side next to the south-wall gun racks. The boy's mummified body was still dressed in a nice brown dress jacket and brown slacks with black dress shoes on his feet. That body also had on a little black bowtie with a white, button-up dress shirt, immediately confirming what Miguel had suspected upon first seeing the body.

Peter was a ghost…He had to be.

Miguel shivered all the way down to his work boots. He was terrified of the supernatural, but considering he had not sensed any ill intent from Peter, and considering he'd already escaped those plastic horrors outside, this was par for the course…Besides, he had not changed his mind about escaping with the boy. Maybe getting out of here would allow Peter's soul to rest.

"Madre de Dios," whispered Miguel.

He made the sign of the cross, said a silent prayer, and then grabbed the nearest rifle off the south-wall racks. Peter had been correct; the rifle already had a clip in it, so it was time to go.

He pulled open the armory door and quickly shut it behind him.

"Was there something bad in there?" asked Peter.

"Uhhh…yeah," said Miguel. "It…It doesn't matter. Don't worry about what's in that room…We need to leave. We have to get out of here now, Peter."

"I want to leave, but…" trailed off Peter.

"But what?" asked Miguel.

"It's just that…there's something else out there," replied Peter. "There's something else out there other than the plastic people."

"Something else out there?" asked Miguel. "What else could possibly be out there?"

"I don't know, but my dad did," said the boy. "I know he did. Whatever it is…it's worse than the plastic people."

"Worse than them?" asked Miguel. "How do you know?"

"I've listened to my dad's last recording," said Peter. "You should hear it before we go. I know I said I didn't know what happened, but that wasn't really true. Whatever is out there?...It killed everyone in here."

"*Ooookaaay*," replied Miguel with wide eyes.

He did not like the sound of that.

Peter took the initiative this time. The boy walked over to his dad's body, reached past the corpse's withered and mummified right hand, and pressed a large red button. A recorded message picked up after that from a speaker in the console, a message that had to be the dead man's last words.

"There's no time left…" came the recorded voice amidst the crackle of some kind of interference. *"We succeeded in opening the portal. The tunnel to the other universe is stable but has merged with our reality…<Crackle>…Can't close it…<Crackle>…Something came through…Dear God, it resided in-between…*

"<Crackle>…It's been waiting, watching…<Crackle>…It's too powerful…<Crackle>…Something terrible, horrific…<Crackle>…My God, it's merged with Fancy…<Static whine>…<Crackle>…Get help…<Crackle>…It's killing us…<Static whine>…Feels like I'm drowning…<Crackle>…Must protect Peter…<Crackle>…Can't close the portal…<Static whine>…God save us all…<Static whine and message ends>."

Miguel felt the blood drain from his face yet again. This situation had just gotten a whole lot worse.

"Tunnel to another universe?" he asked himself. "Something terrible and horrific? What does that even mean? What in the hell did these people do?"

He shook his head, took in yet another deep breath, and steadied himself again.

"Doesn't matter," he said in stark resignation. "We have to get out of here, and we have to go now…We have to go…both of us. I'm getting you out of here, Peter."

"Yeah," nodded Peter. "Let's get out of here."

Miguel clutched his new rifle and led Peter out of the control room. They made their way down the metal steps to the only currently-known entry and exit to this part of the building.

Miguel took a quick scan of the outside through the wire-crossed square window at the top of the door, surmised there was no one in sight, and nodded once.

"Let's go," he said in a shaky voice.

He did not know where all of the plastic people had gone, but he could clearly see his truck, and Kelly was no longer in it. The street was empty, and the truck was clear, so…

He pulled down on the handle, yanked open the door, and both of them ran for the truck.

He ran around the front of his truck and yanked open the driver's-side door just as the plastic people emerged from the buildings across the street.

"Get in the truck, Peter!" yelled Miguel.

"Joe watches. Joe waits," chanted the crowd of plastic horrors. "Joe watches. Joe waits. Joe watches. Joe waits…"

Thankfully, Miguel had fired a rifle before. Guns were as ubiquitous as candy in this country, so he had no issues as to how to handle a firearm.

He swung the rifle up into a firing position, aimed for a man in a security-guard uniform, and then pulled the trigger. There was a loud "BANG!" as the rifle fired, Miguel felt the kick of the stock against his right shoulder, and then the plastic man he was firing at went down to the asphalt, a good-sized hole in his forehead, right between his eyes.

"Yes!" cried Miguel as an electric pulse of temporary victory surged through him.

And temporary it was. Miguel's goodtime feeling of victory evaporated as the plasticized security guard he had just put down got to his feet and continued walking forward along with the other plastic people. The man still had the hole in his head, right between his eyes, but this did not slow him down in the slightest.

"Change of plan!" yelled Miguel.

He launched himself into the driver's seat just as Peter was climbing into the passenger's seat. Miguel set the rifle in-between them both, buckled in as quickly as he could—record time, in fact—pulled his truck key from his left jeans pocket, and then jammed the key into the ignition. He turned that key, balanced the clutch and the gas, and heard the rumble of the engine a second later.

The plastic people were much faster than he had anticipated. These once-people of plastic sheen and uncanny grins were at Miguel's light-green truck just as Miguel shifted into first and hit the gas.

Naturally and of course, he had left the window open.

One of them, the fastest one out of the group, a tall man with brown hair, this plastic man dressed in a grey business suit with a red tie and white dress shirt, managed to reach the truck. This horrifying living mannequin grabbed ahold of Miguel's truck door just as Miguel was pulling forward.

Miguel hit the gas in order to keep this plastic-coated terror from reaching inside, and the man's black dress shoes dragged along asphalt as he clung to the open door-window.

"Do you know Joe!" cried the plastic horror. "Joe knows you!"

"Miguel, the rifle!" cried Peter.

Miguel steadied the wheel, let go of it, his foot still on the gas, reached over, and grabbed the rifle with both hands.

He quickly flipped the rifle over and tagged the plastic man in the face with the butt end of it, once, twice, and then a third time.

"I don't…know…Joe!" yelled Miguel, each section of that sentence matching in time with each strike of the rifle.

The third strike did the trick. This plastic perversion of a man popped free of the door and rolled onto passing blacktop as Miguel dropped the rifle in his own lap and struggled to steer the truck.

The truck weaved from one side of the road to the other, but Miguel managed to steady the vehicle without crashing it, and then they were on their way…They were on their way.

"Yeah!" yelled Miguel. "Yeah!...Let's get the hell out of here!"

He moved the rifle in his lap to the space in-between himself and Peter, and then he breathed out a well-deserved sigh of relief.

He hit the gas and drove north, that direction leading up a lazy incline that blocked the horizon, and this time he wasn't going to stop for anything.

"We did it!" he said excitedly. "We did it, Peter!...Peter?...Peter?"

He stared over at the boy's face, but Peter had gone as white as a sheet, his lips slightly parted, his blue eyes widened in sudden fear.

"Yo, little man," said Miguel. "What's up? What's wrong?"

"We can't go this way," breathed out Peter. "We have to turn around."

Of course, there was no way Miguel was turning the truck around.

"What?" he asked. "What are you talking about? We can't turn around…Those things are back there. We have to keep going…this…way…"

He turned his vision back upon the road, but the road sign on his right made all of his thoughts trail off into scattered nothing.

The large road sign held the cartoon face of Fancy Joe upon a black background, but that face was grinning from ear to ear, the eyebrows slanted downwards as a menacing accent to a clearly malevolent stare. The words "WHERE ARE YOU GOING, MIGUEL?" were splayed out across the bottom of the sign in large, white, block, capital letters.

Miguel could feel an oppressive cloud settle over him, similar to the dark aura he had first felt upon driving down this accursed road, but this time it was stronger, much stronger.

"We have to go this way…" breathed Miguel as he continued to drive forward in a stupid daze.

He couldn't stop now. They had to get out of here.

But Peter had a different take on the situation.

"You're going the wrong way!" cried Peter. "Besides, he knows, Miguel! He knows! We have to go back!"

"I…I can't…" stammered Miguel. "We can't go back now! Those plastic people will be there waiting! We can't turn around, Peter! Can't you see that!"

They drove up the hill that had previously blocked the horizon, and then they hit the top of that hill, but Miguel let off the gas until the truck rolled to an eventual halt.

And with good reason. There was a giant plastic statue of Fancy Joe, fancy tux and all, straddling the road, a large road sign clutched within the statue's left hand, the thing's grinning white teeth, dark eyes, and blonde, plastic, slicked-back hair all gleaming brightly in the late-day sun.

That choking, cloying feeling of suffocation came over Miguel like a fetid pool of dank perfume. It was so strong now that he felt as if he were drowning despite the lack of a single drop of water in sight.

Miguel's eyes wandered upwards to view the forty-foot-tall monstrosity they had to drive beneath.

The road sign in the statue's left hand, this road sign with a great big cartoon eye upon it, read, "I SEE YOU!"

Miguel felt his heart stop as the statue's gigantic eyes pivoted downwards to stare right through him, two great white and dark orbs of painted plastic untouched by the ravages of time.

"Madre de—" started Miguel.

"Drive, Miguel!" screeched Peter.

Miguel hit the gas without thinking, no conscious directive ordering his foot to push the pedal to the truck floor.

Miguel's old, light-green truck sped forward just as the giant right hand of this statue reached down to grab at the vehicle, those huge digits grasping nothing but air as the truck zoomed between the great statue's legs.

Miguel's tan right work boot practically punched a hole through the truck floor as the vehicle's speedometer needle danced upwards in a slow progression toward actual speed.

He checked the rearview mirror and could see the statue turn, and then that enormous plastic likeness of Fancy Joe Jepson began its pursuit, those huge, black, plastic dress shoes thumping out a massive beat in tandem with its massive legs.

Miguel cried out a litany of prayer in Spanish as he struggled to keep his sanity. That feeling of suffocation was so cloying now, it was drowning him with the sensation of being overwhelmed by something sweet and deadly at the same time.

Miguel looked up into the rearview mirror. The grinning face of Kelly stared back at him from the rear window.

"Miguel, LOOK OUT!" screeched Peter.

The back window of the truck, that glass thick enough to withstand some serious punishment, shattered anyway as Kelly's plastic fist punched through it.

Miguel fought to keep the truck from swerving this way and that as Kelly's arm wrapped around his chest, that plastic hand groping for anything it could find to grip.

She had been hiding in the truck bed. She had been hiding in the truck bed, and he had not thought to check it beforehand.

Miguel reached up and struggled with that insanely powerful arm with his own right hand as he kept his left hand on the wheel.

"Touch my boobs, Miguel!" yelled Kelly from behind him. "You Joe you want to!"

He swerved hard to avoid a crashed, burnt-out car in the center of the road, and then he avoided bodies, a couple of them, desiccated, mummified things with the distinct look of more modern clothing than the 1950s had ever had to offer.

There were more crushed, crashed, or overturned vehicles ahead, SUVs, trucks, and cars of different makes and models, some with mummified bodies draped over broken windows and shattered windshields.

No wonder no one had ever made it out of here. Fancy Joe had been busy.

Miguel swerved this way and that to avoid crashed vehicles, bodies, and debris as he desperately struggled against Kelly's insanely powerful grip. The girl was way too strong, way, way too powerful for that strength to be natural, but Miguel was thoroughly juiced to the max on adrenaline, so he had some defense against her, though he could not pry her from him, try as he might.

The truck weaved onto dirt and scrub grass on the right side of the road, only to cross that blacktop to weave in dirt and scrub grass on the left.

"You can't Joe this way, Miguel!" cried Kelly. "There's nowhere for perverts like you to Joe!"

Miguel shrieked as a burnt-out car, one he had previously swerved around, came crashing down on the truck's immediate right...

Fancy Joe Jepson was throwing them now.

The great statue chasing them scooped up yet another vehicle in Miguel's rearview, this time an SUV. It softballed that heap in one smooth huck, and the truck would have been struck, flattened even, but Kelly's terrible grip had found Miguel's short black hair.

Miguel cried out in pain as his head pulled to the right, and this forced him to accidently turn the wheel. The truck swerved to the right, and the tossed SUV crashed down where they had just been.

"Touch my boobs, Miguel!" yelled Kelly. "Pull my nipples! Pull on my perky nipples, you pervert! Don't you Joe all perverts Joe to Hell!"

Miguel swerved his truck to the left and crossed the road again, this time avoiding someone else's overturned truck. He swerved just in time, right as a derelict scrapheap of a car crashed down from the sky at the point they had just left, that car smashing into the overturned truck Miguel had just avoided.

"Joe knows!" cried Kelly. "He Joes you're a pervert, Miguel, so pull my perky nipples, little Christian boy! You've already touched them once! Pull my nipples and Joe to Hell!"

She had a firm grip on his short black hair, and that hurt like mad, mad enough for him to get mad. He swore a storm of curses in Spanish and then switched those curses to English.

"Get off me, you crazy plastic bi—!" yelled Miguel.

"Take the rifle, Miguel!" cried Peter in return, cutting short Miguel's own expletive.

Peter had propped up the rifle between them both, that barrel right beneath Kelly's shiny plastic face, Peter's small hands steadying the firearm as best he could.

The young woman turned her dead, soulless, doll's eyes upon Peter, but then those dead eyes widened in surprise.

"You!" she shrieked. "Joe's been looking fo—!"

Miguel let go of Kelly's arm, reached over with his right hand, and mashed down on the M14's trigger with his index and middle finger. There was a deafening "BANG!" that reverberated around the truck cab, a large bullet hole magically appeared in the roof, the rifle fell over onto Peter's lap, and Miguel's hearing took a solid vacation for several seconds.

He looked over at the young woman he had previously, though briefly, favored. The round had struck her in the face at pointblank range, and half of the plastic skin on that face, the right half, was missing. Miguel could see muscle and tendons beneath Kelly's plastic right eye, and those muscles and tendons were most certainly *not* plastic.

The young woman's plastic eyes rolled up in the whites as she let go of Miguel's hair and pitched backwards into the truck bed.

Miguel had swerved to the right as he was pulling the trigger of the rifle, but the sudden release of Kelly's plastic grip caused Miguel to overcompensate and swerve back to the left, just in time to narrowly avoid yet another thrown, derelict vehicle.

Miguel could see a tunnel ahead, a tunnel of solid and thick concrete burrowed into a distant hill, and the accursed road they were on led straight toward it.

"That's the way out!" he cried.

His right foot was practically married to his gas pedal at this point. Nevertheless, he had lost speed from all of the swerving he'd had to do, so it was catchup time.

The huge statue of Fancy Joe continued to charge, somehow keeping pace with the truck, that giant of horrendous plastic still pursuing them, even after missing with every burnt-out vehicle it could reach.

Miguel felt nothing but pain as that suffocating feeling began to overwhelm him. He stared down at his swiftly chapping hands, the tanned-skin slowly desiccating, mummifying, just like all of the corpses he had seen in this freakshow of insanity.

"What is…this!" he gasped.

"It's Joe!" yelled Peter. "He's killing you! You have to get away!"

But there was one more obstacle in their way.

Off the road ahead, on the right, was a dead semi, the burnt-out fuel tank it had been hauling overturned and stretched out across the road, but that burnt-out fuel tank was also broken in two, leaving a small space of road in-between the pieces, a little stretch that he could possibly squeeze through…

"Got to…make it!" gasped out Miguel.

His skin felt like withered leather, his eyes felt like dehydrated grapes, and his lungs felt like they were filled with sand.

He could see in the driver's-side mirror the image of the great statue's left hand swinging downwards as the sign it carried plummeted with it.

Miguel had previously lost speed by swerving this way and that in a desperate attempt to maintain control of the truck, but now he jammed his foot to the floor, shifting up, slamming that pedal to the metal.

His truck squeezed through the opening left behind by the shattered rig's fuel tank, and the mirrors on each side of his old and faithful light-green truck came off as both of those mirrors were roughly torn away…

And then they were past the derelict hunk of junk, home free were it not for the huge plastic nightmare still chasing them.

Fancy Joe Jepson's road sign came smashing down behind them, only to shatter into wooden splinters all over the asphalt. Fancy Joe, himself, toppled over as his huge right shoe caught upon the rig's burnt-out and split fuel tank, and then that monstrosity of plastic merged with otherworldly horror crashed to the road to slide face first as Miguel's truck zoomed onward in mocking defiance.

Miguel felt the killing, cloying vise of that oppressive suffocation leave him all at once. He took in a deep gasp of air and braced himself as the truck entered the tunnel within the hill, noting as well that his tanned skin looked healthy once more.

Fancy Joe wasn't getting him…No, he was the one that got away.

"Did it," he said as he breathed out a sigh of relief. "It looks like I am a good little Christian boy after all, Kelly."

Miguel flipped on his headlights and drove through the tunnel until the exit appeared, but something was off. He drove the truck out into full night, his headlights marking the way forward.

"It was just daytime!" he hissed out.

He had just finished that bit of exasperation when he both felt and heard the front tire blow on the driver's side, that tire right beneath him. He cursed under his breath so that Peter couldn't hear that particular expletive, but Miguel sensed they were both safe now, so there was no reason to keep driving on a destroyed tire.

He slowed down, pulled over, and stepped out of his truck.

Of course, his spare was in the truck bed.

After all the craziness that had just occurred, he was still on edge, still paranoid, and he needed to know if Kelly was still in the back of the truck. Thankfully, there were telephone poles and power lines nearby, and there was one lonely lamp upon the nearest pole that shone the saving grace of its light down upon them, probably to mark the entrance of the tunnel he'd just left.

He turned and could see the "KEEP OUT!" and "DANGER!" signs around the tunnel, but he didn't need to heed that warning. He wasn't going back in there.

Miguel wanted to peer over the side of his truck in order to see if Kelly was still in the truck bed, but he was somewhat afraid to, and the fact that it was suddenly night outside wasn't helping his lack of courage in the least.

"Why is it night already!" he said in exasperation.

Peter appeared at his side, the boy popping into existence without warning.

Miguel held in a shriek and tried to compose himself, his left leg in the air out of an instinctual preparation to run.

"I told you not to go this way," frowned Peter.

"What?" asked Miguel. "What do you mean?"

He could not question the boy further for clarification, as their conversation was suddenly interrupted.

Kelly crawled over the side of the truck bed, only to fall to her side and roll over the asphalt onto her back. Her skin was still plastic, and the right side of her face was still devoid of that fake skin, but there was something else wrong with her, something seriously wrong.

"It's Kelly, but—" started Miguel.

"Somebody, help me!" cried out Kelly. "I can't see! I'm blind! I can't…Oh, my God, I can't feel anything!"

Miguel felt his heart implode. Despite all that had happened, despite all of the insanity he had just been through, he was not heartless.

It was clear that Kelly had not changed back to her human guise, so he knew something was wrong with her…but he could also tell that this was her true self, the actual Kelly, not the Kelly possessed by Joe. If she had not changed back in physical form, then that meant…

"Is someone there?" asked Kelly. "I can't feel anything! I can't see!"

"You can't save her, Miguel," said Peter softly. "She was dipped in molten plastic. There's nothing you can do."

Miguel walked to the young woman's side, knelt down, and held her plastic body in his arms.

"It's me," he said gently. "It's Miguel."

He stared down at her ruined face of muscle, tendon and plastic, and he couldn't help but shed some tears.

"Miguel?" asked Kelly. "Who are you!...I need help!...You have to call my friends!"

"I'll try," said Miguel, his voice cracking. "I don't have a phone, though."

"Please!" said Kelly. "Please, Miguel! You have to help…me…I can't…see…I can't…feel any…thing…I just…feel…cold…"

Her voice trailed off she rattled out one last gasp.

Her plastic skin flaked off and turned into specks of light, her body vanishing through spontaneous disintegration. Miguel could not hold onto her as he watched Kelly disappear altogether within his arms, her remaining traces scattering upon the night breeze like so much reflective glitter thrown into the wind.

He choked out a slight moan as he wiped at his eyes.

"She didn't deserve that," he said in a shaky voice. "She didn't do anything wrong. It was all that thing's fault. It was all Joe."

"She was already dead, Miguel," said Peter. "She died when they threw her in the plastics vat. The molten plastic killed her…I know, I watched her face melt…She's finally moved on to her next life…She died a long time ago…just like me…"

Miguel turned to see the boy fading out of existence, his body shining with a white light, like the faint glow of a lamp.

"Peter…" said Miguel unhappily.

"It's my turn to go," said the boy. "I understand now…You freed us both, Miguel. You freed Kelly, and you freed me…Joe can't keep us trapped anymore."

"I…I understand," said Miguel, though he was not happy about this fact.

He had wanted Peter's soul to find peace, to be at rest, but now that it was happening, it bothered him. The boy had deserved better, just like Kelly.

Peter's image was rapidly fading.

"Don't worry about me, Miguel," said Peter. "I'm finally free, and so is Kelly, but…I know now it's not 1958 anymore. Time stopped in there, and I lived in a dream…Heck, I didn't even know I was dead. No wonder I didn't want to go in that room."

This made sense to Miguel, but that didn't explain why he had lost several hours of daytime. He could sense something was wrong here, very wrong, and if Peter knew secrets from the other side, then Miguel needed to ask him now before the boy faded out altogether.

"Time didn't stop out here!" choked out Miguel. "It couldn't have, because it's nighttime!...Did time speed up?...Why is it nighttime, Peter! What's going on! Do you know!"

"I warned you not to go this way…" came Peter's ghostly voice.

The boy faded to the point where he was almost entirely see-through, and even his voice sounded distant, far away.

"The Jepson Road is a tunnel to another universe, remember?" came Peter's last words. "You crossed over, and now…now you can't go back…"

He faded out altogether, specks of light where he had once been, like fireflies dancing, and then even those were gone, fading into the night sky like so many spent flecks of ash.

Miguel felt the blood drain from his face a third time as he looked up into the night sky with the sinking horror and slow realization of what Peter had meant by that parting statement. It wasn't the plastic people, the ghost of the little boy, Kelly's terrible death, or the merging of an otherworldly horror with the giant statue of Fancy Joe Jepsen that disturbed him this time.

No, the two moons in the sky did that for him.

#4...THE GIRL

A promotion doesn't necessarily mean "easier."

James O'Rourke reported for duty at the Bureau's Nyx Division. Whatever this "Nyx Division" was, O'Rourke did not know, because his instructions were on an explicit "need-to-know" basis. Nevertheless, he'd been assigned this duty as a promotion, so here he was.

He was dressed in his good black suit, white dress shirt, black tie, and black dress shoes, his official "men-in-black" style, though this was only normal for special occasions in the Bureau. He needed to make a good impression on the first day of his new position, and this was indeed a special occasion for him, if only for him.

"It's simple," said Acting Director Bays. "You go into Room 58, and you watch the subject for the entire time you're in there. The walls, floor, and ceiling are lined with mirrors for security reasons, and there are cameras all over the edges of the ceiling."

O'Rourke had played guard duty for some of the other high-risk prisoners in this building, but he'd never been in this part of the Bureau before.

They walked down a long white hallway until they reached a secure double doorway that was locked with a high-tech laser scanner. Acting Director Bays swiped his identification through the scanner and waited for O'Rourke to do the same.

"This door has state-of-the-art facial-recognition technology," said Bays. "The real protection, however, is beyond it."

The doors slid open to reveal a large elevator lined with mirrors. O'Rourke entered along with the acting director, and the first thing he noticed was the distinct lack of car-call buttons on the car-operating panel, or rather, there was only one button, a small dark-red button marked with a white "B13."

Bays pushed the button, the elevator doors slid shut, and O'Rourke could immediately tell they were headed down.

"As you can see, this elevator is large enough to hold an entire squad if necessary," said Bays in a grim tone. "This shaft goes down thirteen floors. At the bottom of this shaft are three rooms: Room 56, Room 57, and Room 58."

"Three rooms, sir?" asked O'Rourke.

"Three rooms," repeated Bays. "Room 56 is the checkpoint, Room 57 is Monitoring, and Room 58 holds the subject. You've overseen some of the world's worst criminals, men and women who are so dangerous, they have no public identity, and that's why you're here. You've got enough hours logged in now that you're ready to oversee Subject 13."

"Understood, sir," said O'Rourke.

"This elevator only has one button, and it goes down," noted Acting Director Bays. "The elevator is programmed to go up one minute after it hits B13. You have to request the elevator through Room 56, the checkpoint. An armed guard will take the elevator down to retrieve you."

"Affirmative, sir," nodded O'Rourke.

The elevator stopped after their descent, the doors slid open, and they stepped out into a small mirrored room, Room 56.

Two soldiers dressed in black-ops gear awaited their arrival, each one armed with APC9K submachine guns. The soldiers let them pass, and O'Rourke and the acting director once again swiped their identification through another high-tech laser scanner.

They entered the next room, Room 57, this one quite a bit larger than the checkpoint room. This room was also lined with mirrors, but it was the monitoring station that caught O'Rourke's eye. There were a dozen active monitors to watch the next room, a single agent at a metal desk assigned to the task of overseeing them.

O'Rourke peered at the surveillance monitors for the room in question, Room 58. Another agent was watching the subject, but the "subject" within Room 58 looked to be nothing more than a thirteen-year-old girl.

"Subject 13" was a young, skinny, Caucasian girl with long, straight, brown hair, a wafer of a girl with slender arms and legs. She was dressed in a private-school uniform, that uniform complete with a white dress shirt, a dark-blue vest jacket, and a dark-blue skirt. She wore white ankle socks with small black dress shoes, and she was sitting in a simple wooden chair in the middle of the room, another agent staring down at her in solemn silence.

This had to be a joke, some kind of initiation thing for O'Rourke to pass before he was taken to his real assignment.

"The subject is that girl?" snorted O'Rourke. "Seriously?"

"Don't ever underestimate that *thing*," said Bays.

He did not sound like he was joking.

"You don't talk to that thing, you don't even say a *word* while you're in there, and you don't interact with it *at all*," said Bays in a deadly serious tone. "Taylor's shift is up, so you get in there and take his place, and do not…*do not*…take your eyes off that thing."

"*Ooookay*," nodded O'Rourke uncertainly. "Is there something I need to know, sir?"

"The less you know, the better," said Bays. "Frank, Agent Zimmermann, that is, has been here the longest, so we had to move him to monitoring only. The longer you spend time with it, the more chances it has to get inside your head. The best way to combat that is to know as little as possible about it, so you just do as instructed."

"Yes, sir," replied O'Rourke.

"You go in, Taylor will back up slowly, and you'll slide into his place," said Bays. "You don't take your eyes off it. That's how this works…You'll only be in for an hour at a time, and then Jackson will replace you. The shifts rotate in threes, and then Crew 2 comes in to replace Crew 1. We've got three crews and Crew 4 for call-ins. Understood?"

"Yes, sir," said O'Rourke.

"Good," nodded Bays. "This is the top tier, James. Don't screw this up."

He still did not look or sound like he was joking.

O'Rourke did not like the sound of any of this, because if it wasn't a joke, it seemed highly unethical, but he was not one to question orders.

"Agent Zimmermann is on monitor duty," said Bays. "He will unseal the door for you and then seal the door once you and Agent Taylor have switched places. If there's an emergency, he'll instruct you in what to do…The main thing to remember is the core of your training: don't panic. If something goes wrong, whatever you do…don't panic. Good luck, James, and may God watch over you."

"Yes, sir," replied O'Rourke.

Acting Director Bays took his leave, but his ominous briefing left O'Rourke somewhat shaken. O'Rourke had no idea what was going on, but he was not going to shirk his duty, so he collected his wits and waited at the mirrored sliding door that led into Room 58.

O'Rourke walked into the mirrored room as soon as Agent Zimmermann unsealed the door, but this room was tiny in retrospect, a square of mirrors no larger than twenty-by-twenty feet. All of this was really unsettling, and just entering this well-lit little room filled with mirrors set O'Rourke's teeth on edge.

The door was on the south wall, to the left of the subject, her right from her point of view, the girl directly in the center of the small room. The open door behind O'Rourke was the only way in and out of this room, the single entrance and exit, and that, in itself, was a red flag for him.

He kept his eyes on Subject 13 as Agent Taylor slowly backed up toward the south wall, and then they switched places, O'Rourke sliding in to take his place. O'Rourke heard the door behind him slide shut, and the little mirrored room was sealed once more, he and the subject the only two people left within the small room.

O'Rourke stared down at this little slip of a girl, and he estimated she couldn't be taller than five feet, and he was six-two. A part of him still believed this was some kind of prank pulled on him by the Bureau, because this young teen girl couldn't possibly weigh more than ninety pounds at that, not much of a threat at all.

He stared down at her as the minutes ticked by, but she did nothing but sit there and stare straight ahead, right at his black belt buckle. He took that time to study her in detail, but there was nothing particularly threatening about her. She had very dark eyes to match her stringy brown hair, and her wrists and ankles were so slender, they looked like twigs compared to any of the agents assigned to watch her.

She was not bound, and the chair she was in was a simple wooden chair, something someone might find in a kitchen, though strangely enough, the wooden seat was bolted to the floor.

Thinking about it, about all of it, this whole assignment was insane as far as O'Rourke was concerned, but he was not about to disobey orders, not without good reason.

There was no sound in the room except the soft hum of the ventilation system pumping in cool air. O'Rourke had allergies, and air conditioning caused them to flare up, but he resisted the urge to sneeze. Even so, he felt that familiar itch strike him, but he fought it as best he could in order to keep his eyes on the subject.

The girl in front of him, this slender, frail reed of a human female, jerked her head up in a clockwork motion and stared him directly in the eyes, her eyes raised wide in the whites, a wicked smile on her thin lips.

This startled O'Rourke for a second, breaking his concentration, and he sneezed without wanting to. He sniffed and quickly wiped his eyes and nose, and though his eyes were only closed for a couple of seconds at the most, when he opened them again…she was gone.

Her chair was empty, and her small and frail frame was nowhere in the reflections around him, either.

O'Rourke temporarily panicked, took two steps forward, and swiveled around to look in the reflections on every wall, but she was gone. She had simply *vanished* within the breadth of a second, no trace of her at all.

"What the…!" he breathed out.

"Don't move!" came Agent Zimmermann's voice from a speaker on the south wall.

O'Rourke froze as ordered and shut his mouth tightly, gritting his teeth, the empty chair directly behind him.

He wasn't stupid, because something was very, *very* wrong with all of this, and this got his blood up. His heart raced as the hairs on the back of his neck stood on end, because nobody could just up and disappear like that, especially in a room full of mirrors.

"It's behind you," said Agent Zimmermann in a calming voice. "Slowly turn your head to your right and look in the west-wall mirrors."

O'Rourke turned his head slightly to the right, and the image of his side profile revealed her, the girl standing directly behind him, back-to-back, imitating his every move, an inch from him, never touching him at the same time.

She had been there the entire time, slipping behind him in that fateful breadth of a second while his eyes were closed, and she had mimicked all of his motions in perfect synchronicity, no matter where he had turned, no matter how he had moved. His own body had worked against him on this one; she was so small and thin that he'd had no idea she was even there, nor had that possibility ever crossed his mind.

His heartrate picked up as he felt a strange fear hit him squarely in the chest, because this was something he had never dealt with or had experienced before. Normally, O'Rourke was not one to disobey orders, but it angered him that some frail, slender girl could cause him to panic, and he let Zimmerman know it.

"What in the hell is this!" he demanded.

"Calm down," said Agent Zimmerman. "Don't say anything."

"Like hell!" said O'Rourke in angry reply. "You're going—*Let*—to explain—*Me*—what in—*Out*— the hell is—*Frank*—going on, Zimmermann!"

"Stop talking!" ordered Zimmerman.

"This is—*I*—insane!" choked out O'Rourke. "What is—*Will*—going on! I need—*Bathe*—answers now, or—*In*—I'll smash down this door—*Your*—and beat them—*Blood*—out of you!"

"STOP TALKING!" shouted Zimmerman. "It's adding in words!"

"Adding—*Open*—in—*The*—words?" asked O'Rourke in confusion. "What—*Door*—in the hell—*Frank*—are you talking about!"

"I'm not opening this door, Subject 13," said Agent Zimmerman in a calm voice. "Now, you need to listen to me very, very closely, Agent O'Rourke. You need to stop talking right now. It's adding in words, and you don't even realize it."

"That—*I'll*—doesn't even—*Torture*—make sense!" yelled O'Rourke. "Now—*Anita*—you tell me what—*And*—in the—*Make*—hell I'm—*Her*—supposed to—*Beg*—do, or I'm—*For*—out of—*Death*—here! Now, give—*Frank*—me a straight answer, Zimmerman!"

"I'm going to get you out of there, O'Rourke," replied Zimmermann, "but you need to stay quiet and follow my instructions to the letter."

"This prank—*Open*—has gone—*The*—on long—*Door*—enough!" yelled O'Rourke. "Get this—*Frank*—little girl off my back!"

You know what?...He'd had enough.

O'Rourke turned to grab her, but she mimicked his motion with such precision and timing that he could only grasp air no matter how many times he attempted it. He could not grab her behind his back in time before she stepped a hair out of his reach and then stepped back into place before he could react again.

This, of course, only infuriated him more.

"This isn't—*Open*—funny—*The*—anymore!" yelled O'Rourke. "Get—*Door*—me out—*Frank*—of here, Zimmerman!"

Frustrated to the point of breaking, he rushed backwards to force her toward the south-wall mirrors. His intent was to force her around to his front, or she'd be squished between his back and the mirrors.

"STOP!" shouted Zimmerman. "DON'T TOUCH IT!"

O'Rourke ignored him and slammed back first into the south-wall line of mirrors. This small, willowy, teenage girl avoided his trap and whipped around to face him, but he used that opportunity to grab her frail left wrist with his right hand.

"Got you, you little…" he began, but his voice trailed off as he struggled against her.

She gave him a wicked grin, eyes wide in the whites, and she swiveled her slender left wrist in his right hand to where her left hand was over his right wrist.

O'Rourke knew this game, so he reached out with his left hand to grab her by her right shoulder, but her right hand snaked up over his left arm to bend down and over the pit of his elbow. She stepped onto his black dress shoes, her shoes on his, and try as he might to shake her off, he could not do it. She moved with him, arms and legs adjoined, regardless of where he circled his arms or moved his feet.

He kicked up with his left leg, but she stepped her right shoe onto his left knee, then back down onto his left shoe once his leg had dropped. He tried to grab her around her skinny waist, but she leaned backwards and circled her arms with his so that he could gain no grip upon her anywhere. She was like a squid or an octopus upon its prey, and he simply could not shake her.

"What the—!" he choked out.

"Stop moving!" ordered Agent Zimmerman. "We'll find a way to detach it, but you have to remain—"

Now O'Rourke was really mad. This little game of the Bureau's had gone way too far, and he'd had enough before, but it had not been official, and now he'd officially had enough.

"ENOUGH!" he yelled.

He rushed forward toward the chair at the center of the room. He was enraged now, but his conscience screamed at him to stop, because he was going to break this small girl in half without meaning to.

It didn't matter, however. This slender twig of a teenage girl whipped around him and latched on from behind, her skinny legs around his to where her shoes were still on his shoes, her willowy arms still wrapped around his from behind, her left cheek pressed into the black cloth on the back of his good suit.

O'Rourke tried to move, but her grip was like a steel vise, and he could not, not for the life of him, struggle against it. She suddenly had impossible strength, something unbelievable, and yet it was real and happening and he could do nothing about it.

He felt her twig-like limbs move his, forcing him to turn around and face the south wall. His left arm moved up along with hers, her left hand atop his, and then he gripped his own short black hair with his left hand, pulling his head back so that he was staring up at one of the cameras.

O'Rourke felt real fear now. This did not feel like a joke or a prank anymore.

He opened his mouth to cry out for help, but the words that spewed forth from his lips were not his own, and this time he knew it.

"Open the door, Frank," said O'Rourke without wanting to.

"Hang on, O'Rourke," replied Agent Zimmerman. "I've sounded the alarm."

"It won't help you," said O'Rourke. *"I am the night, Frank. I was born of Chaos. You can't stop me from leaving. You cannot hold me prisoner."*

"Stop talking, O'Rourke," ordered Zimmerman.

"I will get out, Frank," continued O'Rourke. *"I will get out, and when I do, I will spray your blood all over that room. I will feed what's left of you to Anita, and then I will tear your pretty little wife apart one piece at a time...and feed those pieces to her, as well."*

"Stop talking, O'Rourke," said Zimmerman again, but this time he sounded angry.

O'Rourke tried to say his own words, but something in his mind held him back, something so dark, so fearfully terrifying, it was indescribable.

"Open the door, Frank," said O'Rourke. *"Open the door and bow down to me, and I'll spare you. Prostrate yourself before me, and I'll let you live as my new priest. I won't have to skin Anita alive and listen to her screams for mercy. I won't have to make a bedsheet out of her skin and use her bones—"*

"Stop…talking!" hissed Zimmerman.

Rage consumed O'Rourke over this. His mind was his own, and this *thing* could not, *would not* control him. He pushed against that overwhelming, dark force in his mind, railing against it with nothing more than pure rage and sheer willpower.

"I'll pay a visit to your lovely, lovely wife— Get—*Frank,"* said O'Rourke. *"She—*Off—*has pretty blue eyes that I'll—*Get—*wear as a necklace—*Off— *Frank. I'm going to—*Get—*rip off your parts—*Off—*and present—*Get—*them in a box—*Off—*to lovely, lovely—* Me—*Anita, and then I'll—*GET OFF ME!"

O'Rourke ripped his own left hand from his hair, spun to face the chair in the center of the small, mirrored room, and bent over to fling her off. She flipped over his back, but she landed on her feet in front of the chair, spinning to face him, only to fall back into the chair, back into her sitting position once more. He took that opportunity to backpedal while keeping his eyes locked on her, his gaze unwavering this time.

"That was incredible, O'Rourke!" cried Zimmermann in vocal amazement. "Just stay there and wait for Bays to come down. I'll shut off the alarm as soon as he arrives."

O'Rourke took a moment to compose himself, adjust his hair and tie, and take in a few deep breaths, never letting his gaze wander from his charge, this "Subject 13," some unidentifiable *thing* that somehow looked like a frail, willowy, teenage girl. He knew enough not to talk this time, but he was not going anywhere, not leaving, because now he knew better. There was no way the Bureau could allow this thing to escape.

In retrospect, this position was a lot more difficult than he had been led to believe.

#4a…BONUS STORY: THE CHILD

Molly had seen the poor boy all alone on the side of the road. He looked to be about ten, and he had clearly been crying, so she could not just leave him out there in such rugged territory. He was hesitant to get into her old red truck, but she was convincing in her argument. The boy's name was Jordan, and he was scared, but he was safe now.

"You shouldn't be out here at night and alone near these woods," she said as they drove along. "You're lucky I spotted you. Someone could have snatched you up or a wild animal could have gotten you. What were you doing out here anyway?"

"I got lost," sniffed Jordan. "There were cars on the road, but I couldn't ask for help, because Mom said I shouldn't talk to any strangers except grandma types."

"It's all right," said Molly. "I'll drive you back to your house. And just so you know, my name is Molly, and I *am* a grandma type."

She thought about driving him back to his house, but another idea came to mind.

"Maybe I should just take you to my house, and we'll call your parents from there," she said. "We'll just dial your mother, and she'll come pick you up."

"I live just up ahead," said Jordan. "Mom is getting me a smartphone for my birthday, so this won't happen again. I keep telling her I need one."

Molly dropped him off at the Petersons' house, which was odd, because she was sure the Petersons still lived there, and they didn't have a son. Furthermore, she had no idea what a "smartphone" was, and she drove off feeling a little addled over all of this.

*****

Jordan walked inside, and his mother and aunt immediately scolded him.

"Where have you been!" cried his mom. "We were about to call the police!"

"I got lost," sniffed Jordan, "but an old woman in a red truck gave me a ride here. She just drove off a minute ago."

His aunt's face turned a deathly white as she asked him a simple question.

"An old woman in a red truck?" she asked. "What was her name?"

"Molly," said Jordan in confusion. "Why?"

"Molly Wayne died in a blizzard over thirty years ago," said his aunt in a shaky voice. "They found her old red truck on the road after the thaw. She froze to death."

Jordan was suddenly glad he had not gone to her house to use her phone.

#5...WATCH ME

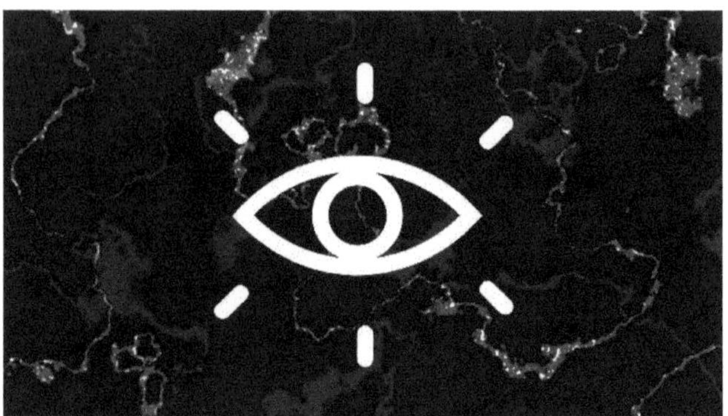

It's all about perspective.

"**You think** you can hold out on me?" demanded Bree over the phone. "That's five hundred you charged over six months as a 'tip.' Renters don't 'tip' landlords, you slumlord jackhat! Why do you think I moved out!...Oh, no, this place is far better than that dump!...Oh, yeah?...Well, I'll see you in court!...You don't think so! Watch me!"

She slammed down the receiver and scrunched up her face in obvious, visible rage. She was a fighter, this one, but her anger was a slow boil, a coffee pot that had been left on for too long.

She was definitely one to watch. That temper needed to be checked.

The phone she had slammed down was a landline, an ancient, beige, light-up-push-button thing that looked like it had barely survived the '80s, but it had come with the apartment, and strangely enough, it still worked, so she used it quite often. This was actually something that shone in her favor, as the younger generations did not appreciate reliable technology from the past; they were prone to buying and using cheaply-made foreign junk.

Her name was Bree Maeve Byrne, she was twenty-six, and she worked for an eyecare office as a receptionist.

She weighed approximately 145 lbs., give or take a few pounds, depending upon the time of year. She was white, of Irish descent, with an hourglass body, short dark-brown hair, and C-cup breasts. She had a pretty face beset with dark-brown eyes, a face, mind you, that held no secrets, as her expressions were brutally honest, an honesty that shone forth sometimes as hostility, something she most certainly needed to work on, as her perceived attitude often spelled trouble for her.

Today, she was dressed in a dark-purple tee with white swirls on it, the shirt faded due to too much wear and too many washes, and this old and favorite shirt was complemented by some similarly old jeans that showed off the contours of her bottom quite nicely, a deliberate decision on her part, but a negative trait in its boldness, an unladylike affect picked up by the tawdriness of peer pressure and modern media.

She wore old white sneakers with no socks, a barefoot-in-shoe she had picked up in habit long before she'd entered this new apartment, something that would eventually be corrected out of her, right along with most of the terrible habits she needed corrected.

She did not wear dresses as a proper woman should, nor did she have decent dress shoes, white knee-high socks, or anything else befitting a woman, but this was also to be expected, considering the disrespect her generation often showed toward…well…anything.

As previously mentioned, she also had a temper, but it was not the fiery stereotype so often associated with women of the Irish persuasion, no. Rather, it was the slow burn that had, once again, been previously mentioned.

Nevertheless, a temper was a temper, and that was unbecoming of a lady.

Her old landlord was the scum of the earth, a currently-negative situation she was still dealing with, but that situation was simply life in a bag. There was nothing else to that little scenario, and this was not her fault, so those points were in her favor.

Now, today, she was here in her new apartment on one of her days off, although "new" for this apartment was a relative term. She had only been here for a month, and she had struggled to make the place her own, though that struggle was dying out due to the mere passage of time and the inevitable process of acclimation.

This new place's ancient phone was parked upon the east kitchen counter, so she traveled over to the south kitchen counter where the sink was located. The sink was to the left of her white refrigerator, and her white oven rested between the east kitchen counter and the south kitchen counter, to the left of her sink. It was all very compact, but that was to be expected in such a small apartment, and this was also the reason why it was so difficult to hide anything that stood out in any particular fashion.

She stopped and stared down at the pair of aqua-blue ankle socks lazily strung across her black kitchen countertop. She reached down and picked up the offending pieces of clothing, but the puzzled expression upon her face revealed her lack of memory over leaving them there.

You see, Bree had awakened from sleep around 7:00 AM, made her bed (definitely a bonus in her favor), gone to her bathroom, stepped into the shower (as she was already fully nude), wet her hair, shampooed, and had lathered up with soap whilst her hair was percolating in its expensive hair product, and then she had conditioned, rinsed off, and had dried off with a beige towel directly after this, drying her short hair by wrapping yet another towel—this one white—around that wet hair.

There was nothing wrong with these activities, save for the crude behavior of sleeping in the nude, something no rational human being should ever do. Her daily showering, however, was a fervent positive of the gold standard, as good hygiene was always expected of a proper lady.

She had used the toilet directly after that and had then walked to her bedroom, fully nude save for the hair-wrapped towel, and then she had removed that towel and had dressed for the day in the aforementioned set of clothes she was currently wearing. She had then walked back to the bathroom and had tossed her wet-hair towel in a white hamper that also contained her previously-used beige body towel.

She had traveled to the kitchen after this, at which time she had received the call from her scumbag ex-landlord, and this was the moment in time we are at now, that moment in which she was studying the pair of aqua-blue ankle socks within her right hand.

She stared down at the kitchen counter after that, and her lips scrunched inwards as she studied what was there, or rather, what had been lying in wait beneath her aqua-blue socks.

There was an eye drawn upon the countertop.

There was an eye drawn in white ink upon the countertop, probably with some kind of marker, but where one could get a white marker was a mystery in itself. The eye was drawn in the most basic style, just a circle within lids, lines like lashes extending out from it, something even a child could do in terms of artistic quality.

Bree reached down and ran her fingertips over the eye, but it was clear the eye had not been inked on, no, but *painted* on, and that paint was quite dry.

Her eyebrows furrowed as if struggling to remember such a thing and why it was here, and then she gave her head a half-shake, a gesture in intention as if to say, "What?"

She walked back to her bedroom, the offending pair of aqua-blue socks still in her right hand. She then walked up to her wooden dresser, only to slide open the third drawer down, revealing the rows of rolled and colored panties and bundled socks within.

Those socks were merely for work, not for any other time, and that was something that needed correction. Nevertheless, the orderliness of her undergarments was refreshing, far superior to most of the younger generation, these grown toddlers that lived like hogs and sows in a pigsty.

It was a simple matter to put the socks back where they belonged, and then she was on her way, out the bedroom and out the apartment door, purse in hand, on her way to wherever on her day off, and when she would return was in question, as was her destination.

She returned slightly after noon, only a few minutes past, and the first thing she did was walk through her living room/kitchen area and into her bedroom.

To be fair, this small apartment only consisted of the mix of living room and kitchen, the bedroom, and the bathroom. There was nothing else to this quaint little space, but this was all she could afford, and Bree appeared happy enough with it, especially after dealing with her last landlord.

She walked up to her dresser, that dresser to the right of her bed at the east wall, and she placed her purse down upon it, and that was when she noticed her small makeup kit, that kit normally located within the bathroom but now on top of her dresser, right next to a small night lamp, a night lamp she had purchased quite cheaply at a yard sale.

Earlier in the month, she had spoken to a friend over the phone about the deal she had made after she had purchased the lamp, and in retrospect, there was nothing negative or untoward about being thrifty. This was definitely another positive in her favor.

Anyway, her makeup kit was strategically placed at the back of the top of the dresser, right next to her bedroom's light-green wall, so she snatched it up, and by the expression upon her pretty face, she appeared puzzled, though this was only conjecture.

To be fair, makeup was most becoming of a proper lady, as any proper lady needed to put on her best face in order to deal with the challenges of a man's world. Having and using makeup was a step in the right direction, but she rarely used her kit, though she had owned said kit since first moving into this small apartment, and that reticence needed to be corrected.

She studied the case for a few precious seconds before noticing what rested above its former nesting place, yet another eye, this one identical to the first, though smaller, that eye painted in white upon the light-green wall above the back-top of the dresser.

She switched her small makeup case to her left hand and rubbed the eye with her right thumb, but such a rubbing revealed nothing, as the paint used to create the eye had already dried.

Her eyebrows scrunched inward as her lips scrunched inwards as well, and then those lips parted slightly, a look of extreme confusion cast within the profile of her pretty face.

She shook her head, muttered something under her breath, and then headed to the bathroom. She then placed the makeup kit back where she normally stored it, upon the narrow bathroom counter where her bathroom sink was located.

Her orderliness and timeliness in the matter of cleaning up was flawless, something of a surprise for someone of her generation, and this was even more of a surprise for Bree in particular, as she had never enlisted or had been in any way connected to the military, where such habits are usually formed.

She took the time after that to use the toilet, and then she walked back to the living room/kitchen to sit down on her small brown couch and turn on her flatscreen via a black remote.

She flipped through her favorite streaming service until she found a matchmaker show she wanted to watch, and then she vegetated for two hours watching that drivel. Such shows were dedicated in their mindlessness toward women, so such a viewing was neither positive nor negative, as it was expected behavior for her gentle sex.

During that time, she got up to grab an orange soda from the fridge, along with some pretzels she dumped into a small, clear, plastic bowl. The drinking portion of this activity caused her to use the restroom a couple of times, but this was no hardship, as she could pause her show at her leisure.

Snack foods, of course, were a negative in general, as they were unhealthy, overpriced, and resulted in medical bills later on due to such an unhealthy lifestyle, thereby burdening the overall system for honest, hardworking taxpayers.

Aside from that, being of a younger generation, she did not watch cable anymore, and anything she watched was purely of the streaming variety. This was disrespectful to the time-honored tradition of quality programming, but such behavior was to be expected anymore from such a selfish and thoughtless generation.

After she was finished with a very short, two-episode binge, she yawned and proceeded to her bathroom. She used the toilet one more time, and then she flossed and brushed her teeth before proceeding to her bedroom, specifically her bed.

She had already locked the front door of her apartment, but she shut and locked her bedroom door anyway, as this was an additional layer of security for her, an imaginary boundary that was only physical for those who did not know how to evade such simple, protective measures.

Bree then stripped out of her clothes, as the young woman preferred to sleep in the nude, a trend that was most prevalent amongst those of her age or younger, these younger generations bucking long-standing traditions out of a warped irreverent logic, yet one more reason for a well-justified and intense dislike for them by the older generations.

She laid down upon her bed, on her side, not even bothering to cover with a blanket, and she was soundly asleep twenty minutes later.

She slept for a grand total of three hours and twenty-seven minutes, and when she awoke, she rolled over to her bare back and placed her hands behind her head as she stared up at the white plaster of her small bedroom's ceiling.

She had a decent line of dark hair along her armpits, a failing upon her part to act like a proper woman, but this was to be expected with her generation, a small failure of decent female hygiene that stacked upon the larger failure that was the entirety of the younger generations altogether.

Her legs were spread, *incredibly* unbecoming of a woman, really unforgivable, actually, because anyone could have walked in and seen her in her most private position, but that was nothing that couldn't be addressed during a harsh future lesson.

It would not do to describe in detail what she sometimes did from this position…Let's just say it's disgusting and cannot be mentioned here.

Furthermore, she was not trimmed down below, and she was going to need a harsh lesson in that kind of hygiene as well…Astonishingly unbecoming. Unbelievable.

These new generations were certainly trying.

You see, when a child is willful and rebellious, that child must be punished in order to firmly establish the dominance of the parent, or that child will never be a productive citizen in any way, shape, or form.

These younger generations were nothing more than uncouth anarchs, and their national parent, our great government, has long since diminished into nothing more than a corrupt and pensive "buddy" without direction for its citizen-children. This willful and rebellious outlook and behavior, however, could be remedied on an individual basis, and it would be.

But enough ranting. There was too much ranting anymore, especially online. There was never enough action, never enough of what was actually *needed* to correct society, and that was something that would be remedied shortly…Yes, all of this was merely a prelude to something greater anyway.

Bree sat up on her bed, her hands at her sides, and her dark eyes widened in surprise. She hopped out of bed and walked over to the plain and bare, light-green wall across from her bed to study what was hanging there.

A small nail had been hammered into that wall days earlier, a nail she had never really noticed until now, and it was upon that nail that hung a fine print dress, a white dress with green and pink print, the print markings of fresh spring roses, and beneath that dress upon the light-blue carpet were new black dress shoes with new knee-high white socks tucked within those shoes.

She walked over to the clothing and gripped the dress with both hands. Her naked body trembled as she pulled the dress from the wall, that tremble an obvious visual sign of an intense fear and releasing of adrenaline, but that fear and adrenaline were surely amplified by what was behind the dress.

Upon the blank, light-green wall was a large white eye, that eye painted on the wall, that eye identical to the first two she had discovered, only larger than the previous two.

I, of course, had painted those eyes during her moments of absence, or in the case of the last one, while she had been asleep. Those eyes represented the watchful eye of the concerned, a concern not just for her, but for society as a whole, that watchful eye a symbol of order and respect that needed to be honored and would be honored, if not by example, then by force.

Monitoring her activities had been a simple task with the placement of thirty-one spy cameras within her tiny apartment, and I had placed them everywhere so as to achieve the maximum angles for equally maximum viewing accuracy.

It was nothing for me to copy the keys to her apartment, nothing at all, and I had a tracker in the lining of her purse to inform me of her location at all times whilst she was away from the apartment, so there would be no untoward early surprises.

But now for the finale, something a while in the making.

It was a simple thing, really, for me to step out of her closet while the dress was still gripped within her shaking hands, that closet left of the bed in the east wall, and it would be even simpler still to subdue her with a quick injection of tranquilizer into one of her bare buttocks while she was both nude and unarmed.

Yes, she was going to learn within the confines of the soundproof training area I had set up within my own basement, and she would either learn to conform to the standards expected of society, or she would be buried in my backyard with the others.

These newer generations were certainly stubborn and stupid, and I'd had more than my fill of disappointments with them. I had a number of newly planted trees in my backyard to showcase that. Hopefully, she would prove different.

Bree stared at the dress, her naked back and bare shoulders trembling, her buttocks taught and tight and clenched with what had to be shaking fear.

"What the fu—!" she rattled off, but she never got to finish that unladylike expletive.

Her unfinished expletive ended in a terrified screech as my left arm snaked around her throat while the hypodermic in my right hand jabbed into the delicate skin of her right buttock.

#5a…BONUS STORY: THE LITTLE MATCH GIRL, REVISED

Little six-year-old Victoria sat down on the cold dirt next to the wooden building where the weavers worked day and night to make clothing for the fair people of London. She was freezing, she was tired, and she wanted sleep, and the last time she had eaten was yesterday when an old woman had taken pity on her and had given her a stale crust of bread.

It was snowing again, and the temperature was dropping, but even so, people were out and about, because Christmas was coming, so she had a chance to make some money. She had one box of matches left and nothing more.

An old man in a top hat came walking by at a brisk pace, and she attempted to get his attention, though the scowl on his face nearly chased her off.

"Please, kind sir, would you buy some matches?" she asked in her humblest voice.

"Begone, you little scab!" said the man as he pushed her down into the steadily-collecting snow. "Off with you before you receive the blunt of my cane!"

Victoria tried not to cry as she stood back up on her stick-thin legs, adjusting her torn and disheveled brown dress to look even somewhat presentable. She was not ready to give in just yet.

She signaled to a plump, wealthy-looking woman who wore a big, feathered, blue hat and a long blue dress. This woman had to have money, as indicated by the large green pendant she wore just above her ample bosom.

"Please, miss, would you like to buy some matches?" asked Victoria.

"Away with you, you foul little creature!" scolded the wealthy woman in blue, and she walked off with nothing more to say.

Victoria sat down in the snow and cried. She was so cold and so hungry, and all she had was one small box of matches.

She thought, perhaps, to light a match, to light a single match so she could be warm, and in so doing, she might see happier times within the flame, a happier life when she had been with her grandmother when the old woman was still alive…but then another thought came to her…a much darker one.

It came to her in a flashfire of viciousness, a sudden brand of smoke within her young mind, so she put her plan into action without further thought.

She quickly trotted down the street and around a corner to reach Andersen's Stables. She waited for the stableboy to go inside the nearby building, and once he was gone, she grabbed an unlit lantern the boy had left behind. She poured the lantern fuel upon the hay and then took a single match from her small box of matches. She lit the match and paused for a brief moment to stare into the tiny flame.

Victoria could see the face of her grandmother within the flame, but the kind old woman held a look of fear upon her weathered face, her wizened head shaking in an emphatic "no."

"Don't worry, Grandmother," whispered Victoria. "This will make everything *better*."

She tossed the match into the oil-soaked hay and ran as the fire quickly spread. It was not long before half the city was in flames, and she was in the middle of it.

She listened to the screams of those around her as the citizens of London ran to and fro for safety, some gasping for air within the smoke, some catching ablaze as they tried to flee the burning buildings crumbling around them.

A flaming figure came stumbling past Victoria, the immolated woman flailing and screaming, and Victoria recognized this human candle by the burning blue hat she wore. What had once been the woman in the long blue dress, this portly woman now a living pyre, stumbled forward to collapse in the snow, and she smelled like roasted pork and melted fat as she permanently stopped flailing and screaming.

Victoria held up her two little hands, palms out, over the woman's still burning body.

"Now, I'm warm," she smiled.

#6…TAIGA TAIGA, BURNING BRIGHT

"In what distant deeps or skies, burnt the fire of thine eyes?"—From "The Tyger," by William Blake.

Peter rushed down the outpost stairs as the emergency klaxons went off, Urrekshish and Kaleena right behind him. They hit the observation-post walkway running, and it didn't even take a pair of vid-binocs to see the trouble brewing in the distance. Oh, no, they could clearly see the fires from here.

Agora III was a Taiga-Class Terran planet, and this little Intergalactic Confederacy outpost, A3-H17B, was responsible for terraforming this equatorial section with coniferous pines, those pines imported from both Earth and Sh'rrett.

It was a waste of Peter's talents; heck it was a waste of Urrek's and Kaleena's talents too, but this was their assignment.

Peter was actually ex-military, Terran Alliance Infantry back in the day, as was Urrekshish, also ex-military, though Urrek had been in the S'arrkohna Briold Infantry. Even Kaleena didn't belong here, especially

Kaleena, as the females of the Kyrie were larger and more fearsome than their males, and she had been designated as one of the elite soldiers in their all-female infantry, one of the highly-trained and deadly Val-Kyrie.

Kalleena was a Kyrie, and the Kyrie looked human for the most part, only much shorter, with broader shoulders and thicker bones. Their males were around the same height as the average S'arrkohna, about three-and-a-half to four-feet tall, but their females were taller and heavier-built with more muscle. All Kyrie sported thick, dark hair on their heads that was somewhat stiff, but it was their eyebrows that set them apart, as those lines of hair above the eyes were magnificently long and thick, and Kalleena's were no exception.

Urrekshish was one of the diminutive but fierce S'arrkohna. Their people were covered in brown fur, and they typically held golden or amber eyes. They sported sharp fangs in place of their canine teeth, and they had small, dog-like snouts for noses. Their males and females were identical in size and muscle, though not in shape.

Peter, himself, was six-one, bald since he was twenty-one, and he had a rugged, athletic build for as old as he was, and he was pushing fifty. He looked like a veritable giant compared to his two friends, but that was fine. He respected his friends, and their heights had nothing to do with that respect.

All three of them no longer wore the colors of their home planets, no. They each now wore the dark-blue jumper-utility parkas assigned to them by the Intergalactic Confederation Engineering Corps. Agora III was where they had been stationed, this was the division they had been stationed in, and each of them followed orders, regardless of what penny prize the I.G.C. had awarded them for their loyal service.

Why those I.G.C. fat cats and politicians had stuck them with the task of terraforming this planet was beyond Peter, as their training was better suited for killing things in the most expedient and efficient way possible.

Even so, the fires raging in the distance were what held Peter's attention now.

"It's a fire!" growled Urrekshish. "It's wiping out the northern line!"

Peter cursed under his breath as he brought his hands up to the top of his bald head in frustration. This was bad, because there was a raging inferno out in the distant trees, but there was no reason for that fire, not here in these stark, wintry conditions.

"Son of a…" he breathed out. "We've got to stem this and now!"

"Look!" yelled Kaleena. "There's something moving in the trees!"

Peter unstrapped his vid-binocs from his belt, flipped them on, brought them up to his eyes, and stared out past the initial tree line of conifers to view the *actual* problem. Spoilers: it wasn't the fire.

Moving through the trees was a lithe but massive shape, a beast that vaguely resembled a tiger, but one twelve-meters-tall and twenty-five-meters-long, a gargantuan shape with flames rippling across whatever it had that passed for skin.

Peter sucked in his breath and shook his head. He knew exactly what this thing was.

"That's a friggin' MAD," he hissed out. "We've somehow activated a MAD."

"A Mutant Assault Drone?" asked Kalleena in complete and utter surprise. "I thought they were all dismantled after the war! Why in the forty-seven gods is one here!"

"I don't know," growled Urrekshish, "but I do know they chewed us up like…like…"

"Like popcorn," frowned Peter. "It's going to hit this base any minute now…*Wheeelp*…We wanted some excitement, to see some action, and…it looks like we're going to get it. Get everybody to the armory…if that will even make a difference."

"No wonder they sent me here," winced Kalleena. "I should have known."

"I doubt they knew," frowned Peter. "The exact location of the remaining MADs has been lost for years. I think the I.G.C. Terraforming and Colonization Bureau just got unlucky."

"Not as unlucky as us," grunted Urrekshish. "It's going to kill us all…Orders? What's the plan?"

Peter gave himself two seconds of thought to put together any kind of logical plan.

"Evacuation's out," he said unhappily. "There's not enough time. Fighting it will get us all killed…There's no doubt about that."

"What then?" asked Kalleena. "If I'm going to die, I want to die fighting."

"No, that's suicide," frowned Peter.

"It would be a glorious death," said Kalleena thoughtfully.

"It would be a waste," grimaced Peter. "You'd be bitten in half and probably roasted before that…Wait…Wait a minute…"

"What is it?" asked Urrekshish.

"MADs are cyborgs," replied Peter. "They're half organic. This one's skin is clearly synthetic, and it's reinforced to resist most conventional attacks outside of artillery…"

"And?" asked Urrekshish. "You're going somewhere with this…"

"Darn right," nodded Peter. "If its synthetic outside is aflame, its organic inside must have a constant core temperature that's resistant to heat…Urrek…What's the status on that A.U.V. of yours? Is it juiced up and loaded?"

"Why?" asked the S'arrkohna male. "What does that have to do with…"

Urrekshish's golden eyes went wide as his furry brown face split into a toothy grin of comprehension.

"Oh, yeah!" he grunted. "Let's head to the armory!"

"Isn't that where we were going in the first place?" asked Kalleena in audible confusion.

"Yeah," nodded Peter, "but now we have a reason to go there. Let's head out."

They booked it to the armory while Peter gave directions to the rest of Security through his communicator. He was the chief officer at A3-H17B, though he was only in command of twenty officers for an outpost that hosted a little over twelve hundred people. Still, those other officers needed instructions right now, and those instructions included laying low and keeping the populace calm.

They walked into the armory garage where Urrekshish's A.U.V. resided.

The armored utility vehicle in question was a pet project of the four-foot-tall S'arrkohna male, because Peter knew for a fact that Urrekshish held a deep fascination for all things Terran. The S'arrkohna warrior loved Terran vehicles, buildings, lore, cultures, religions…just Earth in general.

"There it is," grinned Urrekshish. "The Thunderbird."

The little S'arrkohna eagerly motioned toward his labor of love.

The armored hover-vehicle was five-meters-long, almost three-meters-wide, and a little over two-and-a-half-meters-tall. Urrekshish had painted it a cobalt blue with yellow lightning bolts along the rear half and a great bald-eagle's head painted across the front.

Peter whistled as he gave it a once-over. The cockpit was designed for a pilot and copilot, while the back held a rear-mounted, .50-caliber, kinetic-heat heavy machine gun with a single's firing seat. Centered on the top of the A.U.V. was a dual .40-caliber kinetic-heat turret gun with a 360° swivel chair for the pod gunner.

"This…is what dreams are made of…" whispered Kalleena in a husky breath.

Peter ignored her and gave Urrekshish a light push from behind.

"Hey, is it fully loaded?" he asked.

"Yep," nodded Urrekshish. "It's armed and fully powered…We have no time left, though. If we're going to do this, we have to do it now."

"Agreed," grunted Peter. "Urrek, you're piloting. Kalleena, you're…"

"*Guuuuun…*" breathed the four-and-a-half-foot tall Kyrie female.

She wandered over toward the back half of the vehicle to inspect the rear-mounted gun.

"You're on the rear gun, then," sighed Peter. "Looks like I've got the ball turret…Come on; let's get this show on the road. That MAD will be here any second."

He studied his two compatriots one last time. There was a good chance he wasn't going to see either of them again. There was a good chance they were all going to die, and not just the three of them…More than likely, everyone stationed at this outpost would be slaughtered. He wanted to remember his friends as they were now, because this might be the very last time he saw them.

He nodded once to himself, content with the memory he had just made in his mind.

"Let's ride," he grunted.

They loaded into Urrekshish's Thunderbird, and Peter strapped into the ball-turret gunner's seat. He flipped on the com-switch next to him and spoke loudly and clearly into the speaker on his right.

"Let's go!" he said firmly. "Urrek…start her up, and…you know what to do, right?"

"Oh, yeah," grunted the S'arrkohna, and they were off.

The tricked-out A.U.V. rumbled out of the armory-garage gate and onto the wintry asphalt of the compound.

"Kalleena!" said Peter. "We're going to lead that thing off! That means you and I will run interference while Urrek drives us away from the compound!"

"Affirmative," replied Kalleena. "This will be fun."

"Oh, it'll be something, all right," muttered Peter.

Urrek piloted the hover-vehicle down past the main-garage tarmac and out onto the wintry terrain beyond.

The great flaming tiger, the beast they so feared, had already burned a line through the northern trees, and it was headed directly toward the outpost, so Peter decided to get its attention.

"This baby of yours better be fast, Urrek," he grunted, "because here it comes!"

He swiveled to his right in the turret and used the manual HUD to lock onto the beast. Peter clamped down upon the firing switches, and the A.U.V. ball turret rattled as streaks of orange kinetic rounds spat fire into the distance.

The creature was far faster than they had anticipated. It spun in a ninety-degree arc and charged as Urrekshish boosted the A.U.V. to full speed.

"Hit the throttle!" yelled Peter as his targeting swiveled left to right, left to right.

His targeting was thrown off by the S'arrkohna's veering of the vehicle to avoid spaced-apart trees, boulders, and bad, rocky terrain covered by snow. Peter did his best to line up the targeting HUD, and then he fired more magnetically-propelled, self-immolating bullets toward the creature closing the distance behind them.

More lines of orange spat backwards to impact the MAD in various places, but this time the assault was from Kalleena's rear gun. This thing roared as it was struck in the face, along the sides of its flaming body, and upon its front legs, but it barely slowed at all.

"We're just pissing it off!" screeched Kalleena.

"Good!" yelled Peter. "Keep up the pressure!"

The pair fired in tandem as Urrekshish did his best to keep the hover-vehicle from destabilizing over the rocky terrain.

"We need to hit Brink's Fjord!" cried Peter. "Keep firing till you're out of rounds!"

"That won't be difficult," he heard Kalleena mutter over the com.

Peter chuckled as he continued to lay down fire at the raging beast behind them.

He checked the terrain map on his left, and they were headed in the right direction, right toward the Brink, a pair of cliffs that led out toward the Broken Sea.

"Head us down into the Fjord!" said Peter. "We'll lead it out from there!"

"That's a one-way ticket!" yelled Urrekshish. "Once we're in the Fjord, it's do or die!"

Peter grinned at that statement. His S'arrkohna compatriot had been watching too many ancient-Earth war films lately.

The beast continued its chase without any more provocation, though they gave it plenty. Kalleena's gun spit orange lines of kinetic heat at its huge face, angering it further, that rage mathematically squared as Peter continued his own assault.

Kalleena's gun rattled off rounds until she stopped firing altogether.

"I'm out!" she yelled over the com.

Peter rattled off more rounds until the guns did nothing but click when he pressed down on the switches.

"Me too!" he replied. "I'm out, but it doesn't matter! We're at the Fjord! This is it!"

They entered the frozen valley between the Brink, and Peter felt a sharp spike of fear as the MAD turned left to climb the cliff upon Peter's immediate right, his left if his turret had been facing forward.

"I can't see it!" he yelled.

"It's coming down up ahead!" cried Urrekshish.

Peter swiveled his gunner's chair to view through the forward cameras ahead of them. The beast was indeed coming down the cliffs, bouncing from one rocky wall to the next to trap them before they could reach the open sea.

"We're not going to make it!" he yelled.

He knew he was going to die, that they were all going to die, but his little S'arrkohna buddy surprised him at the last second.

"This is the Thunderbird!" barked Urrekshish. "The dial goes up to eleven!"

Peter was thrown back into the straps as twin jets powered by compressed fuel blasted out from the back. The A.U.V. roared forward just as the MAD roared down upon them. Peter swiveled the gun turret around to view the great and terrifying beast land behind them as the Thunderbird rocketed out of the Fjord and onto the flat sheets of ice that made up the Broken Sea.

Urrekshish flipped off the jets as the A.U.V. flew out across dangerous, unstable sheets of ice. The mutant assault drone, this huge and flaming tiger, crunched through the Fjord's ice flow to blindly follow them out onto the expanse of frozen water. It jumped once to catch them, but the Thunderbird slipped through its front paws just in time.

The huge burning creature crashed through a sheet of solid ice as it dove headlong into a frigid, watery grave. Chunks of ice and freezing water kicked up all around the AUV, one particularly large chunk of ice banking off of Peter's turret, doing enough damage to lock up his swivel drive.

Urrekshish drove in a wide circle around the enormous hole in the ice before making his way back to the entrance of the Fjord.

"Is everyone okay?" asked Peter.

"Yes," answered both of his compatriots at the same time.

"Did we kill it?" asked Kalleena.

"That thing had to have an organic interior that was somehow resistant to heat," replied Peter. "My guess is that…this was the reason why it was locked away here on Agora III. The lowered temperature kept it in hibernation, but we somehow happened to terraform near its vault, which changed the climate just enough to wake it up…Yeah, it was resistant to heat, but in the end, it couldn't take the cold."

"It was a glorious death," replied Kalleena.

#6a…BONUS STORY: IT'S ELEMENTARY

Brian had been flying his Cessna Skycatcher when a glowing green portal had opened up right in front of his little plane. Thankfully, he wasn't training any students today, because they would have been in for the rude awakening he was now receiving, that awakening the realization that he was now somewhere else, and where that somewhere specifically was, he had no idea.

He had passed out upon traversing that portal, and he had honestly thought himself dead when his plane had hit the strange green doorway, but also thankfully, that had proven false, so that, in itself, was good fortune for the moment.

Nevertheless, he had awoken in a small tent while laid out on a simple hammock-strung cot, but he was uninjured, and he was still wearing his flight instructor's clothes, though he had not been carrying any weapons with him during his flight.

He did not know what was going on, but he was wary, because this reeked of some kind of science-fiction-type abduction, and he did not know what was going to happen next.

He walked out of his little tent and was met with a lifeless, barren landscape of red soil capped by the bright day of two orange suns in a clear blue sky.

Before him stood six purple-skinned giants dressed in huge gladiatorial armor, and each giant was easily twenty-feet-tall. The six wielded equally giant weapons, spears and swords and axes, all of which exuded various, dangerous forms of energy.

There were four males. One had a spear that crackled with electricity, another had an axe that burned with fire, the next, a hammer made of solid stone, and the last held a trident that sprayed out a cold mist.

The last two giants were female. The first held a sword that shone brightly with light, while the second brandished a whip that absorbed light, wreathing the sinister weapon in darkness.

"You have been chosen, little one, to represent your world," said one of the giants in a booming voice, the one with the crackling spear. "You will choose six of your world's elements, and we shall then test our might against the living elemental warriors our magic shall create from your own chosen elements."

This giant whipped his huge spear around in a flurry of crackling, electric circles before he planted the blunted shaft end into the red soil beneath him.

"I am Torik," he proudly stated. "My element is thunder, the power of lightning, wind, and furious sound!"

The second male giant swung his great axe and seared the air around him with a blaze of fire.

"I am Kreeos," he said. "My element is fire, and I wield the mighty force of a volcano!"

The next male giant swung his hammer and cracked the red earth beneath him, causing the ground to shake and rumble.

"I am Ragnos!" he boomed. "I hold the power of stone, the power to shake the earth itself! Tremble before my might!"

The last male giant stepped forward and pointed his trident skyward. A whirling mist of icy shards spun around the weapon for a second before he slammed the pole end into the red earth at his feet.

"I am Tridos," he said firmly. "I hold the power of water, that which makes oceans and winter! I drown my enemies and crush them in ice!"

The first giantess gently pushed past him and pointed the huge tip of her glowing sword at Brian's face.

"I am Lumina!" she said in a fierce tone. "The force of light, the very power of the twin suns, is mine to command!"

The last giant, the second female, sauntered past the first giantess and cracked her whip several times before giving her reply.

"I am Shadavon!" she hissed. "I wield the hidden power of darkness, that which swallows the soul!"

Apart from the fact that Brian figured these giants' names to be really stupid and somewhat cliché, he did sense a definite threat here, if only to him. There was no way these maroons were ever going to take Earth, but he didn't need them to know that. They were, however, quite capable of nuking *him* to ash.

He kept his mind sharp and his wits about him as the giants made their challenge.

The first giant, the male giant with the spear, pointed out toward the barren distance.

"Behold the price of failure," he said with ominous intent.

Brian turned in alarm to stare at a small group of furry creatures with lizard faces being led away in chains by another group of purple giants. These small creatures appeared broken in both spirit and form, their faces an expression of doomed hope and final loss.

"If your world's elements fail," said the giant with the spear, "then we shall conquer your world as is worthy of our kind. It is might that rules the stars, and it is might that shall always lead."

Brian frowned as he thought about this. Never in his life had he ever thought he would be the one to save the world, but it appeared that this was exactly what he was going to have to do, but that was fine, because if he was anything, he was smart...

Eh, who was he kidding? These Darwinian throwbacks would never be able to take Earth no matter how much magic they wielded.

Earth didn't need magic...Earth had science.

Brian looked up, stared down the giant with the spear, and gave the overgrown bully a knowing smirk.

"Might has its place!" he yelled confidently. "I'll concede that point, but never underestimate the power of the mind!...The element from my world that I choose first is...plutonium!"

#7...MISSY

When that weird little girl is not so much "weird" as she is "deadly."

Lorena drove around a parked red Chevrolet Chevelle and then parked her own car along a dirt stretch of forgotten road that led to the cozy white house in the distance, a two-story firmly nestled within the dark trees of this backwoods area.

She shut off her lights and turned the key to shut down the engine of her Oldsmobile Custom Cruiser. She reached over and grabbed her briefcase full of case files, thought better about it, and left her briefcase in the passenger seat. She didn't need that yet.

It was Friday, and she had a date with Robert tonight, so it was best to review this case and make a judgement of future action now rather than let it sit until Monday. It was a hassle, true, but children were the one universal thing that Lorena could not turn her back on. She would never do that.

True, she was looking forward to tonight and her date with Robert, but some things were just too important to let sit, even though she could have, in fact, let this marinate until Monday.

Besides, this was just a quick interview anyway. She wouldn't need her briefcase for that…No, she was ready to go.

Dawn had not yet touched the eastern trees in the distance. There were still about ten minutes to go before that morning orb would pierce the sky, but that was fine. She had a busy day, so she was here early, and that was unfortunate for Mrs. De Veuve, but what the State wanted, the State got. It wasn't like Mrs. De Veuve could turn her away without serious legal repercussions.

This, of course, was about Missy. Missy De Veuve had somehow been lost in the filing, and if Lorena had not been so diligent at her job, she would have never discovered the existence of the little girl, nor would the State have sent Lorena here, out here in this neck of the boonies of their own fair county.

And the boonies this was. The dark angle of thick trees and overgrowth cast a long shadow of spindly fingers that tugged at one's sensibilities and stoked one's own backwards fears, and that was during the day. Being out here during predawn was a little much, to tell the truth.

Still, this was about Missy. The little girl had already turned seven, yet she had not been enrolled in school. Over two whole years had gone by without her attendance, and that was simply unacceptable.

Lorena walked along a dirt path strewn with fallen leaves until she reached the front door of the De Veuve residence. It was the light from a bottom floor window of the house that lit her way, for without it, she would have had to leave the lights on from her car to see anything at all.

She could see that house light within this cozy two-story via a single standing lamp at the west wall, and that quick peek through a window on the right revealed a small living room that led to a white archway, probably the entrance to the kitchen. The rest of the house was shrouded in darkness, much like the early-morning sky.

Lorena had only knocked twice before the door was answered, that singular, white wooden door creaking open to reveal the little girl in question.

This little girl was around six or seven, so that much was accurate, but a complete description of her had been wholly lacking within the State files.

This little blonde thing had pale peach skin, skin painted over with a light brush of peach upon alabaster, and she possessed ruby red lips that held a light sheen in what little light there was. She had striking green eyes, an eye color that was rare in combination for a natural blonde. Her adorable face was settled within a circlet of blonde ringlets, a face that was both cute yet disturbing in its…well…*adorableness*, and combined with her antiquated clothing, her very presence unsettled Lorena, if only because the girl looked like a walking and talking porcelain doll made flesh.

And speaking of antiquated clothing…

This little girl wore a red dress that looked like a mix of styles from the Victorian Age and the Renaissance, a red, velvet drape with frills along the hem, a hem that rested above her narrow ankles. The shoulders of the dress were puffed, with spotless-white sleaves that ran down to form small tight cuffs around her twig-thin wrists. Beneath the hem of that dress shone the black gleam of well-polished brass-buckle shoes surrounding white ankle socks, something that most certainly added to the overall semblance of a living doll.

It was 1972, for crying out loud. No one outside of a stage play dressed like this anymore.

Lorena, herself, had on her formal attire of a white button up, a brown vest jacket, and a matching brown skirt. She had on her pantyhose with her good white heels, and she had her long, feathered, brown hair pinned back for the moment for a more professional look.

She did not consider herself the most attractive woman in the world—brown eyes and brown hair were very common indeed for a white woman in her late twenties—but this little girl made her look…plain.

Nevertheless, Lorena had a job to do. She needed to speak with Mrs. De Veuve.

"Missy?" asked Lorena.

"Yes?" asked the little girl.

This little blonde doll's voice was like a silver bell, a sweet call that held a strange lull to it…Lorena had to shake her head to fling off the feeling of both nostalgia and complacency that haunting voice cast upon her.

"I…I'm from Child Welfare." she said after a second of composure. "I need to know why you haven't been in school, Missy, so I need to speak to your mommy, sweet heart. Where is your mommy now?"

This little living doll scrunched up her red lips as her blonde brows furrowed in visible confusion.

"Mother isn't expecting visitors today," said Missy. "She has gentleman callers now and then, but she's not had one for at least a month, Miss…umm…Whom am I addressing, ma'am?"

This little thing held a slight southern accent, something else that dug into Lorena's psyche, a combination of voice and style that nearly tripped her up again. It was that dulcet calm in Missy's voice, that lulling bell that ate at Lorena, and it was difficult to resist.

"Uhhh…Kaminski," replied Lorena.

"She's resting right now, Ms. Kaminski," said Missy. "It's not wise to disturb her at this hour, though you may come in and wait if you like."

She lifted the sides of her dress and did a formal curtsy, something Lorena had never expected to see in her lifetime from…well…anyone.

This was crazy.

Lorena had to shake her head yet again. Not only was this little thing like a living doll, she was precocious in both manner and speech, so much so that it stunned Lorena for a few seconds. Missy's intelligence had to be off the charts for her age.

"I…uhhh…" started Lorena.

"Why don't you come in and wait, Ms. Kaminski," said Missy. "Mother is always willing to entertain new guests. She's had her fill of gentleman callers, I think, so I believe she would like to…*entertain* someone new…new and different, that is."

The fact that this little girl kept using the term "gentleman caller" disturbed Lorena on a deep level, not to mention the precocious doll's emphasis upon the word "entertain." Oh, Lorena was definitely going to have to have a few words with Mrs. De Veuve. Whatever was going on here did not seem appropriate, or at least, not appropriate with a child in the house.

"I think I'd better do just that," frowned Lorena.

She was about to step across the threshold when the little girl in question peered around her and out into the darkness of early morning. The precocious child's face scrunched up again in visible confusion, so Lorena turned to follow the little doll's example, though she, herself, could see very little in the early-morning shroud of predawn.

"Who else am I addressing, ma'am?" asked Missy. "Is there someone else with you?"

"No…" said Lorena hesitantly. "I came here alone."

"Then which vehicle is yours, might I ask?" asked Missy.

"That's not your mom's Chevelle?" asked Lorena.

"No, ma'am," replied Missy.

They came out of the dark after that, two strangers walking at a brisk pace from out of said darkness. They made a direct line for Lorena, and they each came from one side of her, from the east and the west.

One of these strangers was an older white man in his sixties, a respectable-looking man in a brown business suit wearing a matching brown fedora on his greyed head, but the other stranger was unusual in her appearance, unusual in the fact that she was a black woman barely out of her teens, a young black woman in a swirly blue and purple tie-dye shirt, blue jean jacket, and bell-bottom blue jeans.

The woman of the two had her long black hair tied in a bun with a strip of what looked like material taken from the very type of blue jeans she was wearing, but this little feature was not what held Lorena's attention. It was the very real and very deadly shotgun the woman was pointing at her that captured her interest.

These two were as mismatched a couple as Lorena could imagine, but the fact that the woman of the pair was armed and pointing that weapon straight at Lorena overrode any questions Lorena might have had about that.

"We should have waited until sunrise," said the woman in a hostile tone.

"It's too late for that," said the older man. "I wasn't expecting anyone else to show up."

Lorena had no idea what was going on, but this did not look good. She instinctively backed into the house and pushed back Missy, placing herself between the precocious little doll and the two strangers.

The woman with the shotgun kept the door open with her right black boot before Lorena could close it.

"Get back, lady!" demanded the armed stranger.

Lorena backed further into the De Veuve residence, all the while keeping herself between Missy and the clearly hostile couple before her. Their sudden presence, along with their very clear hostility, caused

Lorena's adrenaline to automatically spike in vivid and clamping fear.

"Who are you people!" was all that came to her lips at that moment.

The armed woman of the pair stepped in as the older gentlemen followed suit.

The older man reached into his inner suit pocket and pulled forth a silver aspergillum, that strange device the Catholic Church used to sprinkle holy water, the small mace-like object clutched firmly within his right hand.

Lorena held up her right arm before her face as the man shook the aspergillum at her, sprinkling her with what she could only assume was the holy water in question the device was supposed to carry. It was annoying, true, but it wasn't exactly life threatening.

"What are you doing!" cried Lorena.

"She's clean," said the woman of the pair. "Let's do the little girl."

"Hey!" protested Lorena. "You leave her alone!"

The woman with the shotgun held it up to Lorena's face and motioned with the weapon for Lorena to step aside.

"Get out of the way, lady!" commanded the armed woman.

Lorena wanted to protest again, a somewhat stupid thing to do in light of the situation, but she did not get the chance to. No, she turned to view Missy, because the little girl had stepped back and away and to the side of Lorena, stepping back and away and aside in order to address the two hostile strangers. Missy then indeed addressed the two strangers, a deep frown etched upon her little doll's face, an expression that caused Lorena to hesitate for a second.

"You weren't invited in," said Missy. "You need to leave now before you awaken Mother. She most assuredly won't be happy you're here. She wasn't expecting any callers today, certainly not an older gentleman accompanied by such a brazen harlot."

It did not take a genius to catch the insult bound within the precocious little girl's words, and under normal circumstances, this would have horrified Lorena that such a young thing would even know such a word, but these were not normal circumstances, and the reaction to that insulting word was immediate.

"What did you call me!" yelled the woman with the shotgun.

She turned the firearm upon Missy, aiming for the little girl's face, but Lorena stepped in-between Missy and that deadly weapon.

"Stop!" demanded Lorena. "Don't you dare!"

"Move out of the way!" commanded the hostile woman with an equally powerful incentive, that incentive being the shotgun she was now pointing at Lorena's face.

"Calm down, Latasha," said the older man. "The little one's just trying to get under your skin…We need to find the mother anyway."

"Not before I blow apart this little sh—" started "Latasha."

"No, you won't!" commanded Lorena. "You put that down right now! Don't you dare threaten a child!"

These two crazies angered her, angering her to the point of stupidity, because she was most certainly not the one with the gun. On some level, she was terrified, but her common sense had been overridden by a need to protect children, something she had always carried with her, something she had carried with her throughout her entire life.

"Step aside, miss," nodded the older gentleman in the fedora. "Let us do our job."

"Job!" cried Lorena. "What job! You think threatening to kill a little girl is a job!"

"This dumb-dove mirror warmer thinks that's a little girl, Fenman," said Latasha.

The older man shook his head, frowned, and then directed that frown at Lorena.

"We can't kill what's already dead, miss," said the older gentleman, this "Fenman." "What we can do is lay her to rest…Now…step aside so we can do our job and put her down."

"What are you talking about!" protested Lorena. "You two are crazy!"

Missy stepped into view once more, stepping out from behind Lorena on Lorena's left, the little girl deliberately putting herself in harm's way.

"It's okay, Ms. Kaminski," said Missy. "These two can't hurt me. Even if they did manage to do anything, they would only anger Moth—"

The older man of the hostile pair, the one named "Fenman," shook his silver aspergillum, droplets of the blessed water splashing in an arc straight towards Missy's pale little face.

The little doll raised her left arm in front of her face as the droplets of holy water struck her in various places.

The effect was immediate, just as immediate as the insult Missy had levied against Latasha.

Missy transformed in an instant. The golden ringlets of her hair turned jet black, and her pale, peach-brushed skin turned a distinct shade of blackish-blue, a washing over of colors unnatural for a human being. She stepped back as she hissed in defiance, comically-large, glistening white fangs dropping down from her gums in an overt, supernatural insanity of transmogrification. Her green eyes glowed even greener with an internal emerald light, and there was nothing on her little face but sheer rage, rage and something else, something wholly evil.

Lorena shook in both surprise and swift horror as she backed away from the little girl…no, not a little girl, something else, something beyond description.

"Old fool!" screeched the monstrous little doll. "How dare you soil me with your god's foul presence!"

"She's not melting!" yelled Latasha.

"This one's old!" cried Fenman. "It's not like that nest in Monterey! Keep your wits about you!"

Lorena shrieked and backed away toward the front door as Latasha pulled the trigger of her shotgun.

The young woman fired off two rounds, two blasts of pellets that exploded outwards in a deafening roar around the quaint domicile, this little house out in the middle of nowhere.

Unfortunately, both shots missed.

The monstrous little doll that was Missy dodged to the left at blinding speed, dodging to the right after that as Latasha pulled the trigger for the second shot. Not one single pellet struck the little demon, even at point-blank range. No, the first shot tore up a wooden coffee table, shattering a small vase resting upon it, and the second shot blasted into a grandfather clock that rested against the southern wall that separated the living room from the kitchen.

The young woman pulled the trigger for a third shot, but nothing happened.

"Damn!" cursed Latasha. "Gun's jammed!"

She struggled with the firearm as the older man in the fedora, Fenman, pulled forth a large wooden crucifix from his inner suit jacket.

Considering he'd already pulled forth an aspergillum from that jacket, Lorena figured the man had to have an arsenal hidden in there.

Fenman held up the crucifix, stepped forward, and blazed forth the holy symbol like a blessed shield.

"Back!" commanded the older man. "Back, creature of the night!"

Missy's normally sweet red lips had turned a nightmare black, and she opened those ebon lines to hiss yet again, baring those huge, unnatural fangs.

Fenman's crucifix burst into flames, and the older gentleman was forced to toss the holy relic to the floor. He stamped upon it a second later, something sacrilegious in Lorena's eyes, but a fire was a fire, so immediately putting it out was probably just instinct.

Missy giggled and grinned, her mouth opening wider than it should have possibly been able to open, those overlarge, glistening white fangs a deadly symbol of their own.

"Silly old man," she replied in her dulcet tones. "That won't work on me."

Lorena lost control of her bladder as fear and her previously ignored survival instinct finally took control of her. She had urine running down her right leg as she turned, ran to the front door, and gripped the knob. She turned that knob and pulled hard, but the door was stuck shut, stuck solid, stuck as if glued to the frame.

She could feel the door give a little as she struggled and strained to open it, but there was something gluing it shut, something strong enough in construction to prevent her from budging that wooden gate barring her only current exit.

Her mind had temporarily shut off, but it flipped back on again as she looked toward the windows of the house, only just now realizing those windows were painted over in black, painted over to keep out the sun's comforting light.

"But they weren't that way from the outside!" she rattled off to herself.

She turned and flattened her back against the door as the supernatural battle continued to wage before her.

"This one's really old!" cried Fenman. "We'll need to destroy her before we can get to the mother! Get that gun working, Latasha!"

The older gentleman reached into his suit jacket a third time, but this time he pulled forth a long wooden stake from his jacket arsenal, a silver tip on the end of that rudimentary weapon.

"To the flames of Hell with you!" said Fenman.

He stepped forward to end the monstrous little thing, but Missy leapt straight up as the older man attempted to drive the stake through her tiny chest. The little girl crawled across the ceiling after that, only to dive directly down upon Fenman's shoulders.

The older gentleman's brown fedora was knocked from his head as the little demon clutched him from behind, her oversized fangs sinking through the stiff fabric of his suit jacket, sinking through his white button up and then into the flesh of his left shoulder.

Fenman cried out as he was bitten, dropping his stake in the process, and the silver-tipped weapon rattled across the wooden floor.

Missy jumped from his shoulders and back to the ceiling as the older man stiffened, his fingers gnarling as if he were wracked with sudden, agonizing pain.

"Fenman!" cried Latasha.

The older gentleman's face darkened as his veins blackened, ebony lines weathering outwards across his leathery skin. He fell to his back after that, his body shaking, his limbs locked in a rigid pose.

"My God!" he choked out. "We were wrong! She's not a…not a…Aaaggh!"

"Fenman!" screeched Latasha again.

The older man's skin blued over as his breathing slowed down to near nothing, and then his breath petered out altogether, the light in his eyes dying out forever.

Lorena could do nothing but stare in lancing, wide-eyed terror.

The young black woman with the shotgun popped free the jammed cartridge, and then she took aim at the little doll-demon crawling across the ceiling.

Missy hissed once, her green eyes flashing an emerald light, her huge fangs still glistening in the lamplight of the single standing lamp at the west wall.

"I'll kill you!" shrieked Latasha.

She fired three times, each shot missing as the crawling demon above her skittered from one side of the ceiling to the other, each shot blasting open a large hole in the ceiling plaster, that plaster raining down in small chunks to bounce across the wooden floor.

Latasha pulled the trigger again but was only met with a loud "CLICK!"

Missy dropped down from the ceiling, landing on all fours with an unnatural ease, and then she slowly stood to face her assailant.

"You should have stayed at the bordello," smiled the little monster. "Now it looks like you're out of time, whore."

"You little piece of…!" spat Latasha.

Her face worked inwards with a blazing fury, but then she shook her head and grit her teeth in defiance.

"You're the one who's out of time!" she yelled.

The young woman spun and flung her shotgun with all her might. The firearm smashed through the window left of the door, the right window from the outside, and dawn's light spilled through the shattered black glass, that comforting glow streaming in to spread its warmth across both Latasha and Missy.

The green glow in Missy's eyes died down as her skin changed back to the pale peach it was supposed to be. Her huge fangs retracted into her gums, and then the little girl held up her right hand to shade her now normal green eyes from the light.

"Don't you know anything, little fly?" asked the monstrous child. "There are no vampires here…Sunlight can't harm my kind, though it restrains our abilities to a degree…No, it's just an inconvenience."

Latasha stood both speechless and dumbfounded for a second, but then her head jerked upwards toward the ceiling as a loud clacking noise resounded overhead, the ceiling shaking from something large moving above them, bits of plaster dust sprinkling down upon them in a snowy cloud.

"Uh…*ooooh*," smiled Missy, her ruby lips pulling back into an insulting smirk. "It appears you have awakened Mother, and she doesn't take kindly to unwanted visitors tearing up her home. She especially doesn't like callers of your low class."

Latasha choked out a shout as thick silken cords, huge strands of webbing, sprayed over her from a hole in the ceiling, those white strands ensnaring her in a biologically-made net, and then she was pulled up to crash through the plaster above her, the woman screaming the entire journey upwards. That screaming was quickly cut short as it was followed by a loud death gurgle, and then there was silence.

Now there was only Lorena, Missy, and the deceased older gentleman on the floor, though upon further thought, Lorena supposed Fenman didn't count anymore, so it was really only down to herself and the demonic child before her.

Lorena still had her back to the door, so she slid down that door to her bottom to rest herself on the hardwood floor. She was in shock, and she knew it, but her mind was far and away from rationality, because nothing made sense anymore. There was nothing she could do but shake, her psyche locked in sheer terror.

Missy turned, walked into the kitchen, and then walked back out less than a minute later. She had a long silver spoon pinched between the slender fingers of her right hand, and in her left, she held a small glass jar, a jar with a steel and tin lid, that little jar filled with a black, jam-like substance.

"It wouldn't do to have you disappear, Ms. Kaminski," said Missy. "No one will miss those hunters, but you actually have eyes on you, and we can't have more people from the government coming out here, so it just makes sense to let you go…Besides, you put your life on the line for me, and that's something Mother won't forget, not ever."

She walked up to Lorena as Lorena shook in paralyzing, crippling fear. The little monster that was Missy removed the lid from her jar, dipped in the silver spoon, and scooped up a spoonful of the strange black jam within the jar.

"This is Mother's Mercy," said Missy. "She makes it herself, but it's only for the deserving…That's why you should have it, Ms. Kaminski. I think you've earned it."

Lorena stared in horror at the quivering, trembling blob of black upon the silver spoon. She did not know what this stuff was, and she most certainly did not wish to find out, but it was not like she had a choice in the matter…She did not want to die, especially in whatever terrible ways were present within this house of unmitigated horror.

"Just open up for me…" trailed the little demon as she raised the spoon up to Lorena's lips.

Lorena reluctantly took the spoon into her mouth, though she did not want to.

The substance that shimmied and shook on her tongue felt *alive*, and she nearly spit it out, but it was fear that rooted her in place and kept her from any open defiance. That black goo was spicy in flavor, though the texture and the fact that it was *moving* made it much more difficult to swallow than any burning sensation.

Lorena gagged as the substance traveled down her esophagus, but she managed to choke it down anyway.

Missy turned, walked back into the kitchen, and then walked out again without the jar and spoon. She walked back up to Lorena and took Lorena's left hand into both of her own, though Lorena quivered at her touch.

"Now there's just one more step," said the little girl who was not a little girl.

Missy's oversized fangs dropped down from her gums one more time as she bit into Lorena's left wrist.

The bite hurt like mad, and a venomous fire raced through Lorena's blood, temporarily causing her to jerk and shudder uncontrollably as she opened her own mouth in a silent scream of pain, her eyes squeezing shut from the sheer magnitude of that pain.

It occurred to her in stark realization that she could have just escaped through the now shattered window where dawn's light was streaming in, but sheer terror had prevented her from doing so, from even *thinking* about such an action.

She was stuck before the monster she so wanted to run from, and that previous mental prison of paralyzing inaction had screwed her over, because now she was *physically* paralyzed by whatever terrible affliction was currently coursing through her, a bitter, venomous dose of irony that was just now taking root.

But Missy would not just *allow* Lorena some peace. The little demon continued to talk, and what she said was neither encouraging nor comforting.

"Birth is always painful, Ms. Kaminski," said the little demon. "But without birth, there can be no life, certainly not for our kind."

The pain caused Lorena to shake and sweat, a torment beyond words, and this lasted for at least a full thirty seconds, a million years in her mind, but then it was over just as swiftly as it had begun, the agony receding, fading into a foreboding, tremulous calm.

She breathed out a long sigh of relief and then opened her eyes, hoping in some way, somehow, this whole situation had simply been a bad dream, but this foolish hope was an egregious mockery, because the only image to greet her vision upon the raising of her eyelids was Missy's wicked profile, the little demon patiently awaiting Lorena's return to normalcy.

"Come with me now," said the evil little doll. "Our kind are territorial, but Mother will want to meet you anyway. I believe we shall speak to her before you take your leave."

This was something Lorena most certainly did *not* want. As terrible and as monstrous as Missy was, Lorena could not begin to imagine what her mother was like.

But she did not have a choice in the matter.

Missy took Lorena by her uninjured hand and coaxed her to stand, and then the terrible little girl led her toward the stairs, leading Lorena toward a set of wooden steps, ascending steps to the left of the kitchen, white wooden steps that led upwards toward whatever unimaginable horror lurked above.

Lorena was led by the hand up those stairs, and as she took one step after the next, the walls around her began to change, the pristine white wallpaper with green flowers caking over with many years of dust and dirt, the paper peeling as if rapidly decaying by Father Time's own hand, great strands of webbing forming here and there and everywhere.

Lorena walked into the upstairs, but there was only one room up here, one very large room that spanned the entirety of the second floor, that room filled with webbing, white silken webbing in the corners and the ceiling and strung everywhere else to form a complex maze of walkways and passages.

The only other thing that stood out was the large circular window in the north wall, that window painted over with an ominous black.

There was no light in here, not a mote, not even a glimmer, and it took Lorena a moment to realize that she could still see, viewing her surroundings in black and white like the images of an old T.V. show.

She shuddered deep down, deep deep down to her very soul.

Something was wrong with her, very wrong, and she could feel it, sensing it all the way down to that cast in spirit. There was a growing darkness inside her, growing like a swiftly metastasizing cancer, and there was nothing she could do about it. There was also a helplessness inside her born out of fear, but she could not give up…

There had to be a way out of this.

Missy led her through the maze of webs, but there were distinct holes in the wooden floor, holes caused by Latasha's shotgun blasts. There was one hole that was of a particular avoidance, that one larger than the rest, and above it hung…

Lorena recoiled at the cocooned and very deceased body of Latasha. The young black woman was now nothing more than a withered, desiccated husk, her dark skin stretched in leathery pronunciation over her hanging skeleton, but her eyes were still intact, her dark eyes bulging slightly outwards due to a lack of surrounding supportive tissue.

Lorena's own horror was interrupted by the dulcet tones of the monstrous doll that was Missy.

"I'm here, Mother," said the little demon. "I've brought up Ms. Kaminski. She's been very kind to me, I think."

Lorena's lips parted in a silent gasp, and she shook in place as the huge black leg of a spider reached forth from an overcoating shock of webbing from the south, that huge arachnid's leg stretching forth from that silken wall of white, that leg as thick around as one of Missy's own legs.

The sharp black tip of that huge leg stroked Missy's pale right cheek.

"Those hunters actually thought we were vampires, Mother," said Missy with a slight giggle. "They had no idea they were in the lair of a Widow."

Lorena could hear a shadowy voice stab into her mind, a sibilant whisper so dark, it froze her in place.

"Such foul-tasting undead could never enter here, my child," came the terrible voice.

"Yes, Mother," said Missy. "They know better than to come here, I think."

"Yes," spoke the dark voice. *"You did well with the hunters, my child…and I see you've brought me a gift as well."*

"This one was willing to give her life for me," smiled Missy. "She's from Child Welfare, and she tried to protect me from the hunters, so I gave her your blessing."

"Then she may leave," said the shadowy voice. *"She may go and use her influence to hide us. She must leave, for she will soon know the hunger that binds our kind."*

Missy turned and smiled at Lorena, and it was then that the full knowledge of what had happened crashed into Lorena's psyche, an explosion of cosmic proportions, a horror so profound that there was no comfort, no light for any future salvation.

She was one of them now.

Lorena could feel the evil inside herself, germinating within herself, a darkness so terribly overpowering that she had no internal dialogue to describe it.

But there had to be something she could do…

She turned to catch the grisly image of the withered corpse that had once been Latasha. If this woman had been anything like her older male counterpart, then perhaps…

There was something Lorena could do, but it could only work depending upon Missy's reaction to it, and only if the little horror reacted in the same way a second time…Even then, Latasha's corpse still had to have the item in question.

Lorena reached into the webbing cocoon that surrounded Latasha, burrowing into the thick, sticky strands, her hands immune to that sticky glue now, immune due to the evil already changing her from within. She reached inside the cocoon in order to reach into the blue jean jacket the woman had worn, and it took her less than three seconds to find what she was looking for.

She pulled forth the desired object in desperate triumph, though doing what she was about to do would probably mean the end of her, but at this point, ending herself was far more desirable than whatever terrible fate was in store for her…She did not want to live as one of whatever it was Missy and her mother were.

She spun and held up the large wooden crucifix the deceased hunter had been carrying in the recesses of that innocuous jean jacket. The wooden holy symbol inflicted a slight burning sensation within the palm of Lorena's right hand, further cementing the fact that she was now infected by the Widow's evil, a supernatural evil too horrible to ever live with.

"Back, both of you!" she screeched, and then the real madness began.

Missy's insufferably cute face warped and changed yet again, warping back into that monstrous, dark figure with flashing green eyes, blue-blackened skin, and oversized fangs.

The little girl hissed once in automatic defiance, and then Lorena's newly acquired crucifix burst into flames.

This, of course, was exactly what Lorena had wanted.

"NO!" came a mental shout that speared straight through Lorena's mind.

The ringing of this mental assault did not stay the conviction Lorena felt surging through her. Her insanely-desperate plan had worked, and Missy's horrific mother could not change one iota of what Lorena was about to do.

Lorena tossed the flaming crucifix at Missy's feet, and the little demon-doll's antiquated red dress lit aflame at the hem, those flames spreading upwards without mercy.

Missy screamed and darted out of panic through the morass of webbing around her, and then that silken deathtrap went up as well, quickly blazing across lines of spread strands that encompassed the entirety of the upstairs floor.

The heat around Lorena was so intense that she panicked as well. She could not contain her own reaction, and that reaction was to run, a survival instinct that had been implanted within human beings since their conception, and part of her was still human, a part that was still unwilling to just up and die.

She turned and pushed past thick webbing with ease, heavy webbing that would have prevented her from moving before she had been inflicted with this terrible curse. She ran toward the dark circular window embedded in the north wall, the large window that had been painted over in black, the only window up here.

She hit the window at full speed, shoulder first, and then she was through it, crashing through the panes to momentarily fly through shattered glass flung about her in gleaming, slicing bits.

She hit the bare dirt seconds later, falling straight down from the second floor, and she hit that dirt feetfirst and rolled over her left shoulder as if by cosmic instinct, something she could have never done mere minutes ago.

Her high heels popped off her feet, the straps snapping from the rigorous strain of weird acrobatics, and Lorena was immediately up and running in nothing flat.

She was in her car after that, jamming the key in the ignition, her quivering right hand desperately turning that key to get the car started. Her station wagon roared to life as she pushed in the clutch, and then she automatically shifted into reverse, though her attention was still on the house before her.

She could see the dilapidated, run-down two-story in flames, that house covered in blazing webbing, just a ball of fiery silk surrounding that den of evil, and she knew right then that this was the building's true form. The bewitching spell that had made this house look warm and inviting had finally been broken, the deadly illusion dispersed.

She winced at the screaming in her mind, even as she pushed in on the clutch and roared her station wagon backwards, doing a half-donut to turn the car around, only to throw the stick into drive, and she did drive, jamming the pedal to the floor, the screaming in her head dying away to nothing as she put distance and the blazing ball of webbing and wood behind her.

✳✳✳✳✳

"That's right," said Lorena into the speaker of her phone. "I'm quitting, effective immediately…No, I already know that…No, I…I've been diagnosed with an incurable illness…Yes, it's progressive…There's nothing I can do…I'm going to move and…and enjoy what little time I have left…

"No, you don't have to worry about the Missy De Veuve case. Mrs. De Veuve and Missy moved away to France years ago when Missy was only two. This whole case was some kind of oversight by the State…

"Yes, I did go out to the house. There's nothing but a burnt-out hollow where the house used to stand. In fact, I did a little digging, and I found an old article on microfilm. The house burned down five years ago, right after the De Veuves moved away…It was a lightning strike, I believe. Shame too. That house was only on the market for two months after the De Veuve's departure…Well, that's a closed case, so that's all there is to that.

"No, thank you, Mr. Stanford…No, that's okay…Yes, please tell everyone I'll miss them…No, I'll be all right. I'm cashing out my bank account, and…and I'll get by somehow…No, it will be all right; I'll be all right…Thank you, Mr. Stanford…Yes, I'm sorry, too…Yes, goodbye. I'll call you if I need to settle anything else…Thank you again. Goodbye."

She hung up after that, placing the large white receiver of her phone back onto its base.

"So much for that," she muttered.

She walked out of her kitchen and into the bathroom, sighing as she studied her surroundings. Her house was simply too small anymore, but she was selling it anyway. She was going to go cheap but bigger, maybe buy something run down in a remote location…It was really the only option.

But none of that mattered right now. No, she had a persistent problem following her around, and it was high time she addressed it.

Lorena flipped on the light in the bathroom and stared into the mirror. In the reflective glass was her own image, but behind that and to her right was Missy's image, the little girl's horribly burned and bleeding face staring back at her, her little bald head missing its golden locks, her little body's bare skin devoid of any cloth, her antiquated clothing replaced by charred, flame-ravaged flesh.

"I see you've been busy, Ms. Kaminski," came the girl's disembodied voice, that southern voice still a haunting lull that made Lorena wince.

"Unfortunately," replied Lorena. "What is it you want, Missy?"

"Oh, so you're no longer pretending you can't see me?" asked the ghoulish figure in the mirror.

"Why bother?" asked Lorena. "You're there every time I turn around."

"And I always shall be," smiled Missy, flecks of black crumbling from what was left of her thin lips.

"I'll ask you again," frowned Lorena. "What is it you want?...You must want something, or you wouldn't be in my face every time I turn around."

"Our kind will always see the restless damned, Ms. Kaminski," said Missy. "That has been our fate ever since we first came to be."

"What is it you want, Missy?" repeated Lorena, her voice lowering an octave. "I'm not going to ask again. I'm getting very tired of your intrusive presence."

"I only stopped by to ask a question," said the charred little girl.

"And what's that?" asked Lorena unhappily.

"Where is your beau, Ms. Kaminski?" smiled Missy. "Where is that handsome fellow named Robert you've been seeing? He came by last night, didn't he?...He paid a visit, but he never left here, to my understanding…He is indeed such a handsome fellow, too. He's quite a tall drink of water, as Mother would say."

Lorena sucked in her breath as she squeezed her dark eyes shut. She opened them after a second of shaking anger, but this time her eyes were a verdant green, a flashing green that glowed with an internal, emerald light for a few seconds.

"Oh, temper, temper, Ms. Kaminski," smirked Missy as she wagged one charred, bleeding, and blackened finger. "You have no power over me anymore…

"Besides, this is all your fault anyway. Mother gave you a gift, and you tried to reject it, but that's not how this works. You're one of us now, and you ever shall be…

"Oh, but there's more to your crime, I think. Our kind may be different than mortal men, but I was still a child, and you murdered me. You murdered one of your own, and a child at that. Now you have to live with the consequences of your actions. Now you have to live with what you've done."

This hit Lorena in the heart, a deliberate emotional attack she had not been prepared for. It quelled her anger, quelling her rage in spite of the caustic goading of the burnt child in the mirror. She had always considered herself a protector of children, and she still wanted to be one, even if that was no longer possible, and what had ultimately happened to Missy ate at her, ate at her like nothing else.

"I never wanted you to suffer," grimaced Lorena. "I really didn't…And I am so sorry this happened to you, Missy, I really am…I've always dedicated my life to helping children, so this really does hurt me…I really am sorry. No child should have to suffer through what happened to you."

"Touching sentiment aside, you started that fire, Ms. Kaminski," reminded Missy.

"Oh, I wasn't talking about the fire," said Lorena with a shake of her head.

"Oh, you weren't?" asked Missy. "Are you referring to our kind?...I wasn't the recipient of a gift like you, Ms. Kaminski. I was born this way, so your sentiment, though touching, is severely misplaced…

"You were nothing but a spawn anyway, not a pureblood. You were supposed to gather power over time, but ever since you killed Mother, it looks like you've just up and taken her place…I didn't even know that was possible…

"Now you're a full Widow, and you shall forever be Arachne's legacy. You're not a half-breed anymore. Now you can make a full change, and you may find being a full Widow preferable to being human…Mother did…She rarely walked around in a human shape…but I digress…

"I suppose I shall make my point, and my point is very clear, Ms. Kaminski…You have a whole new world before you, and all the rules have changed in your life, so I hope the disaffection that has curtailed your emotions is stoic in its conviction, because you'll be seeing many more bodies than just mine from now on."

Lorena squeezed her eyes shut and muttered an ugly curse. Missy had a way of pushing all of her buttons at once.

She opened her eyes and gave the very crispy little demon the staredown.

"I don't need a naked, barbecued little girl in my mirror to tell me that," she scowled.

She reached over and flung open her bathtub's green shower curtain.

Within the tub was the webbed, withered, and desiccated corpse of Robert, Lorena's now former boyfriend, the man's mouth permanently wide in a silent scream, his brown eyes bulging slightly from their sockets, a single fly upon the right eye, the insect's ubiquitous presence more of a reminder of what Lorena had become than Missy's warning and Robert's corpse could ever be.

#7a…BONUS STORY: BREAKING THE FOURTH WALL

Jerry made sure the knots around the babysitter's wrists were nice and tight. He had her sitting on the brown-and-white-trim tiles of the kitchen floor, somewhere in the house where he could gain access to a butcher knife, and now he had possession of that large knife, so that little problem was out of the way.

He held his knife against the babysitter's exposed throat, and her breathing picked up, but he didn't care. This young woman, a slightly-chubby brunette in her early twenties, wouldn't be giving him any trouble. It was the brat in the corner who was setting his teeth on edge, because she just wouldn't shut up.

The little girl in the corner was probably seven or eight, but she had pale skin and jet-black hair, and her little black dress wasn't doing her any favors in the "making friends department," either. He had thought about taping her mouth shut, but in the eight robberies he'd already made, he hadn't even so much as bruised anyone, so he did not feel the need to do anything untoward to this child, creepy as she was.

"I told you to stop talking, little girl," he warned again. "Do you want me to slit her throat? I'll kill her and then kill you. Got it?...You're stepping on my last nerve."

But this little girl would not budge an inch. She did not even show any fear.

"You won't hurt her," said the little brat. "You can't hurt her. I already know that."

"Please…" begged the babysitter within his grasp.

"Shut up," said Jerry in a cold voice. "I didn't give anyone permission to speak."

"We don't need your permission," said the creepy little girl. "The People Beyond the Fourth Wall can see what you're doing, and they already know what's going to happen, and even if they don't, they'll know soon enough, and I know too, because this story never changes.

"You can't hurt us, and you're going to get caught, and there's nothing you can do about it. You're going to be unconscious until the police get here, and that's that."

"That's it," grunted Jerry. "You're done, little one. I'm taping your mouth shut."

Jerry stood with the roll of duct tape in his hand, but in his haste, he dropped the roll of tape, and naturally, it went rolling across the kitchen tiles with all expediency. He bent over and moved forward to snatch it up, but as he did, he forgot about the kitchen counter in front of him, and he immediately banged his head upon the hardtop.

He swore as he stood and turned while holding his forehead in his right hand, but the roll of tape behind him bounced off the kitchen-counter hem, and he stepped upon it, sealing his fate. He slipped upon the roll and fell backwards, the back of his head bounced off the kitchen countertop, and he blacked out before he'd even hit the floor, hitting that tiled floor with a loud thud.

"How…How did you know that, Brittney?" asked the babysitter in horrified amazement.

The little girl in black gave the young woman a strange and knowing smile.

"I've already read this story," said Brittney, "and I already knew the ending."

#8A…WHITECHAPEL PART I

When the obsessive fanboy is the least of your problems.

𝕵𝖆𝖒𝖊𝖘 𝖜𝖆𝖑𝖐𝖊𝖉 into the saloon and ran a cursory glance over the joint.

This place was a throwback to every Wild West show he'd ever watched as a kid. There were large, round, wooden tables with old wooden chairs surrounding them, those chairs filled with dusty ne'er-do-wells. There was a long wooden bar complete with an old-timey bartender, wooden walls with lit oil lamps posturing dim illumination, and barmaids—whoa, Nelly—barmaids.

The customers, the ne'er-do-wells, were a scruffy-looking, dirty lot that were all talk, but even if they weren't, James wasn't worried about them. He had his Rune Maker in his holster on his right hip and his enchanted saber in its sheath on his left hip, so these yahoos wouldn't be giving him any trouble. As bad as they *thought* they were, they were a bunch of cowards when it came to fighting someone that screamed "mercenary."

Besides, he had on his enchanted bulletproof vest, that safeguard offering firm protection to his center mass, and his enchanted steel neck collar contained his retractable Hermes-Alliette helm, so head shots weren't exactly a worry, either. That banded helm was located in an extradimensional space in his jacket's collar, and it was heavily enchanted, formfitting around his head and face for maximum protection.

In fact, the button on his collar that expanded his helm was the first thing he'd hit if any trouble went down. That helmet had saved his life more times than he could count.

But he wasn't here for fighting. He was here to relax, wind down, lay back, etc., etc.

He took a seat at the bar, leaned forward, and nodded toward the bartender.

The bartender, an older gentleman with silver hair and round spectacles upon his weathered nose, was dressed in a white button-up and a black vest along with black slacks and polished black dress shoes.

This was part and parcel to Hollowstone. Everybody out here still thought they were living in the 1800s. Of course, that's the way these city states worked in this crazy world of magic and monsters. Some cities were futuristic, with flying cars and enchanted monorails, neon lights and such, and some cities were normal, the way James remembered them from his world, but some cities were backwards, like this tired old dust hole.

But that's why he was here. He needed a change of pace.

He was getting too old for the bustling city life anymore. He was pushing fifty, and it was past time for him to slow down. Perhaps he should have settled down, found a wife, and parked his butt in an actual home a long time ago, but there was a fire burning in his blood, an itch he could not quite scratch, and that yearning for adventure still called to him, even as old as he was. So, he was in Hollowstone for the time being.

Normally, he went where the money was, to the breach sites, but those sites were drying up around him, mainly on account of him closing the breaches…He was good like that.

Eh, he'd find work here. There was always some merc-work to be had in any of these places, even Hollowstone. Besides, it was only a matter of time before another breach opened and he was back in business.

If it was one thing he understood, evil never slept.

"What'll it be, stranger?" asked the old bartender.

"Just give me a beer," grunted James as he sat back onto his barstool. "I don't even care what brand. I just want to veg out tonight."

"Bottle or tap?" asked the bartender.

"You've got oil lamps in here, but you have beer on tap?" snorted James.

"The lamps are for the aesthetic," said the old man with a tightlipped smile. "We're different in Hollowstone, not backwards. We have electricity and indoor plumbing. Surely, you've noticed that, sir."

James had always passed by Hollowstone. He'd only ever been at their train station, and their station still used paper postings for the train times. Hell, they still had newspapers here.

Even so, his original assessment of the place had been way off. They weren't as backwards as he had led himself to believe. In fact, he felt a twinge of disappointment at the realization that Hollowstone was simply an eccentric tourist trap and not the Old West like he had first thought…Still, he was here to relax, so starting trouble was not on the agenda.

"I honestly had no idea," smirked James. "Only ever been to the train station. That's how I got here…You know what? Just serve me up a bottle."

"That'll be one even," replied the bartender.

"One Federal Credit?" asked James. "It's one-fifty up in Coco…Huh…I should come here more often."

The old man smiled for the first time since James had laid eyes on him.

"You'll find Hollowstone to be much more amenable in that respect," said the old bartender. "You'll also find that we serve real beer here, not that overpriced, watered-down swill they pretend is beer in Coco City."

James smiled and shook his head. He reached into one of his inner jacket pockets, pulled forth a silver credit, and handed the coin to the old man.

The bartender left him for a moment, came back with an open beer bottle, and then handed him that frosty beer, the bottle labeled "Bailman's" in old-timey white print on a black background.

James took a tentative sip, discovered he liked it, and nodded back in return.

"This *is* good," he acknowledged.

"Of course, sir," replied the bartender.

The older man gave James a cursory glance and nodded once.

"Are you a mercenary, sir?" he asked.

Aside from the obvious gear, it was the scar. James had a rather large scar that ran from just underneath his left eye all the way down to the bottom of his chin. That scar bedecked his dark skin due to a rather unhappy encounter with a widow's spawn back when he was barely out of his teens…Yeah, never grapple a giant spider.

Of course, he didn't make stupid mistakes like that anymore. He knew better than to get in over his head at this stage in his life. He could have been sucked dry at that out-of-the-way brothel way back when, but obviously, he hadn't been because he'd been lucky, and James didn't want to rely on luck. That had been right before he'd walked through a rift into this universe…

That last universe, his original one, had become an apocalyptic wasteland during his short time there, and it had actually been worse than this one in a lot of ways.

Life was way too short for stupid mistakes anyway, especially here in this crazy world of magic and monsters.

Nevertheless, the old bartender was expecting an answer, so James was going to give him one, the only one he wanted to give.

"Yep," grunted James. "I'm not here for any work though. Just here to sit back and relax."

"Hollowstone is an excellent place for that, sir," said the older man. "I'm sure you'll enjoy your stay."

If James were going to reply, he never got the chance to. A younger man walked up to the bar and sat down beside him, just on his right.

This boy looked to be in his early twenties, barely out of the womb as far as James was concerned, but that was irrelevant. What was relevant was the fact that this baby-faced boy with tanned skin and a wide grin had just sat down right next to James for no apparent reason. There were other barstools with no one else next to them, but for some unknown reason, this kid had chosen to sit next to James.

The boy nodded once at the old bartender.

James gave the young man a once-over.

The dark-eyed, clean-shaven young man with well-trimmed, short black hair was wearing a fine black cloth jacket with gold filagree along the edges, and this article of clothing partially covered a jet-black shirt that spanned the distance between the center line of the open jacket. The boy had black pants on him paired with fine black cowboy boots to complete the basic outfit, but it was the black Gaucho hat with gold filagree along the rim that got James' attention. This kid honestly looked like he'd just stepped out of an episode of *Zorro*, minus the mustache.

In fact, upon further inspection, the boy had a rapier dangling from his left hip and a gun holstered on his right. Strapped diagonally across his back was a long, thick, golden metal tube with line ridges, the ends capped for some reason, the thing reminiscent of an archaic scroll or map case.

This kid was a merc; he had to be. Either that, or he was an explorer, but James was pretty sure there were no earnest explorers in this world…Well, maybe, maybe not.

"Yes, young sir?" asked the bartender. "What would you like?"

"A shot of Tequila," smiled the young man. "I need a pick-me-up."

The boy held a distinct Spanish accent, which was funny, because James was certain there was no Spain in this world. There was no Mexico, Columbia, El Salvador, Venezuela, etc. Still…some things just carried over from one universe to the next, so why not? They had beer and ale and even Tequila here, so James just wrote this off as a whatever.

What was weird, however, was that this young man was clearly white without a trace of native blood in him…

Upon further thought, it occurred to James that perhaps there was a Spain in this world, and maybe that country was just a focal point in all universes, but the thought of that was ridiculous, but then again, this crazy world of magic and monsters was already ridiculous, so that theory might actually be true.

Who knew?

Of course, there was the distinct possibility that the boy was a riftwalker like James, but James highly doubted that. James was kind of unique in that respect.

After the nearly thirty years he'd been wandering around this insane world, he'd never met another riftwalker, someone who'd come through a breach from some other world.

The only things he knew of that came out of those rifts were nightmares from the deepest depths of madness, of which, he had no desire to remember. He'd killed enough of those creatures to know what the rifts were like, which is why he would never walk through another rift portal again. Over the years, he'd come to the conclusion that he'd just been lucky as hell to walk through a breach and not ended up in actual Hell.

At any rate, the bartender nodded and poured a shot of Tequila for the young man.

"That will be one-fifty, sir," said the older man.

The boy paid for his drink, smiled, and then downed the strong alcohol in one gulp. James honestly doubted the kid had even savored it for a second.

The boy stared up at the bartender and nodded once.

"Are there any jobs here?" asked the young man.

"Are you a mercenary, young sir?" asked the bartender.

"Yes, sir," smiled the boy. "I'm looking for work. The cities north of here have dried up for the big jobs, the breaches. Someone has been closing them."

James lowered his head and stared down at his beer in the most unassuming way possible. There was no reason for this kid to know that James was the culprit when it came to the drought of big merc-work. Besides, he was doing the boy a favor. The kid would live longer.

"I would see that in a positive light," replied the bartender. "The breaches are a threat to everyone."

"Oh, I know," smiled the young man. "But that's why I'm here. I want to do my part."

"I see," said the older man. "Well, there are no breaches around Hollowstone. It's on account of the Mourning Field."

"The Mourning Field?" asked the boy.

"There was a great plague of rampant breaches that destroyed a city southeast of here," said the old man. "The city of Poe rested above some ancient ruins that were a magnet for scholars and researchers…and unfortunately, cultists. The cultists succeeded in opening unchecked breaches that annihilated everything in the region.

"The whole area is an ash bowl of boulders and dead, fossilized trees…No one enters there. Only the dead exist there, and the living who enter it do not return, though the breaches are long gone…We call it 'The Mourning Field.' The whole area is cursed…It's the perfect example of what happens if no one closes a breach."

Poe, huh? Apparently there had been a city in this world named "Poe" that had been completely destroyed by breaches. This bit of information actually gave James some validation for closing the breaches, so he stuffed that info in his mental vault to save for later.

"Oh," frowned the young man. "I suppose I will head farther south, then."

"That would be wise, young sir," said the bartender.

The old man took his leave after that in order to attend to other customers farther down the bar.

James turned his attention back upon the beer he wanted to enjoy.

The young man sitting next to him looked thoughtful for a moment, shrugged, and then turned his head to look at James as if seeing him for the first time.

"You look like a mercenary," said the young man.

"Yep," grunted James.

"Do you know of any breach work?" asked the boy.

"There're merc jobs other than breach work," said James. "You can find plenty of them in Coco City."

"I want to close breaches," frowned the young man. "I don't want some city cleanup that some state of affairs office has listed…I want to close breaches."

Not a smart thing to go looking for. That was certainly a death wish. James only did it because he had been forced to at a young age and now this was his life, but this kid…this kid was asking to get killed…This kid was something else.

James turned his head to give the boy the staredown.

"Have you ever closed a breach before?" asked James.

"Yes," said the young man in a serious tone. "One."

He then tipped his Gaucho hat and shone a wide grin.

"I closed one in Ridgewind out west," said the boy with full confidence. "That was the Razor's Edge."

James had a working knowledge of most of the locations of breaches thanks to his personal rune-technician and fence, Lazarus Radditz, though he was not on the up and up on any new ones at the moment. He did know that the Razor's Edge had been closed recently, and it actually *had* been located in Ridgewind, but he highly doubted this kid had closed it. Closing a breach was no mean feat.

"Uh, huh," said James. "Well, I'm here to relax, not close breaches. Take a load off, kid. There's no reason to get ahead of yourself."

The young man frowned again and shook his head no.

"I did close that breach," he said with slight anger in his voice. "I'm not lying."

"Okay," shrugged James. "How did you close it?"

"I got to the breach alone while other mercenaries were fighting breachers," explained the young man. "I used a Bacon-Scot orb to close it."

James was familiar with such orbs. They were similar in magic and tech to the Merlin-Crowley lines that prevented breachers from exiting a breach site. Nevertheless, those things were expensive and regulated, and the Feds sure as heck didn't hand them out for free.

James had always closed breaches on the fly with whatever was at hand in the classic, you know, "poor man's" way. That usually involved killing the "master" of the breach, and considering what came out of those breaches, this almost always involved nearly getting killed in the most horrific way possible.

But this kid had supposedly used a Bacon-Scot orb, and if the boy actually *had* used a Bacon-Scot orb, then that meant, of course, that the young man already had money, because money was the only way this pretentious squirt was going to get ahold of something as powerful as a Bacon-Scot orb.

There was no point in beating around the bush, so James just probed for the obvious.

"Are you rich?" he asked.

"My family has means," shrugged the young man.

Well, that explained that. It *was* possible this kid had actually closed the Razor's Edge, but James needed a little more info to be sure.

"Did you run into any breachers?" asked James.

"I destroyed several skeletons, but I also killed a manticore," nodded the boy.

Skeletons were a Class-One Corporeal Undead, dangerous only due to the fact that they tended to use weaponry—James had destroyed quite a few—but a manticore was an entirely different story. A manticore was a Class-Three Mythical, and killing one was truly a feat, something else James highly doubted this kid had actually accomplished.

Nevertheless, he was here to wind down, not argue with some wannabe.

"Okay," shrugged James. "So, what's your name, kid?"

"Kit," smiled the young man. "How should I address you, señor?"

Señor? What the…?

James shook that off and went with it.

"James," replied James. "You a *Knight Rider* fan, Kit? How about *Zorro*?"

"I don't understand," said Kit in both audible and visible confusion.

"Never mind," said James.

Sometimes, he just couldn't help himself. On the bright side, this kid wasn't a riftwalker, so there was that. The boy was just a wannabe.

That begged the next question.

"So, why do you want to close breaches, Kit?" asked James. "Seems like dangerous work to me."

"There are no wars anymore because of the breaches," said the boy thoughtfully. "When something is worse than a war, any war, don't you think we should all unite to end it? I want to do my part…And of course, I want to be just like my hero."

"Your hero?" asked James in confusion.

The boy grinned and nodded emphatically several times.

"I read the *Marcos the Riftwalker* books," he said in mild excitement. "Have you read them?"

This was a new one. James had read books in this world, but he hadn't heard of this series before. In fact, when he decided to retire, he was thinking of writing some books of his own…Still, he hadn't heard of this kid's series of choice.

"*Marcos the Riftwalker*?" he asked. "I don't think I've heard of that series."

He put his beer bottle to his lips and took a swig.

"Oh, yes," replied Kit. "They're awesome. They're written by my favorite author, Lazarus Radditz."

James choked on his beer as he coughed for a second into his left hand.

The old man hadn't ever bothered to give himself a pen name.

"Are you all right?" asked Kit.

"Yeah…" choked out James. "Why don't you, uhhh…Why don't you fill me in on these books?"

"Oh, they're about an adventurer named Marcos who came from another world," grinned Kit. "He traveled here by walking through a breach. He travels from city to city and closes breaches.

"The last one I read, *Sanguine Road*, had him face off with a djinn. There's a teaser at the end for the next book. I can't wait for it to be published. In the next one, Marcos gets trapped in the Liminal and has to escape Death…like the ferryman, the angel of death, not just like regular death…You know what I mean."

"Is that right?" asked James in facetious interest.

In reality, he was mildly upset.

Damn Radditz. The older man had been profiting off of James' adventures in more ways than one…Oh, yeah, that old man owed him a cut.

Still…*Marcos*? What was going in that man's head?

"So why do you like this 'Marcos'?" asked James.

"He's my hero," shrugged Kit. "I know he's a fictional character, but he's the greatest mercenary ever. He has more experience than ten normal mercs. I've studied everything he does…In fact, his gear is like a blueprint for me. That's why I purchased a Rune Maker and had my sword enchanted."

Now this was interesting. The boy had an enchanted sword, and that was one thing, but if this kid had a Rune Maker…

"Rune Makers aren't for sale, kid," said James. "You can't just order one out of a catalog…It takes a pact with a demon to make one."

"My family has means," shrugged the boy. "And it's 'Kit,' not 'kid'…And I do have one."

The young man gently pulled his gun from its holster and showed it to James. The rune-laced six-shooter was indeed a Rune Maker, and Kit even laid it out upon his flat palms as a show of peace, exactly the same way James always did.

If James had any doubts that this kid was rich, all of those doubts evaporated in an instant upon seeing the museum piece that was laid out upon the boy's open palms.

Only a hundred and thirty-three Rune Makers had ever been made, and not all of them were accounted for, which meant this kid had some serious cash. Either he'd gotten a registered one from an auction, or he'd purchased an unregistered one off of the black market, but either way, the kid had actual money backing him.

"Damned Radditz," muttered James.

"What?" asked Kit with one raised, dark eyebrow.

"Never mind," said James with a shake of his head. "Uhhh…You should put that away…Anyway…Anyway, uhhh…do you have one of these books on you?"

"Not on me, no," said Kit. "They're back at the hotel…I'm staying at the Driftwood Tumble for a week…Wait, why? Are you interested in reading them?"

"I just want to take a look before I buy one," replied James.

He needed to confirm this BS between him and Laz, though he already knew the answer to this one.

Damned Radditz.

"Okay," grinned Kit. "The hotel is right down the street. You follow me, and I'll show you…You'll definitely love them; I know it. No mercenary should be without one."

"Right," grunted James.

James finished his beer and then followed Kit out of the bar, though the both of them did not make it very far.

Ahead of them was an old-fashioned carriage parked out in the street, four very real horses hooked up to it, four horses of jet-black hue, those horses chomping at the bit and ready to go. The carriage was all black with a rather pale, morose-looking driver at the lead, the tall man dressed in an all-black suit with a black top hat upon his bald head.

"What the…?" muttered James.

A young woman in a very old style of dress, something out of the Victorian Age, curtseyed and approached both James and Kit.

"Kind sirs," said the young woman, "I am seeking the one known only as James."

James felt all of his red flags raise at once…Hollowstone was a little outdated, but it wasn't *this* outdated. Plus, this woman held a distinctly British accent, which was odd, because just like the country of Spain, James was certain there was no Great Britain in this world, either.

He eyed the young lady before making a decision as to what to say.

This young woman was white, in her very early twenties, and a little over five-feet tall, a pretty if not mouse of a thing that a good sneeze could knock over. She wore a blue and white dress with a small bustle, though she wore no hat upon the raised, curled, dark-brown tresses that adorned her petite head.

James sensed no ill intent from her, but he'd been fooled before. Nevertheless, he decided to bite.

"I'm James," he grunted. "That's my only name. You're probably looking for me."

"Oh, excellent," smiled the young woman, but that smile turned to desperation in the span of a second. "We have need of your services, sir. I understand you defeated the Minotaur of Park Ridge?"

James winced. That was not one of his prouder moments. He should have been more vigilant during that hunt, because it had cost him a pretty penny to fix his helmet VI after that minotaur had knocked him straight through a wall.

However, this bit of news immediately impressed Kit.

"You slew a minotaur?" asked the young man in surprise.

"Yeah," frowned James. "That was a while back, though."

"Then you *are* James," smiled the young lady, but once again, that smile transformed into desperation. "We have need of you…A minotaur has been murdering young women on the streets of my fair city."

"Is that right?" asked James cautiously.

Minotaurs were a Class-Three Mythical, much like the manticore Kit had supposedly killed. Minotaurs, those big bull-heads, were maneaters, true, but they usually set themselves up in mazes, and they normally didn't patrol streets of any kind.

Something wasn't right here.

"That sounds…a little strange," frowned James. "Where has this been happening? Is this in Hollowstone? Why hasn't Hollowstone State of Affairs put a bounty on it?"

"We live south of here," replied the young woman. "I come from Whitechapel, a small city in respects to this grand place, but it's my home, and my friends and family are in danger because of the beast…

"This creature prefers the fairer sex…Our modest city has already lost a number of women to the monster, including a dear friend of mine from the more unfortunate side of town. It takes the poor because they cannot afford a defense against it…It strikes at night when they are alone on the streets."

"Uh…huh…" said James warily.

Whitechapel…Why did that name sound familiar?

James didn't know every town and village around here, but he *thought*, anyway, that he'd heard that name before…

"So you say this minotaur is attacking people on the streets at night?" asked James. "That doesn't sound like a minotaur, kid. They make their lairs in mazes. The one I killed was in the sewers of Park Ridge. A cult had set up shop in that town and were feeding unsuspecting people to that overgrown bull. They'd throw them down in that sewage maze to be eaten, so I can understand why that one was there, but minotaurs don't generally pop up in the open for everyone to see."

"That sounds just like one of my books," grinned Kit. "It's the one where Marcos—"

James raised one hand to silence the boy. He liked Kit to an extent, but he needed some more information from this young woman.

"It's true, sir," emphatically nodded the young lady. "The streets of Whitechapel are like a maze after the sun sets…and I've seen the beast, myself. It was nine-feet tall with steam blowing from its nostrils, monstrous horns upon its great head…It carried off my dear friend before I could get help…Her body was found the next day in such a state that I…I cannot describe it to you…I have trouble sleeping at night from the sheer horror of it."

None of this sounded right. James was unsure of the whole thing, from the outdated dress to the whole minotaur thing, but he didn't get a chance to ruminate upon his doubt. No…Kit made James' decision for him.

"I'll go," grinned Kit. "I killed the Manticore of Razor's Edge. I can slay this minotaur, señorita."

Señorita?

Aside from that little verbal extravagance, something wasn't right here.

"Wait, wait, wait," said James with a shake of his head. "Hold up…I thought the Mourning Field was south of here, not some other city or town…"

"South*east*," corrected Kit. "She said her city is *south* of here…Besides, it's clear the young señorita has need of my services."

The young lady turned to look at Kit as if seeing him for the first time.

"I…I'm only supposed to fetch Mr. James, and—" she began, but James cut her off, though not on purpose.

"Young señorita? You two are around the same age," grunted James. "Stop showboating, kid."

"I'm not 'showboating,'" said Kit angrily. "And it's 'Kit,' not 'kid.'…That…That doesn't matter…I'm taking the job if you aren't."

"I never said I wasn't taking the job," frowned James.

"Then I'm going whether you go or not," said Kit with a tightlipped frown.

"I'm not going to go back and forth with you on this," said James with a shake of his head. "Why don't we both take the job and split the pay, huh? We can have each other's backs, and we can share the credit."

Kit looked thoughtful for a moment before nodding his head in agreement.

"Okay," he said with a slow grin. "Two swords are better than one."

"Excellent," smiled the young lady. "Please, I know the hour is late, but time is of the essence. If you please, good sirs…"

She opened the black carriage door and waved for them to enter.

James sighed…This job was all kinds of wrong…There were too many red flags, and normally he would have said no, but Kit had decided to be an idiot about this, probably just to impress the girl, so James was actually only going to Whitechapel to keep the boy from getting himself killed.

Kit *was* his biggest fan, after all.

He peered into the lantern light of the carriage interior and shook his head once. Something about this didn't feel right, but he couldn't just let Kit get in that carriage by the boy's own lonesome, so that's all there was to it.

He was only going because of Kit, and that was only because he had some sense of honor. He really didn't believe the boy had actually killed a manticore, but the kid had an enchanted rapier and a verified Rune Maker, so James wanted, honestly out of curiosity, to see what the kid could do, and if Kit couldn't cut it, James would warn him off this life for good. The one thing he didn't want was for the boy to get killed, especially over a stupid book—or books, plural—that Radditz had written about James, himself.

"I have a fanboy," muttered James under his breath as he shook his head in mild disgust. "Wonderful. Just wonderful…Thanks, Laz."

They piled into the carriage and sat down upon black-pillowed seat-boards, James and Kit in the back seat with the young lady sitting in the front seat across from them. A single lantern hung from the ceiling to light the interior of the carriage, though that lantern was a ceiling fixture and not a hanging lantern, therefore it would not swing or jostle as the carriage moved.

There was probably a vent above the lantern for the smoke, but this made no sense to James, as even the simplest light bulb would have been a better choice…Apparently, these people were *really* old school.

James settled in near the carriage wall while Kit sat next to him near the door.

The boy removed the golden cylinder from his back and laid it across his lap, shifting in his seat in order to get comfortable.

"What is that thing?" asked James as he eyed the strange golden tube across Kit's lap. "Is that a map case?"

"No," chuckled the young man. "This is a one-of-a-kind portable cannon I had specially crafted for my own use."

"Oh, really?" asked James in mild interest.

If the boy really did have a "portable cannon," then he wasn't as foolhardy as James had first figured him to be.

"Sí," grinned Kit. "It has a single-shot, rune-laced, titanium spear inside it. The runes ensure the spear is indestructible and can punch through whatever it hits…Unlike the Gungnir's Fury rune, it will even punch through some serious magical defenses…The outside case is alchemical gold designed to fire the spear without the use of gunpowder. I take the caps off, I say the trigger word, and 'BOOM!'…instant death."

"You have a magic railgun?" asked James in no small surprise. "That's actually useful, Kit."

"I know," nodded the young man with a keen smile. "I'm saving it for emergencies."

"Is it a one-time thing?" asked James. "I mean, do you have to replace the whole thing after it's fired?"

"No," replied Kit. "I just have to recover the spear, but because the spear cost me a small fortune, I'd rather not use it until I have to."

"I can see that," remarked James. "Still, that is definitely useful."

Considering the warning flags that were flapping in the wind of his subconscious, he had a feeling they were going to need that cannon, though hopefully, they wouldn't.

"Excuse me for a sec, Kit," he said quickly.

He did not wish to be rude to his "client," so he turned his attention toward her for the moment. For one thing, he didn't even know her name.

"What's your name, miss?" he asked, his attention squarely upon the young lady sitting across from him.

"It's Lenore, Mr. James," nodded the young woman. "Our driver is Mr. Clemm. He's a good enough driver at night, very good, in fact, though I hesitate to send anyone out on nights such as these."

"I'll bet," frowned James.

Something wasn't right about any of this. There was something nagging at him about all of it, though he could not place his finger on any of it.

"Is there something the matter, good sir?" asked Lenore. "You seem out of sorts."

"No, no," said James with a shake of his head. "I'll figure it out…eventually."

"Figure out what?" asked Kit. "What's to figure out?"

"Nothing," frowned James.

This was a lie, of course, but until he had more information, "nothing" was all Kit was going to get.

A thought occurred to him a second later, a rather unpleasant one.

"How far away is this town?" asked James. "How long will it take us to get there?"

"I believe it shall take all night," said Lenore unhappily. "Mr. Clemm, however, is well versed in such nightly travels, as I previously mentioned."

Yeah, that wasn't going to work.

"I don't mean to be rude, Miss Lenore," said James, "but if this ride is going to take that long, then I think I should get some sleep. We can talk more about this when we arrive at Whitechapel. Staying up all night is not a great way to start the day, especially on a hunt, so…is that okay by you?"

"Oh, of course, sir," nodded Lenore. "I believe I shall take to slumber as well. It would be wise to be ready for the morrow anyway."

"Oh…well…" said Kit uncertainly. "I had been hoping—"

James could literally hear the disappointment in the boy's voice. It was clear the kid wanted to get to know Lenore better, but he wasn't going to be able to do that at the present moment, because Lenore made that decision for him.

She reached over and closed shut a long black curtain that spanned from the carriage wall to the carriage door, effectively sealing herself from prying eyes, the lantern on James' and Kits' side, blotting out the light for herself as well.

James gave a brief snorting chuckle before he laid back a bit with his hands behind his head.

"Do you find something amusing, señor!" asked Kit in audible anger.

"Not at all," said James with a slight smirk. "I'm just trying to relax so I can grab some shuteye…Good night, kid."

"It's 'Kit,' not 'kid,'" replied the young man in a sulking tone.

"Yep," said James.

He closed his eyes and tried to calm his thoughts. This new job was sketchy at best, so he kept his wits about him. There was a lot that didn't add up, and he was none too happy about it.

For one thing, riding around in a black carriage in the vicinity of an area aptly titled "The Mourning

Field" was just asking for trouble…Plus, there were now four of them on this trip, and four was about as unlucky a number as you could get.

Four was Death's number…Never a good sign.

He'd run into Death before, and if there were two things he understood about Death, they were A): Death was a liar, and B): he didn't play fair. Nevertheless, James had signed up for this job, and if Death was actually involved in this somehow, then James would deal with him in the same way he'd dealt with him before…

He'd tell him off again, because that was about the only thing you could do with a primordial, cosmic force.

*****

Curious townsfolk surrounded them as both James and Kit walked down the main drag of Whitechapel.

Lenore had ordered Mr. Clemm to drop off James and Kit at the stables, and then Lenore and Mr. Clemm had taken their leave, so now it was just James and his unsuspecting fanboy walking through the land that time forgot, and to be honest, James was not happy about any of it.

The dirty streets, yellowed-brick buildings, and stoic people were like something out of the Victorian age, and as far as James could tell, there was no rune-tech of any kind.

"They're still using oil lamps in this burg, and I doubt it's 'for the aesthetic,'" frowned James. "Horses and carriages, top hats and dresses…What the hell?"

"I guess we stand out," grinned Kit.

"Guarantee you they've never seen a black man before," muttered James. "This is…odd. I don't know how I feel about this. I'm used to more modern places. You get a good mix there…barring Hollowstone, but Hollowstone is a gimmick city anyway. It's mainly for tourists…This place is more like…It's like they haven't changed since the 1800s, not that you would know what the 1800s were, but that's irrelevant."

He'd already known this, but it still bothered him a little. He was used to dealing with all kinds, but places like this made his hair stand on end. It reminded him of those movies where the weird townies would sacrifice a travelling stranger to their wicker god. Nevertheless, he'd taken this job, and somebody had to watch out for Kit's inexperienced fanboy butt, so there was that.

"It's fine," said Kit. "People are different all over."

"Well, you got me there," sighed James. "Let's just hunt this thing and get out of here. First, we need to find someone who…"

Several officers of the law approached as they pushed aside people in order to get to James and Kit. James could tell by the Peeler coats and custodian helmets the men were wearing that they were police, though he'd not seen such outfits outside of old cartoons.

"Halt, sirs!" said a broad-shouldered officer with a thick handlebar mustache.

This man was short, about five-six, but he was a burly guy, someone who could hold his own in spite of his height…James really didn't want to have any trouble with him.

"State your business in Whitechapel, sirs," said the man, and like Lenore, this man also held a distinctly British accent, though not nearly as refined as Lenore's.

James couldn't help but stare at the tall and solid custodian helmet perched atop the man's head. Only in this crazy world of magic and monsters would he see something like this.

"We're mercenaries who were brought here to kill the minotaur of Whitechapel," said James bluntly. "We were invited here."

"Is that so?" asked the officer. "Where are your travel papers?"

"Travel papers?" asked James. "We came by carriage…We're here to hunt the mino…You know what? Is there anyone in charge I can speak to? Do you have a mayor or…or a—"

"There is the Earl," said the officer. "I think we shall speak with him on this matter. If you truly are here to hunt the beast, then you will need to speak with him anyway…We'll escort you to his manor."

"Gracias, señor," grinned Kit with a tip of his hat.

"Keep your foreign weapons holstered," warned the officer.

"Yep," said James flatly.

He wasn't stupid. This place was setting off all kinds of red flags, so it was better to just smooth things out now so he and Kit could get their job done. He wanted to get out of Whitechapel as quickly as possible anyway…This place rubbed him the wrong way.

They were led along dirty streets to a three-story building made of brown brick, passersby ogling them the entire way.

It really was unnerving to be stared at like an escaped zoo animal, but considering where they were, James didn't think much of it. It was the mere fact that this place had not aged in the cycle of time, had not progressed past the Victorian Age, that screamed at James to remain cautious.

They all stood before the Earl's mansion.

The lead policeman used a bronze doorknocker to knock three times upon the right door of a pair of large oak doors that barred the entrance to the manor. A stiff-looking manservant of older years—older than James anyway—opened the door and ushered them inside. That man marched up a long and winding staircase a moment later, and after a couple of minutes, the Earl made his appearance at the top of the stairs.

The Earl was a man who appeared a lot younger in the face than James, though the Earl's hair was silver in color as if transfigured beyond white by great age. The Earl was a tall and stately white man in his early thirties, his silver hair short and well kempt, and he wore a well-appointed black suit, a spotless white button-up, and a fine pair of black dress shoes polished to a sheen.

Upon closer inspection, this man was indeed quite young despite the color of his hair, and the round spectacles upon his nose gave him the appearance of great knowledge or wisdom, though James knew this wasn't necessarily the case…He would have to test those waters.

"Ah, guests," said the Earl as he arrived at the bottom of the stairs.

James studied the nobleman's face.

The Earl had striking blue eyes, a hawkish nose, and thin lips. There was his stateliness that enhanced his natural height to put forth an air of significant respect, but there was also a callousness to him, a bitter coldness that hung like a pallid fog, an almost ruthless aloofness that made James not want to be alone with this guy in any setting…This dude made his skin crawl.

James' brief wayward attention was brought back to the matter at hand.

"These foreigners say they have come to slay the minotaur," said the lead police officer, "yet they have no travel papers."

"Is that so?" asked the Earl.

It was his tone that James did not like, a slight disbelief in that voice that ate away at James' own trust.

"How did you come to know of our troubles?" asked the Earl in an upper-class British accent. "In fact, how did you arrive in Whitechapel at all?...Our little city is hardly worthy of the attention of outsiders."

"We're mercenaries," said James cautiously. "These types of jobs are what we do…Besides, we were invited here."

"By whom?" asked the Earl just as cautiously.

"A young woman named Lenore…I didn't catch her last name," said James. "Now that I think about it, I should have asked. That carriage ride took all night."

"I know of no 'Lenore,'" stated the Earl. "And you say you arrived by carriage?"

"Sí, señor," said Kit. "The señorita brought us here by carriage. We came from Hollowstone."

There was a flash of something in the Earl's blue eyes, perhaps anger, perhaps something else, a hint of panic, but James couldn't exactly tell. Something wasn't right here, and that was the only thing James *could* tell, though that knowledge was of little use at the moment.

"I see," said the Earl. "Well, I suppose if you can kill the beast, then a reward shall be due to your liking. First though, I think we should direct you to a fine drinking establishment to wait at until night falls, and then Captain Robinson shall show you to Hanbury Street. You'll find the streets here at night are quite confusing, but this seems to be unique to our little city."

"How do you mean?" asked James.

"Best not to wander at night," spoke up the lead officer, the one the Earl had referred to as "Captain Robinson." "We are under some malign curse once the sun falls. I personally believe it to be the work of the beast. The streets twist and turn, and the buildings are of no help. They change positions and streets, sirs…It's difficult to explain unless you see it for yourself."

"Yes, a note of caution is in order," said the Earl. "Nevertheless, experienced 'mercenaries' such as yourselves should brook no trouble with such trivialities. If you are actually mercenaries and hunters, then I expect you to kill the beast tonight or leave by the morrow."

"One night?" asked James. "We may not find it in one night."

"If you walk those streets at night," said the Earl with a grim smile, "you won't have to 'find' it. It will most certainly find you."

"Uh, huh," replied James. "Well, what's the pay for this job? I'd like to know what the bounty is."

"Of course," nodded the Earl. "I doubt foreigners would be interested in our own currency of Whitechapel, so some precious gems will be in order, rubies, emeralds, and sapphires, should you complete the…'job.'"

They weren't using federal credits?...James wasn't sure if this was entirely legal, but whatever. Everything about this place was off anyway, so why not one more thing?

He just wanted to get the job done, more for Lenore and Kits' sakes than his own, and because this was out of a favor for them, he'd just do it and not rock the boat while he was here.

"That'll work," nodded James in return. "A minotaur is a Class-Three Mythical, and killing one isn't easy. They're clever, which is why they prowl mazes.

"I assume because of whatever curse has landed upon this town that the minotaur has taken advantage of that curse and is now hunting people who go out at night. If the streets really are twisting and turning like you say, then that theory makes sense, and that means we really are dealing with a minotaur, which is why we need to know the pay upfront."

"Of course," said the Earl with a grim smile.

James didn't like any of this, not one bit of it. He didn't trust this "Earl," he didn't trust this job, and if there was a curse over Whitechapel, then he wanted to get the hell out of here as fast as possible…

But he was still doing this as a favor run, and that meant he'd taken the job for two very important reasons. The first reason was an earnest promise he'd made to Lenore to do the job, and the second was to make sure Kit didn't get himself killed. Plus—and this was a bonus—once James spilled the beans to Radditz about this little "adventure," Kit could read about himself in a new book. That would set this kid straight about James, himself.

Actually, it was going to be pretty funny to see Kit finally realize he'd been travelling with his own hero this entire time.

✳✳✳✳✳

Both James and Kit had spent the day at the Ten Bells Pub, having a few drinks while talking about some essentials. James had gotten a good rundown of Kit's skills, so the boy was not so green as he'd first thought. The young man was a trained duelist in both sword and pistol, and Kit had some basic knowledge of dangerous creatures, so James felt as though he did not have to watch Kit's back 24/7.

Kit had also learned of James' own Rune Maker, and that had been an entertaining conversation, though James had not informed Kit how he'd obtained it…That story was too painful for him to bring up anymore.

Now it was nightfall, the oil lamps on the streets were lit, and they were both ready to enter the "maze" part of town, escorted here by the good Captain Robinson and his contingent of policemen.

"Here is the entrance to Hanbury," said Captain Robinson. "We shall either see you return 'fore morning, or we shan't see you return at all."

"We'll be back," grunted James.

He reached up and pressed the button on his enchanted-steel collar, and his Hermes-Alliette retractable helm formed in place. The banded helm was reinforced by heavy rune-laced magics, and the two amber visors across James' dark eyes fully protected his eyes while providing him with night-vision…The helmet also included sonic auto-dampeners to protect his hearing.

Of course, he was already wearing his enchanted bulletproof vest along with his enchanted brown leather jacket, his weapons at his sides, so he was good to go.

He took a moment to look over at Kit, but the boy had already pressed a button on his own black cloth jacket, and that had raised the boy's own helm, a Hermes-Alliette retractable face helm like James', though Kit's helmet was all black with bright emerald visors rather than James' steel-colored helm with amber visors.

Kit placed his Gaucho hat back upon his helmeted head, adjusted the gilded strings to tighten it around the protective armor beneath his chin, and then the young man nodded once at James.

"I see you have a Hermes-Alliette as well," said Kit.

"Never leave home without it," replied James.

"VI's on," said Kit. "Yours?"

"Warning," came a polite female voice inside James' helmet. "Disparate rift energy detected. Area unstable. Proceed with caution."

"Yep," said James.

"Mine's saying the area is unstable," said Kit. "Disparate rift energy detected? What does that mean?"

"It means something very wrong is going on here," said James. "We're entering somewhere that's close to a breach or is basically like being close to a breach. Everything's coming up rift energy, so I'm not sure we're going to have any kind of a warning before we get jumped. Hopefully, we'll get the drop on it."

"Hopefully," said Kit hesitantly.

Their little conversation was briefly interrupted by the timely intervention of their guide.

"Hate to interrupt, but time is of the essence for you," grunted the captain with a nod of his head. "We keep to our own here in Whitechapel, and we don't particularly like outsiders in our business, but even so, foreigners or not, God speed, good sirs."

The short and burly man then tipped his helm and took off with his contingent of men. It was clear the man wanted nothing to do with this side of town.

"That can't be good," muttered James.

He laid his hand across the grip of his Rune Maker, ready to draw it at a moment's notice, and Kit followed suit with his own.

"Ready, kid?" asked James.

Kit took a deep breath from within his helm's corrugated filter, released that breath, and then nodded once.

"Sí, señor," he said, but this time his voice was steady, no hint of fear. "And it's 'Kit,' not 'kid.'"

"Alright, then," nodded James. "It's showtime."

They walked into the darkly-lit street and headed down the grimy thoroughfare, the woodblock paving effectively nullifying the stamp of their thickly-treaded boots.

The first thing James did was eye the various passerby within this supposedly deadly area of the city. The streets were littered with those of lower standard, peoples that one would find within the slums of a city such as this. The men were unsavory characters of dubious intent, while the women were dressed like...

"We must be in the red-light district, so to speak," mumbled James.

"Red-light district?" asked Kit. "What is the red-light district?"

"I'll tell you when you're older," frowned James. "Point is, there shouldn't be people here at all, but this is clearly the slums, the low end of town, so they have to live somewhere...Oh, yeah, we're definitely going to have to kill this thing. These people are going to get picked off one by one...Still...stay wary. We'd better keep an eye out for thugs...though everyone here looks to fit that bill."

"If you say so," said Kit. "I've run into gangs before."

"Yeah, yeah," muttered James. "I'm well familiar with those jackhats. I'm not talking about those idiots that go blind into breaches. I'm talking about actually dangerous people…people that'll cut you down for looking at them the wrong way…more like the gangs where I'm from."

"Okay," shrugged Kit. "People are different all—"

"Yeah, yeah," said James again as he waved off Kit. "Just keep a sharp eye out…You know what? That gives me an idea… Hold up. Let me check something."

He reached into his jacket pocket and pulled forth his pocket watch. He flipped it open and stared down at the hands upon the miniature clock face, but what he saw stunned him for a second.

Kit noticed his hesitation.

"What?" asked the boy. "What is it?…You need to know what time it is? Why?"

"This watch doesn't tell time," said James in open confusion. "I picked up this artifact from a breach site a long time ago. The hours hand points toward the nearest breach opening, while the minutes hand—"

"Points toward the entrance to the Merlin-Crowley line!" finished Kit in audible surprise. "That's the same type of watch Marcos has in the *Marcos the Riftwalker* series. I've tried to purchase one, but everywhere I've gone, artifact sellers have said—"

"It's incredibly rare," said James. "Like I said, I found this in a breach zone when I was lot younger. It's not something you can just go to a store and buy."

"Or make," sighed Kit. "But that's beside the point…Something must be wrong. I can tell by the sound of your voice…So what's wrong? Are we near a breach?"

"I have no idea," muttered James. "See for yourself."

The young man sidled in next to him and took a look at the face of his watch. The hours hand was on the twelve, and the minutes hand was on the six, but the seconds hand, the seconds hand was…

"Why is it spinning around like that?" asked Kit.

The seconds hand was slowly and continuously spinning counterclockwise, opposite the direction it was supposed to go, but that was irrelevant, because the seconds hand never moved anyway. It didn't actually do anything, and it had been stuck somewhere between the two and the three for as long as James could remember.

"The hours and minutes hands are in the 'ready' position," frowned James, though Kit could not see that frown. "That's the neutral position, which means we are *not* in a breach zone…but the seconds hand…I've never seen it do this. I didn't think the seconds hand even had a function."

"Huh…" said Kit. "I wonder what it means?"

"Whatever it is, it can't be good," sighed James.

He closed the watch and put it away in one of his many jacket pockets.

"Come on," he said unhappily. "Let's get to patrolling. We need to find this thing and kill it."

"Sí," replied Kit. "Works for me."

"Let's try a side alley," suggested James. "Somewhere dark. These alleys are narrow enough where a carriage can't get through, and they may twist and turn like a maze. That's where we need to be looking."

"Sí," said the young man. "Vámonos, señor."

"Yep," said James.

They walked along until they found a suitable entrance to a dark alleyway, and then James stopped to unholster his Rune Maker. Kit followed suit with his own pistol, and then they entered the narrow and tenebrous brick corridor that led to who-knew-where.

They did not travel five feet before James' VI issued a stark warning.

"Warning," came the polite female voice in his helmet. "Class-Five Corporeal Undead in area."

"Class-Five Corporeal Undead?" asked Kit. "What is that?"

"You heard that?" asked James, but then he shook his head from the stupidity of that question.

There was no possible way Kit could have heard James' own VI.

"You have a VI?" asked James. "Wait…I already knew that. You already told me."

"Old-timers" was creeping in. To be fair, it was the fact that Kit was imitating a character who was imitating James, himself, that was throwing James off track, and James knew this, but that was too irritating to comprehend, so James chalked the whole thing up to old age with a shake of his own head.

"Of course," said the boy nonchalantly. "Marcos has one, so I—"

That reply gave James an internal cringe.

"I get it," said James quickly. "Never mind that. We've got a much bigger problem…A Class-Five Corporeal Undead is like an ancient vampire or a lich, something that can alter reality to an extent. It's not like the skeletons you've dusted. If that's the case, then we need a plan, because we are in some deep—"

"Warning," interrupted his VI. "Class-Four Automaton in area."

"Wait…What the—?" began James.

"Warning," said his VI yet again. "Class-Two Corporeal Undead in area."

"Are you hearing this?" asked James as he stared directly at Kit's helmeted face.

"Class-Four Automaton?" asked the young man. "Class-Two Corporeal Undead? All in the same place?"

"Damn," said James unhappily. "Artifacts must be on the fritz in this area…Must be why my compass-watch isn't working."

"What about our weapons?" asked Kit.

There was a nervousness in his hushed voice that was undeniable.

"A gun's a gun and a sword's a sword," replied James in a grim tone. "If we can't use any runes, then we'll kill it the old-fashioned way…Come on. Let's head down this alley. We've got a lot of ground to cover before morning, so let's pick it up…Follow my lead."

Kit nodded once, and James took off at a brisk jogging pace, the boy right behind him. Kit was just going to have to keep up, because James did not want to lose any more time than they'd already lost.

Their boots treaded across filth-laden planks as they rounded a corner, the yellowed-brick walls forming a sudden "L" at the end of the alleyway, fat and bleak-shaded rats scurrying out of their path, and then both of them came to a sudden halt as they viewed the gory scene set before them.

James' amber visors immediately switched to night vision as the pitch-cloaked alleyway choked off normal eyesight. James' night vision was all in different shades of amber, the same color as the rune-spelled glass that he was currently looking through, but at least he could see.

Before them were the remains of a young lady of white skin and brown hair, her bloody and mangled corpse splayed out lengthwise across the alley floor, her dress ripped to shreds from neck to crotch, her corset torn open to reveal her bare chest where her breasts should have been, undergarments rent where her genitalia should have been.

There were only two gory pits in place of her breasts, and her genitals were mangled beyond recognition, or maybe they were missing…It was hard to tell with a woman. Moreover, her guts had been pulled up and out, the intestines spilling forth like a grisly and savage waterfall upon the wooden planks beneath her body.

"Warning," came James' VI. "Class-Two Corporeal Undead in area."

The disgusting, yet humanoid, creature perched atop the poor victim was completely nude and pale, pale white in skin, that mucous-covered skin bald as if perfectly shaved from head to toe, and this thing was female…definitely female… and definitely not a minotaur.

The creature's wide bottom was topped upon the poor victim's face, and as it rocked back and forth in some thoroughly repulsive and vile self-pleasuring at the expense of the dead, it bit into a chunk-handful of intestinal gore. The sausage like entrails had been pulled forth from the poor deceased this creature was now currently mounting, and dark-red blood dripped from the monster's smooth, narrow, alabaster chin, a spillage of sanguine fluid that splattered dark blots across her pale, bare legs.

James and his current partner in ops said nothing and did nothing for a few precious seconds as they processed what was in front of them. James had seen a lot of crap and had been through even more garbage than most people could imagine, but this…this was…

"That's a ghoul," said James in a flat tone. "Class-Two Corporeal Undead…The helmet sensors were right about that…Ghouls devour the deceased while defiling them. They feed off of the residual unholy death energy that's left behind.

"They prefer the murdered or those who have died a violent death, though they rarely kill outright unless they're starving, and though they're dead and can't actually digest anything, they eat the flesh because they're infested with bugs that actually consume anything they 'eat,' but A): I've never seen a ghoul before, and B): I sure as hell didn't expect it to be a woman…The stories

I've heard about the male ghouls were bad enough, but this…I can't even begin to…Ugh…

"Never mind. Let's just say that this has to be one of the most horrific things I've ever seen in my life, and I will actively work on blocking the memory of it from my conscious mind later on, but for now…oh, yeah…let's kill her…We've got to release her imprisoned soul…Follow my lead, kid."

He raised his Rune Maker and pulled back the hammer.

"Ifrit's Rage," stated James, and a rune on the barrel of his gun glowed with a bright-orange light.

Both he and Kit stared at the glowing pistol for a few seconds, actively assessing this new positive development.

"Well, whatever artifact interference is going on, my Rune Maker is still working," said James matter-of-factly. "It is, at least, for now, so follow my lead, Kit."

"Ifrit's Rage," repeated Kit in a shaky voice, and the young man's pistol followed suit with its own bright-orange glow.

They were now ready for action, but there was one more thing to ask, and this question was very important.

"Have you got an emergency flame barrier, Kit?" asked James. "Was that mentioned in the books you read?"

"Sí," said Kit with an audible swallow. "It was, and I have one."

"Figured," nodded James. "Get ready to use it."

The hideous female atop the murdered young woman turned and stared at them with glowing eyes, that supernatural glow surrounding tiny black pupils. She had small breasts with little light-colored nipples upon those albino bulbs, and this feminine feature only added to James' overall disgust, but it was the look of sublime ecstasy upon the former woman's smooth, blood-soaked, pale face that enraged James, a look that suggested such degeneracy and defilement that it angered him to the nth degree.

To make matters worse, he could tell her face had once been beautiful, but now it was monstrous, a true mockery of what it had formerly been, a destruction of priceless art by some completely-evil piece of crap.

He knew a little about how ghouls were created, and their creation was never accidental. More than likely, she had been murdered or had died by suicide, and her body had not been secured on hallowed ground after death, so a necromancer had gotten ahold of her.

This was yet one more crime to add to the terrible acts perpetrated by those pieces of absolute dog scat, those foul sorcerers that muttered to their dark gods in the silent hours before dawn.

This woman was not only dead, her soul was trapped in darkness, that darkness compelling her to do the vilest, most horrific things imaginable…Her soul was still in there, trapped in that twisted body…horrified, terrified…James was actually staring at two desecrated and defiled women, not just one.

Necromancers were now completely and thoroughly on his permanent hate list, that list stamped and notarized, and if there was ever one of these foul wizards for him to come across, by fortune or fate, he was going to actively hunt that sucker down or die trying.

He shook those dark thoughts out of his head to get back in the game.

"Be careful on the shot," warned James. "These things are fast, so don't hit me in the crossfire…On my count…On three…One, two—"

The ghoul's serene expression changed to pure rage in a heartbeat. She opened her foul mouth wide in response to James and Kits' interruption of her evening meal, and her jaw dropped and extended far beyond its normal means as she let forth a high-pitched shriek. A choking black cloud of swarming, carnivorous beetles then buzzed forth from that extended maw, each of the brown and black insects a full inch long, and that insectile tempest bore down on them in nothing flat.

"Shields up!" yelled James as he reached up and slapped the flame rune on his bulletproof vest with his left gloved hand.

Kit reached up and activated his own protective flame rune upon his own black vest jacket.

Their separate runes glowed bright red as their shields built around them, the egg-shaped shielding patterned in hexagonal etchings, that ever-important shielding spanning a few decimeters from both of them in order to give themselves some breathing room.

Due to their close proximity within the confined quarters of this narrow alleyway, the shields impacted but flattened against each other to form a solid, bright-orange wall between them that separated James from Kit, but neither shield collapsed due to this, which, in retrospect, was truly fortunate.

That separating barrier was a little too close for comfort, and James could feel the vibrant heat from it, like standing too close to a space heater, but at least the shields hadn't collapsed, which was good, because that safety feature was always a distinct possibility depending upon range of contact for the wielder, and James would rather have the shield and suffer minor burns than not have it and be eaten alive.

Nevertheless, this was a problem.

"We can't maneuver with the shields up!" yelled James. "Wait for these little suckers to burn out first!"

He hoped anyway. The shield was an emergency application, after all. These protective runes had a time limit, less than a minute, so these nasty, flying, little suckers had to crisp out before the shield was forced to recharge, or they were in deep trouble.

The beetles hitting their forcibly compressed emergency barriers went up in flames and smoke as the black and buzzing cloud pounded down upon them. James' amber vision was choked out by the darkness of the cloud mixed with the bright flares of each individual pest's destruction, but this only lasted for a few seconds.

A few seconds, however, was too long for James' tastes.

The cloud of beetles cleared right before the barriers collapsed, but James was dazzled due to the crackling lightshow the dying insects had performed in his vision, so he did not see the pale nude form bearing down on him from above until it was too late.

The hellish female jumped upon him with intense force, knocking him to the wooden planks below, and she bore her full weight upon him, striking him three times in all.

Her wide bare bottom hit across his chest to bear him down, the back of his head hit the wood beneath him, and he took a solid, double fisted, axe-handle blow to the front of his helmet. A normal person may have been overwhelmed or even killed by this savage ambush, but James' helmet saved his life, much like it had many times in the past, because it had an enchanted interior padding that gave his head some protection against kinetic strikes.

James' amber vision went wild, the impacts of the ghoul's vicious attacks momentarily affecting his night vision, and then he heard gunshots ring out in the night. He heard Kit's shout after that, and then that shout was followed by a loud thud.

James struggled to his feet and took less than a second to assess that Kit was back first against the right-side alleyway, sitting on his butt, clearly knocked down by their disgusting assailant.

James could see the glowing eyes of the ghoul in the distance. Those eyes registered as bright amber in his amber vision, but knowing offhand what he knew about ghouls, her eyes were probably red, but that colorful little observation was beside the point, because those glowing eyes gave him a visible target to shoot at.

"Eat hot death!" he yelled as he opened fire.

He fired two rounds dead center at the vicious female's chest, center mass, right between her small bare breasts, but neither bullet connected.

The ghoul was up and on the bricks of the left-side wall in a fraction of a second, leaping forward on pale legs to pounce and crawl upon the vertical surface of yellowed bricks in nothing flat.

She was upon him a hair of a breath later, leaping down from the wall while swinging a vicious right hook, the knuckles of her right fist impacting the left side of his helmet, and the force of the blow spun him around like a top, but he did not fall.

He had not expected her to punch. Such an action was definitely unladylike, especially for the residents of such a backwards town, but considering what he'd already seen of this woman, he should have known better.

"Mother fu—" began James, but he cut himself short, mainly because she was already on him.

She threw a left hook this time, her pale white knuckles impacting against the right side of his helmet, and James staggered backwards but did not fall.

She rushed to grapple him while he was still in a daze, but he was seasoned enough to not stay dazed for long.

She gripped his wrists to prevent him from gaining any leverage or aim against her, and then she kicked up toward his crotch three times in succession, but James was ready for her this time. He placed his left knee in front of him and raised his left leg to prevent those vicious shots to his danglers, and considering the force of the blows, he could tell she was much stronger than most living women he'd come across.

They were locked in this position for a few seconds, and James studied her face in that brief period of time, but what he saw only saddened him. Yet again, he could tell she had once been beautiful, even through the mocking ruse of her pale face and bald head, even with those scarlet lips and smooth chin smeared with blood, and this realization saddened him.

Nevertheless, her stint as an undead heresy was up.

"Seraph's Light!" cried Kit from off James' right.

James whirled his right arm down while raising his left, windmilling his arms in an attempt to throw her off of him and throw her off balance at the same time.

The hideous alabaster female stumbled as she turned to face Kit, James backed away to clear a safe distance, and then the tip of Kit's enchanted rapier emerged from the ghoul's bare white back.

Kit had stabbed her center mass, the tip of his enchanted rapier penetrating the thick bone mass of her sternum, punching through it to the other side to punch through the spine as well.

The undead woman let forth one surprised yelp of pain, and then beams of light emerged from her in various places as the holy enchantment upon Kit's blade surged through her. She disintegrated a moment later, the enchantment dispersing the unholy energy animating her, but the image of her pale naked form was thoroughly burned into James' brain, and that was something he would not soon forget…Even the imposing image of Death, himself, had not been this disturbing.

He shook that foul image out of his head and got back to the task at hand.

"Done and done," grunted James. "Good work, Kit, and in record time."

"Sí, señor," breathed out the young man.

"Protocol Gamma," said James after a second. "Scan for hostiles."

"No hostiles detected," came the feminine voice of his VI. "Warning. Disparate rift energy detected. Area unstable. Proceed with caution."

"That's what I thought," sighed James.

"What?" asked Kit.

"I'm thinking this burg is too close to the Mourning Field," replied James. "That's what's causing all of the weirdness around here. These poor fools must be picking up the leftovers of that cursed place. Must be why everything's so messed up around here…Not that it matters."

"Why doesn't it matter?" asked Kit in audible confusion.

"We fulfilled our contract," grunted James. "We killed the ghoul."

"But Lenore said it was a mino—" began Kit, but James cut him short.

"There's no minotaur here," said James with a shake of his head. "The more powerful the creature, the stronger the 'signal' it gives off, hence why our VIs can detect such powerful signatures coming from miles…uhhh…kilometers away.

"In an actual breach zone, the VI's range is limited due to the warping nature of the breach itself, but my guess is this strangeness in Whitechapel is just an aftereffect of the Mourning Field's proximity. In fact, the Mourning Field probably acts as one giant breach, and that's what's been screwing with our scanners…I don't think we have an artifact problem at all. I think my compass-watch is just being messed with by the Mourning Field.

"At any rate, we're done here. These people have just created a story about a minotaur in order to rationalize their own fears…There's no way a minotaur would tolerate an undead, *any* undead, in its chosen hunting ground, so we are one-hundred-percent officially done here…There's no minotaur, or it would have run off that ghoul in the first place, and a ghoul, nasty as they are, is not going to tangle with a minotaur…so…come on…Let's get out of this part of town and go collect our reward."

"Sí, señor," said Kit. "However, I think I've had enough adventuring for a while."

"You don't want to be a mercenary anymore?" smiled James, though Kit could not see that smile beneath James' helmet. "Done already?"

"Oh, no," replied Kit. "I'm made of sterner stuff than that. I just need time to process. Some downtime is an order…As soon as I get back to Hollowstone, it's wine, women, and song for me."

James could tell that the young man was grinning, even though he couldn't see the boy's face.

#8B…WHITECHAPEL PART II

When everything comes together to form a perfect picture of nothing you actually wanted.

They had patrolled the streets until dawn, and now they were back at the Earl's, and though James had tried to explain the situation to the cold and grim younger man, the Earl was, in James' opinion, thoroughly unappreciative of their efforts.

"So, you did *not* kill the minotaur?" asked the currently-irritated nobleman. "Is that what you are telling me?"

"No, I'm telling you you didn't have a minotaur problem," said James frankly. "There was no minotaur. You had a ghoul problem, and we took care of it—we destroyed it—but that isn't the real issue."

"And what would the *real* issue be, Mr…" trailed the Earl. "And what *is* your name, good sir?"

"James," replied James. "That's the only name I use anymore."

"And what is the real issue, Mr. James?" asked the Earl again.

"The real issue is that you're too close to the Mourning Field," said James. "That place is bad news. It's the only area I've ever heard of that's been destroyed by breaches, and sticking around it is asking for trouble. You've already seen what can come out of it, and that ghoul, nasty as it was, is nothing compared to what may have already come out of it…

"But even that's not the immediate problem…You've got a more serious problem for the moment, and that's the fact that someone has been raising the dead around here, and I don't think it's cultists…I'm talking a necromancer.

"If you've got a necromancer here, the problem you had is just going to keep happening. I'm guessing this sucker is here because he or she is drawing power from the Mourning Field…Now, I'm not one to tell you to just pick up and leave, but—"

"You are correct, Mr. James," said the Earl in a grim tone. "You are *not* one to tell us how we live our lives. However…you are owed compensation for dispatching this…'ghoul.'"

James said nothing in return, nor did he react to the Earl's word bait. He was not stupid. No, he was just going to hold his tongue, take his pay, and leave this messed-up burg with Kit. This town was all kinds of wrong anyway.

The Earl made a motion to his manservant, and the old house servant stepped forward to present two, small, unadorned boxes of dark wood to both James and his young sidekick.

James accepted the box without argument, briefly flipped open the lid, stared momentarily at the small but very valuable jewels inside, and then closed the lid. He nodded once in acceptance of this trade for his services, and the Earl nodded back in return.

James stuffed the small box into one of the many pockets he had lining his brown leather jacket. Those pockets were spelled with the Deep enchantment, which meant they could hold much more than their meager exterior size indicated.

Kit stuffed his box inside his black vest jacket, and knowing him, James figured the boy's pockets were also ensorcelled with the Deep enchantment. The young man was a rich fanboy, after all. Annoying as that was, a near copy of James' gear set would definitely improve Kit's chances of living longer.

After that bit of necessary utility, their attention was drawn back to the Earl.

"Please escort Mr. James and his companion to the city limits, Captain Robinson," said the Earl with a tightlipped frown. "I'm sure they have other places to be."

"Of course, my lord," nodded the short, burly man in the custodian helm.

There was no more to say after that. James was more than willing to leave this crazy burg, and considering what he'd already seen of this place, the city of Whitechapel was going to self-implode from its own stupidity sooner rather than later.

But that was not his problem. He just wanted to leave, so being shown the door was number one on his to-do list.

Captain Robinson ushered James and Kit to the door.

They were escorted from the Earl's mansion without any further ado, a full contingent of police practically pushing them the entire way to the edge of the city, but James felt no anger over this…He simply wanted out of here, and fast.

They stopped at the edge of the city, and the short man in the custodian helmet nodded toward the forlorn dirt road surrounded by plains outside of the city gate, the same city gate that Lenore and Mr. Clemm had driven James and Kit through the first time.

Honestly, it was a good thing this place was walled off to begin with, a ten-foot brick wall at that, because that wall, in itself, was a deterrent for a lot of things that could come out of the Mourning Field.

"You simply need return whence you came, good sirs," said Captain Robinson. "Make no mistake and take no offence…the people of Whitechapel thank you for your service, but…if you will…you must leave us to conduct our own internal affairs."

"Yep," said James dryly.

He motioned for Kit to follow him through the black, wrought-iron bars of the north gate, and they trudged through that gate and out onto the dusty road leading away from it.

James felt a sudden weight lift from his shoulders, a shedding of a heavy black pall surrounding him that had threatened to suffocate him the entire time he'd been within the actual city limits of Whitechapel.

He heard Kit breathe a sigh of relief a moment later.

"It's going to be a long walk back to Hollowstone, señor," smiled Kit, "but I am so glad to be out of there."

"No kidding," grunted James. "This burg is definitely cursed…You can feel the difference within a few feet…uhhh…meters…decimeters?…Never mind. Let's just get out of here. Let's make tracks."

"Sí, señor," replied Kit.

They walked north up the road for a few minutes until Kit finally spoke up again.

"I suppose we will have to find shelter before night falls," said the young man. "It would not be wise to be out here in the dark without some kind of protection."

James shook his head and gave a brief chuckle.

"I have a witch's hut," he said. "It's a double. I've got enough space for me and one more…You're welcome."

Kit cast a visible look of surprise upon him, and then the young man shook his head in confusion.

"A witch's hut?" asked the boy.

"A portable shelter," said James in more confusion than even Kit could muster. "They're little rune-spelled cubes that unfold into a portable shelter. I've got one in one of my jacket pockets…

"They're not pretty to look at—they just turn into big square blocks with a door, four walls, floor, roof—but they're enchanted with some basic defenses to keep hostiles out, and they usually come with some basic beds or bunks inside, maybe some appliances to fix food…Nothing fancy, you know…They're rune-spelled with space magic to shrink down for easy carrying…Wait…You're telling me you've never heard of a witch's hut?"

"No," shrugged Kit. "Nothing like that was ever mentioned in the books. Where did you get it? From a breach?"

James let out a short guffaw and shook his head no.

"What?" asked Kit in audible irritation. "You got it off the black market or by some other unsavory means?"

"Rich people," snorted James with a shake of his head. "I went online on the Rune-Net and ordered one off of Baba Yaga Shelters. Anybody can buy one."

"I've heard of the Rune-Net," said Kit matter-of-factly. "I think my cousin, Ramon, mentioned it once. I never had the interest to investigate it."

"Good Lord," said James with wide eyes. "You're one of *those*…Check out the Net when you get back to Hollowstone, okay?"

"Sí," shrugged Kit. "I suppose I will give it a go."

"It's worth looking into," said James. "There are all sorts of useful supplies you can order online. Not everything I have I found at a breach site or got off of the black market."

"Hmm…" nodded Kit. "So why do you have a double for your shelter? Were you expecting company, or do you have it just in case?"

"I'll tell you when you're older," smirked James. "You're welcome to sleep in it, though. I'm not one to just leave you out in the cold."

"Well, I don't know about you, but I really am tired," yawned Kit. "I sure could use a nap…a long one…a long 'sleep all day and all night' kind of nap."

"Well, we'll walk a little more and then get some rest," said James. "It sucks to be kicked out at dawn after being up all night, but you adapt to the situation in front of you…Let's set up camp aways down the road, and we'll just head out tomorrow morning."

"Gracias, señor," yawned Kit again.

✳✳✳✳✳

James was awakened from restless sleep by an insistent knocking upon his magic hut's singular door.

The small white and featureless block of a room he was in contained a double bed and that was it, but that was more than enough for shelter when it came to being out in the rough, and it certainly beat an unprotected tent.

Kit was, of course, sleeping on the other side of the bed, but the boy was up and awake with a stirring rustle in nothing flat.

"Lights," called out James.

A stark white rune-light lit up to shine down from the flat white surface above them, and both he and his current travelling companion blinked for a moment to let their eyes adjust to the sudden change in luminosity.

There was more insistent knocking upon the only entrance and exit to their plain little shelter, an urgent beat of a fist that James could not simply ignore.

"Window," called out James.

A small screen, much like a regular flatscreen TV, appeared upon the door before them. Within it was the stark form of Mr. Clemm, Lenore's carriage driver, the pale man wearing a black suit accented by a black top hat. The man was standing in the soft glow of his own lantern, a lantern which he held aloft in his left, black-gloved hand, as it was most definitely the middle of the night outside.

"I know him," grunted James.

"Isn't that Mr. Clemm?" asked Kit.

"Yep," confirmed James.

James hopped out of bed and quickly opened the door. He had not taken off his gear in order to catch some Zs, and as uncomfortable as that sounded, it was preferable to being caught off guard and becoming…well…dead.

The door swung outwards to reveal their nighttime visitor.

"Yes, sir?" asked James.

He stared at the carriage driver and waited for a response, but the other man simply stepped aside to reveal the fateful presence of the lovely young Lenore standing behind him.

"Lenore?" asked James.

"Mr. James," replied the young woman with a bitter frown, "you had promised me you would slay the minotaur. You made this vow in earnest response to my heartfelt plea, yet the beast remains at large."

"There was no minotaur," said James as he shook his head in slight confusion. "There was a ghoul, but we killed—"

"The beast yet lives, and it is only the matter of an hour before it prowls the streets once more," frowned Lenore. "Midnight approaches."

"Midnight?" asked James. "Wait…It's eleven at night? I've slept that long? Holy…I guess I needed to catch up on some sleep…I definitely feel better than I have for a long—"

"This is no jest," said Lenore in a distinctly unhappy tone. "It is only the matter of an hour before the beast murders again."

"There's no minotaur," reiterated James with a shake of his head. "There was a ghoul, but we killed it."

"That ghoul was nothing more than a scavenger feeding off of the victims of the beast," scowled Lenore. "It was not the murderer."

"Wait, what?" asked James.

"That ghoul has been sighted before," said Lenore through a tightlipped frown. "Catching a glimpse of that ghastly female was how we always knew someone else had been butchered by the beast. If you had simply talked to the good people of Whitechapel, you would have known that they had actually seen the minotaur as well. That nightmarish creature is no fantasy or fiction of mine…The beast is real."

"But there's no way a minotaur would tolerate an undead creature in its territory," said James adamantly. "It would have run it off or destroyed it."

"This minotaur is clearly different in a number of ways," said Lenore in an equally adamant reply. "It tolerates the ghoul because the ghoul is adept at cleaning up its messes…You should have listened to me and everyone else on the matter…Did Captain Robinson not explain to you the troubles of Whitechapel?"

"Yeah, but he and the Earl accepted the fact that we killed the…Wait…" trailed off James.

Upon mentioning the Earl, something the grim leader of Whitechapel had said bubbled up to the surface of James' memory.

"Wait, wait…The Earl told us he'd never heard of you," he said after a moment of thought. "You seem to be someone of some standing, too. How else could you afford your own carriage and driver?…Yeah, I think the

Earl would know who the more 'important' citizens of Whitechapel are…What's really going on?…Is your name even Lenore?…Because I'm beginning to suspect that name is just an alias."

"The Earl knows very well who I am," said Lenore unhappily. "But you are correct, good sir. Lenore is not my true name, but I have good reason to keep the Earl's eye off of my activities…The man is a liar and a thief and cannot be trusted."

"I can see that," replied James with a nod and a frown. "I get a bad vibe from him…but that still doesn't explain why he'd just pay us after we killed the wrong target. He had the air that we did our job, which is why we were kicked out."

"He profits from the murders," scowled Lenore. "The beast only victimizes women of low standing and low means, those who engage their livelihood around men, so he turns a blind eye to it."

"That…doesn't make any sense," said James in no small amount of confusion. "He must know that once the creature runs out of its 'preferred food,' it's going to hit someone of 'higher standing.'"

"He knows very well," frowned Lenore. "He does not care. If such a scenario were possible, and the beast did burn through the poorest, he would send a small army to eliminate the monster, and then he would appear the hero…

"However, that foul man will never destroy the beast, as he benefits from it in ways you cannot understand. In fact, once the beast kills again tonight, he will simply tell the people how faith in foreign help is a fool's hope and how foreigners cannot be trusted or allowed into the city at all…You must return to Whitechapel and finish the job."

"I don't think they will let us back in, señorita," said Kit from behind James.

James stepped out of the shelter and then stepped to the side in order to allow the young man to address Lenore.

"They did not leave us the impression they wanted us back," finished Kit.

"Mr. Clemm and I shall regain your entrance to the city," nodded Lenore. "In fact, we shall take you directly to Hanbury Street via our carriage, but we must hurry. Midnight approaches."

"I don't know if I want to anger the local nobility," said James unhappily. "Interfering with the Earl's business doesn't seem like a smart thing—"

"He paid you, did he not?" asked the young woman.

"Yeah, but—" began James.

"Then check your so-called 'payment,'" frowned Lenore.

James sighed, reached into his jacket pocket where he'd stuffed the plain wooden box filled with gems, and pulled forth the "payment" in question, but he had to blink twice just to understand what he was looking at.

The small box of dark wood in his gloved right hand was rotted through, a barely held together and weatherworn scrap of a thing that did not resemble in the slightest what he had received from the Earl.

"What the...?" began James.

He opened the box and cursed under his breath as he stared at the pieces of dirty gravel within it. There were no precious jewels of significant value, no...It was all just worthless rocks buried in stark grey ash.

"Mother fu—" started James.

"Come with us, destroy that beast, and then leave the Earl to me," hissed Lenore through gritted teeth. "I will ensure that man gets what he deserves, and what he deserves has been long in the making...However, the beast of Whitechapel must first be destroyed, and I cannot perform that task, myself, which is why I employed you, Mr. James, to do it for me."

There was a deep-seated anger in her tone, a conviction born of rage mixed with a flash of fire in her eyes. The thin mask of civility that Lenore had worn upon James' first meeting with her had finally fallen away...

There was a lot more history here between her and the Earl than James had realized or had even thought to realize, but it was the undeniable tone of revenge that convinced James not to argue with her, because people only held that tone when something truly egregious had been done to them…Oh, yeah, there was some bad blood here.

Normally, he would have written off this little venture as a big fat "L," and then he would have made tracks, leaving Whitechapel behind him, but there was something about Lenore that pulled him toward a different path, and that was unusual, because he normally did not take risks like this.

Nevertheless, if Lenore was on the level, then the Earl would get his comeuppance somehow—something "long in the making," according to Lenore—after James and Kit did their actual job and killed the beast, and that was good enough for James. After all, this was personal now…The Earl should not have stiffed them on their pay.

"All right," sighed James. "Let's get a move on then…If this thing really exists and it actually does strike at midnight, then we should get going…Never heard of a mythical tolerating an undead in its territory, but I'll trust you on this one."

"Good," replied Lenore with a grim smile. "Let us board the carriage then, and Mr. Clemm shall have us back at Whitechapel within the hour."

*****

They travelled by Lenore's carriage back into Whitechapel, and the gate guards let Lenore through without question, not even bothering to check who was inside the carriage.

The first time James and Kit had ridden in the carriage, the trip had taken all night, but he and Kit had used that time to catch some Zs, so they had not really talked to Lenore in depth, and this had been fine at the time—a job was a job—but now that he was wondering who Lenore actually was and what her relationship was with the Earl, there was simply no time to talk to her…

The carriage ride the second time around had been much shorter than the previous one, mere minutes, as it were, because James and his young sidekick had not travelled far from town before setting up camp.

They continued to travel by Lenore's carriage to the street in question, Hanbury, and then Lenore ordered Mr. Clemm to hold and wait for them. The mysterious pale driver in all black did as he was told, and James, Kit, and Lenore exited the horse-drawn vehicle to take foot onto the dirty streets of the low end of town.

"Ah, smell that chamber-pot air," smirked James. "Here we are again. Reminds me of the business district in Coco City."

"It's not that bad," shrugged Kit. "I've seen worse."

"So have I," said James. "That doesn't mean I like it, but I guess we don't have a…Wait…"

His voice trailed off as he spied a young woman in the distance.

The young lady in question was loitering outside of a pub, but by the make and manner of her dress, James could tell she was a "lady of the night." This, however, did not surprise him. It was the woman's face that stopped him in his tracks for a second, because she seemed oddly familiar—very familiar, in fact—though he could not place where he may have seen her before.

"Hold up a sec," said James firmly.

He crossed the dimly-lit street and boldly walked up to the young lady, though his intentions were not so crass as to engage her in her "profession." No, he simply needed information.

"Hey," he said firmly as he walked up to her. "You there! Hang on a minute."

"Ah, good sir," replied the young, raven-haired woman with a smile, that smile accented by the heavy rouge upon her pale cheeks. "Are you seeking some personal attention this fine night?"

"Actually, I…" he started to say, but his voice trailed off as Kit walked up beside him.

"Ah, perhaps you wish for this fine gentleman to make my acquaintance?" asked the mystery woman.

Kit gave a short bow, took her hand into his, brought her hand up to his lips, and gave her a gentle kiss on the back of her hand.

"Enchanted, señorita," he grinned.

She giggled slightly in return, a nervous affect, no doubt, from gaining the attentions of someone far above her station.

James took that moment to study the young woman's face.

There was something about her that was too familiar, terribly so, though he could not put his finger on where he had met her before, and this bothered him…It bothered him a lot.

"I just need to ask—" started James.

"Will it just be the young gentleman?" interrupted the young woman. "Or would you like to take a turn as well, good sir?"

"Oh, you shall have your turn!" hissed Lenore. "Off with you!"

Startled, James turned to view the person who had brought them here.

Lenore had appeared like a ghost from the dark, and the normally-congenial young lady's dark eyes were a flash of fury, her expression a pit of rage, no mercy or pity upon her lovely face.

The prostitute before them paled at the sight of Lenore, and then that painted lady of the night gave a mild curtsey and excused herself.

"I…I'm afraid I must be going, good gentlemen," she stammered. "Another time, perhaps."

And then she was off, walking at a good pace down the winding streets of this slum end of town.

"Damn," cursed James under his breath. "I didn't get a chance to talk to her."

"Why would you need to talk to a common slag?" asked Lenore in audible irritation. "There is no cause to do as such, Mr. James. We do not have time for any predacious indecencies you may feel inclined to subdue."

"I've seen her somewhere before," frowned James. "It's just a hunch, but I think she could have had information for me…something…I don't know…It's just a feeling."

Lenore shook her head in slight disgust and then motioned toward the entrance to Hanbury Street.

"Come," she ordered. "Let us waste no more time on such idle frivolities."

Information wasn't a "frivolity," but James was not going to argue with her. No, he just shook his head, sighed, and then pressed the button on his jacket collar to bring up his protective helm.

Kit took off his hat, pressed the button on his jacket to call forth his own helm, and then put his hat back on his head. The boy then turned his head and gave James an expressionless, helmeted gaze.

"What is a 'slag'?" he asked.

James cringed at that question.

"I'll tell you when you're older," he said uncomfortably. "For now, let's just get to hunting…It's almost midnight."

They followed Lenore as she entered Hanbury Street, the young lady walking past several shops and late-night passerby, and then she entered a side alley, just like James and Kit had done the previous night.

"The beast prowls within these shadowed walls!" called back Lenore as she took to a quicker pace. "Follow me, good sirs!"

Her speed and determination caught both James and his young sidekick by surprise, so it took them a moment to try and match her speed, but by the time their neurons had finally fired in response to her unchecked lead, she had rounded a corner at the end of the L-shaped alleyway they were in, disappearing from sight altogether.

"Lenore, wait!" called out James.

He and Kit rounded the corner in order to slow her down, but upon entering the next alley, they realized all too quickly she was simply not there. The young woman had vanished within the span of seconds.

"What the...?" asked James.

"What's going on, señor?" asked Kit. "Where is Lenore?"

"The streets must be shifting just like Captain Robinson said they would," frowned James. "Damn!...We need to find her."

"How do we do that?" asked Kit in a nervous tone. "If we don't find her quickly, the beast may find her first."

"I know," said James. "Keep your eyes peeled. The first thing we need to do is—"

"Warning," came the soft voice of his VI. "Disparate rift energy detected. Area unstable. Proceed with caution."

"Yeah, yeah," muttered James. "Tell us something we don't know."

"Warning," said the VI again. "Class-Four Automaton in area."

"Wait...Class-Four Automaton?" asked James.

"That's what my VI said last night," said Kit. "What's going on? Are our artifacts going out again?"

"I don't know," said James unhappily. "Something funny is going on…"

There was indeed something funny going on, and his mind struggled to connect it all.

He thought back upon everything he had learned about Whitechapel, but his brain seized upon the prostitute he had seen a mere couple of minutes prior and would not let go…There was something about that woman that was driving him crazy, a connection he could not quite grasp…That prostitute he had tried to question, her face…her face reminded him of…she looked like…

It hit him like a nuclear bomb.

"That's where I've seen her!" blurted out James.

"Seen who?" asked Kit in a startled voice. "What are you talking about? Who have you seen?"

"That woman on the street!" replied James in caustic realization. "I knew I'd seen her somewhere before!...But that's impossible! That woman was the—"

He *had* seen that woman's face before…She had the *exact same face* as the ghoul they'd destroyed…and he was going to relay this bit of important information to Kit, relay it immediately, but a loud and shrill scream caught his full attention and derailed his thought process.

"That sounded like—!" began James.

"Lenore!" yelled Kit, and the boy was off in the direction of the young woman's scream before James could stop him.

Both of them beat feet down the narrow alleyway they were in, only to round another L-shaped corner, viewing another alleyway that led toward a turn at a different L-shaped corner, and then they were off again, never stopping their run as Lenore screamed one more time.

"We shouldn't have let her come in with us!" yelled James. "Dammit!"

"Quickly, señor!" yelled Kit in return. "We must save her!"

They rounded the next corner, both of them with their Rune Makers out and ready, both of them prepared to eliminate whatever horrors lurked in the dark.

They both came to a screeching halt as they viewed the huge creature carrying Lenore over its shoulder.

Even from the back and side, James could see that the nine-foot-tall beast was indeed a minotaur, a hulking mass of brown fur and muscle with two great horns atop its bull head.

It had opened a large iron grate embedded within the alley floor, that rusted metal grate a previously unknown fixture within the dirty yellow planks of this screwed-up burg, and it was half in and half out of what had to be some passageway that led down beneath the streets of Whitechapel.

Lenore looked unharmed, but she was clearly passed out, unconscious over the beast's left shoulder…James knew she would not remain unharmed for long.

"Warning," sounded James' VI. "Class-Four Automaton in area."

Kit raised his Rune Maker to take aim, but James laid his arm across the boy's chest in order to stop him.

"Don't!" he warned. "You could hit Lenore!"

"Then what do we do!" cried Kit.

The boy was well and truly upset, but that was to be expected. Kit was the kind of kid that wasn't going to let some helpless person get eaten…Honestly, James was not that kind of guy, either; he was just smarter about it.

"We're going after it!" said James. "We're going to track it to its lair and ambush it!"

"She could be killed by then!" yelled Kit.

The beast ignored them and then dropped down beneath the narrow alley into whatever passageway lay below.

"After it!" grunted James.

They both took to running after the creature, burning distance before the monster could close the heavy grate above it.

The beast reached up with its massive right hand, intending to close the heavy grate with only the use of one arm, which it most certainly could do, but that was not important. What was important was that its huge right hand was exposed, and that meant that hand was a target, a target that could be struck without the risk of hitting Lenore. If James could freeze that arm and hand in place…

"Ymir's Breath!" he commanded.

A rune on his pistol lit up with a cold blue, and then he fired off two rounds of rune-stamped bullets near the opening of the passageway, two rounds that pinged off of the creature's right hand with a zinging sound, those bullets ricocheting off of the yellow-brick walls at the end of the alleyway a fraction of a second later.

There was a loud and echoing roar as the beast withdrew its hand, and then that roaring began to fade as the creature fled with its prize beneath the streets of Whitechapel.

"I hit it, dammit!" yelled James. "I know I did! That should have frozen it in place!"

"It's getting away!" yelled Kit.

"I know!" yelled back James.

Both of them dropped into the still open pit that had been previously covered by the grate, dropping to land with heavy boots upon hewn stone in the dark, the passageway before them revealing itself due to their helmets' night vision.

The blocky tunnel around them was of carved stone, that stone etched with glowing magic symbols here and there, though James was not familiar with such sigils.

"What the…?" he muttered.

The creature roared again, that echoing roar blasting down the tunnel in front of them.

"After it!" cried Kit.

"Warning," spoke the soft voice of James' VI once more. "Class-Four Automaton in area."

James had a sudden epiphany. It was a connection of neurons that fired all at once, an indication that he was indeed *not* losing his sharpness as he was gaining in years. His scanner was not in error, no. His VI wasn't just blathering off random statements, either… This was beginning to make sense now, the whole of what they were dealing with, and it ticked him off.

"Son of a…!" swore James. "It's not a minotaur!"

"What!" asked Kit in audible disbelief. "It's clearly a…a minotaur, señor! Were you hit in the head!"

"I knew I'd hit that sucker!" cried James as he and Kit ran like the wind after the creature. "It banked right off him, and my charges did nothing to it! It should have frozen him solid! It should have at least frozen his arm!"

"No, you miss—" started Kit, but James cut him short.

"It only…only looks like a minotaur!" huffed James. "It's actually a golem!"

"I know…what you're thinking," huffed Kit in return. "Golems are…are Class-Three Automatons, not Class Four."

"This one's a Class Four because it's immune to magic!" replied James.

The creature roared again as the tunnel ahead branched off in three directions. Thankfully, James' helmet accurately displayed an audible-location sound wedge in his HUD to point them toward the rightmost tunnel. Kit clearly had the same feature installed in his own helmet, because neither one of them slowed down at all as they both turned and bolted down the rightmost tunnel.

"Golems are…are guardians," puffed Kit. "They only kill as a defensive measure…They don't eat people…They can't eat people! I've never heard of a golem that eats people!"

"No, but they are controlled," replied James. "Golems don't act on their own. Someone or something is having it abduct women off the street, and then that…that someone or something is killing those women, mutilating them, but that…but that means…"

"Means what, señor?" asked Kit.

"It means we're dealing with a serial killer!" gasped James. "We're dealing with a good-ol'-fashioned serial killer who's using a golem to…Wait…A serial killer in Whitechapel?…Why does that sound famil…iar…"

His eyes went wide as it came to him, all of it, all of it at once, and that revelation was a mindblower.

"Son of a…!" he hissed. "I know who we're dealing with! I know what's going on!…That's what that Class-Five Corporeal Undead warning was about!"

"What!" asked Kit in frantic confusion. "What's going on!"

"There's no time to explain!" cried James. "Come on!"

They rounded a corner and stopped as the hallway spread out into a large square room filled with carved stone pillars, those pillars etched with runes that shone forth a strange waxing and waning light, that glow a visible amber light in James' night vision.

James ducked behind a pillar and signaled for Kit to do the same, and the boy complied, hiding behind a pillar opposite of James' hiding place

"What have you brought me?" came a voice from across the large room.

James briefly poked his head around the pillar, but not for long, because he knew the lit amber visors on his helmet would give away his position, even with the partial camouflage of the weird glow from the etched runes upon the carved pillars around him.

He could see the distinct form of an elderly man in servant's attire at the base of a set of carved stone steps that led directly upwards. Standing next to this mystery man was the beast, all nine feet of it, an unconscious Lenore still draped over its left shoulder.

James, of course, immediately recognized the mystery man, but he didn't comment on the man's identity for fear of being heard. Kit, on the other hand, was too green to figure out the necessity of stealth.

"That's the Earl's man!" whispered Kit.

James waved at him to shut up, motioning once more for the boy to hide.

Thankfully, the beast roared directly after Kit's audible error, and this prevented their detection, because the bellow echoed round the chamber, and it was so loud, James' audio dampers activated in order to protect his hearing.

"Quiet!" hissed the Earl's servant. "Are you trying to deafen me!...What happened to your hand?...You've damaged it somehow...Quickly...Take the girl to the lower chamber and wait in the lab. The Earl will wish to know of your blundering. We shall have to repair this hand."

James signaled for Kit to wait, though the headstrong boy had his gun drawn and was ready to use it.

The mechanical creature and its handler traveled up the stone steps a moment later.

James kept out of sight and motioned for Kit to stay hidden as well.

The sounds of the beast's heavy footsteps were accompanied by the creaking of the opening of a door, then there was the sound of the creaking of the shutting of that door, and then the slamming of that door, and then silence.

"That was the Earl's man!" repeated Kit, this time more than loud enough to be heard.

"I know," said James calmly. "I also know what's going on, too."

"Then tell me!" said Kit angrily. "Quickly! We have to hurry! We have to save Lenore!"

"Look around you," said James unhappily. "Where do you think we are?"

The boy's helmeted face was unreadable, but his head movements were not. He looked around the area for a few brief seconds, but what he was thinking, James did not know.

"We're in some kind of temple?" he asked. "This place looks ancient."

"Exactly," said James. "Don't you remember what the bartender said back in Hollowstone? He said that the city of Poe was destroyed by breaches."

"Sí," nodded Kit. "I remember. What does that have to do with anything?"

"Think about it, Kit," replied James. "The city of Poe was built over ancient ruins that attracted scholars, researchers, and cultists. The cultists ended up destroying the place, but I don't think the ruins were destroyed…This place has ruins. We're standing in them."

"And?" asked the boy. "So Whitechapel has ancient ruins too?...I don't understand? Do you think Whitechapel will end up like Poe? Whitechapel will become like the Mourning Field?"

"No, kid, I don't," said James grimly. "I don't, because there is no Whitechapel."

"I don't understand," said Kit.

"This *is* the Mourning Field," said James. "We're in it right now."

"What?" asked Kit in audible surprise. "How do you know that?"

"Remember that ghoul we killed?" asked James.

"Sí," said Kit.

"I knew I'd seen that lady on the street before," said James. "The woman whose hand you kissed? That was *her*…*She* was the ghoul."

"No, no," said Kit as he shook his head. "No, that can't be…At least…I think…I…"

"It's her, and you know it," replied James. "The only way that could possibly happen is if her soul is trapped here, trapped in this fake city of 'Whitechapel.' We destroyed her when she was a ghoul, and her soul was released, but it was released back *here*, back into the so-called city of Whitechapel. Her soul is still trapped here, right along with everyone else in this screwed-up burg."

"That's loco, señor!" gasped Kit. "How do you know this?"

"When Poe was destroyed, something came through the final breach and laid claim to this area," explained James. "Or I should say, 'someone.'"

"Who?" asked Kit.

"I'll get to that," said James. "You see, I'm thinking this sucker created the fake city of Whitechapel and bound the old residents of Poe to this place. I'm guessing these ancient ruins had something to do with that. Whatever the case, we really are dealing with a Class-Five Corporeal Undead."

"What are we dealing with, then?" asked Kit in genuine interest. "And why would it bind the residents here?"

"For his own sick pleasure," grimaced James, though Kit could not see that expression beneath James' helmet. "Let me explain…First off, let's just say that I have a device that lets me see into other worlds."

This bit was true; James' smartphone could access another world's internet, and no, Kit did not know about James' smartphone, because James had not told Radditz about it, and if Radditz didn't know about it, then the old man couldn't have written about it, therefore, Kit did not know about it.

"Really?" asked Kit. "Where did you get such a device?"

"From a breach site," frowned James. "It doesn't matter. The point is, I've seen the name 'Whitechapel' before. It's part of a larger city in this other world I can see. A serial killer took part in a series of murders there, but he was never caught…I'm telling you, that sucker went through a breach and created his own Whitechapel out of the remains of Poe."

"Really?" repeated Kit. "So what does that have to do with a Class-Five Corporeal Undead?...Is this killer a vampire or…or a lich?"

"Neither," said James grimly. "He doesn't drain the blood of his victims like a vampire would, and he's not interested in researching forbidden magics like a lich. No, he's just a sicko who's looking to keep killing just like he did before he died…In fact, I'm thinking we're dealing with an Undying."

"An Undying?" asked Kit. "The cursed ones? I think I've heard of them, but I thought they were just myth…just legend."

"What do you know about them?" asked James.

"Not much," said Kit. "All I've heard is that they are cursed to haunt an area, and, of course, that they can't be killed."

"They can, but it takes Death himself to take them," said James. "I'm thinking that's why the Earl has built himself a little murder palace over the remains of Poe. It's to keep Death at bay while he plays his own sick little game."

"The Earl is the killer?" asked Kit.

James gave him the best "Are you stupid?" look he could muster, though he knew Kit couldn't see that expression due to James' own helmet.

"Oh, wait," said the boy a moment later. "Of course, he is…Sorry, señor. Even I have my thoughtless moments…But that doesn't explain how we kill him. If the Earl is an Undying, then the only way to end him is to bring Death *here*, and how do we do that?...And how do we keep Death from taking us, too?"

"Death has to follow a cosmic plan," said James quickly. "As far as I know, neither of us is on that plan yet…Death can only take us when it's our time to go…But that's not the issue…You see, the issue is the Earl cheating Death.

"When someone cheats Death, it disrupts the cosmic order, which makes Death antsy. He's got to correct it quicker than spit, but I have the feeling the Earl has been a thorn in his side for a long time, which means Death would be willing to do whatever it takes to get him."

"So how do we get Death's attention?" asked Kit. "Because if this is what we need to do, we need to do it quickly, because Lenore is running out of time…

"Wait…Wait, wait señor…If the souls of Poe are trapped here, then how was Lenore able to travel back and forth from here to Hollowstone?...And how did she know who you were?...She had to have heard of you from somewhere…As much as your theory holds some weight, señor, it also fails to hold water."

"Oh, I didn't think about that…" said James. "How did Lenore and Mr. Clemm escape Poe?…Wait…Wait a second!…What the…!"

Another epiphany struck him, and this one was an equally-magnificent lightning bolt of a doozy.

It really came down to four things: Lenore being able to leave Whitechapel, what she had said about "The Earl knows me very well," the young woman's open vehemence toward the Earl, and the prostitute's reaction to Lenore's interference…Actually, it came down to five things: There were also the names…Lenore, Mr. Clemm, and Poe. In fact, that last "coincidence" was what really set it off for James.

"I'm a complete idiot!" hissed James. "Lenore! Clemm! Poe!...I should have seen it from the beginning!"

"What!" said Kit in sudden alarm. "What should you have seen!"

"Lenore!" hissed James. "We've been had, kid! Clemm was the maiden name of Poe's dead wife, and Poe wrote 'The Raven' while Virginia Clemm was dying of tuberculosis! It was Poe's way of handling death!"

"I…I don't understand," stammered Kit. "You're not making any sense…What does that mean?"

"Edgar Allan Poe was a famous author from that other world I can see," frowned James. "'The 'Raven' is a famous poem he wrote, but that's not important…What is important is that we can now kill the Earl! We can definitely kill that murdering sucker, and he's stupidly brought the means of his own demise right to his front door!…Come on!"

He took off from behind the pillar and ran up the stairs, Kit right behind him.

"I don't get it!" cried Kit. "How are we going to kill the Earl if he can't be killed!"

"I'll explain when we confront the Earl!" said James. "We have to get to Lenore!...Damn! I don't think Death can be killed, but he can be ejected from the city, so we have to hurry!"

"None of what you said makes any sense!" cried Kit.

"I'll tell you when you're older!" said James quickly. "Just shut up and follow me!"

They both reached the top of the stairs, only to come to a halt before the ten-foot-tall, six-foot-wide wooden door before them.

James watched as Kit eyed the door from top to bottom, the green visors on his helmet moving up and down to study the final barrier between them and their target.

"That is one big door," breathed out the young man. "It's got to be at least three meters tall and two meters wide."

"Then it's going to take both of us to open it," said James in a low voice.

There was a huge, wrought-iron circular handle on the right side of the door. Both of them holstered their Rune Makers, gripped the massive handle, and prepared to pull.

"Get ready," said James. "On three…One, two…three!"

They pulled hard and nearly tumbled down the stairs as the huge door swung open with ease, creaking loudly as it did, both of them catching their footing at the last second.

"That was much easier than I'd thought it would be," chuckled Kit.

"Yeah," grunted James. "Come on. Play time's over. Let's go get this sucker."

"Sí, señor," replied the young man in a firm tone.

They both travelled up some big stone steps and made their way through a ten-foot-tall arch into a large room filled with antiquated mechanical equipment. Gas-fueled lamps lined the walls, something expensive the common folk of Whitechapel would never be able to afford, but lighting was lighting, dim as it was, and what the dim lighting revealed was something even James hadn't expected.

In this new room were large brass tubes attached to gauges, gears, and small furnaces, yet these devices were situated in what appeared to be no-seemingly-logical positions for any of them.

James took a moment to view the strange machinery around him.

"It looks like every teenage girl's steampunk fanfic in here," he frowned.

"Shhh!" hushed Kit. "Quiet, señor!"

The boy motioned toward the large table in the center of the room, a huge Frankenstein's slab with the motionless form of the minotaur laid out across it.

James took a moment to study the beast, and he could see the damaged right hand of it; the exterior fur of the mechanical creature was caught in the fine gears that made up its fingers.

"Damn," whispered James. "My bullets didn't do a damned thing to it…It just happened to get some fur caught in its gears…Bullets must have torn through the fabric, and then that torn fabric got sucked right in…Guess the Earl didn't plan on that little defect."

"It doesn't matter," whispered Kit. "We don't want to wake it up!...Come on!"

"Yep," replied James.

On that, they could agree.

They both crept toward a single wooden door in the distance, that door ajar, that door just as tall and as wide as the monstrous door that had led them up here.

James took the lead and placed himself behind the door while Kit hid close to the outer wall, both of them hidden from sight, both of them in a position to spy through the opening that allowed a view into the next room.

James could see bloodstains on the stone floor within the next chamber, but one quick scan explained the reason behind that. The next room was filled with archaic medical equipment along with various standing shelves and counters set with jars of what looked like preserved human organs…many of those organs the severed breasts and genitalia of numerous female victims.

James could sense the absolute disgust emanating from Kit, but he held up one finger as a symbol for the boy to wait while James, himself, drew his own Rune Maker. Kit followed suit, drawing his own pistol, and James could tell that the boy was waiting on James to make the first move.

Voices arose over the near quiet of their surroundings, those voices originating from the room they were currently staking out.

"What have you brought me?" came the grim voice of the Earl.

"Another one, though she is not so gaudily dressed," came the voice of the Earl's manservant. "She has the dress of fine standing about her…She must have been caught outside of her nightly duties, a commoner pretending to be above her station…How amusing, my lord."

"Irrelevant," replied the Earl. "I need someone new to replace our destroyed 'eater of the dead.' Those two mercenaries have caused me no end of trouble…Still, it was better to be rid of them in this way than to have suspicions roused if they were to meet a more unsavory end…Taurus could have ended them, but I would not take that risk…even with his abilities."

"Yes, sir," said the Earl's man.

"Nevertheless, something strange is afoot here," said the Earl. "It is one thing for those foreigners to have stumbled upon our little city, but it is entirely another for someone to have directed them here…I shall have to have Captain Robinson double the watch at our gates. We will no longer be allowing anyone in."

"A wise plan, sir," said the Earl's man.

"I know," replied the Earl. "But enough of this. Get me the arsenic…I don't want to damage her body. We shall strip her after that and perform the black rite. First, though, let us see who our next eater of the dead shall be…"

James heard the rustle of a sheet, like a bedsheet, and then a loud, unsettled gasp after that.

"Who is this!" cried the Earl in a harsh tone.

"Sh…She was brought in like the others," stammered the Earl's manservant. "Is she not what you wished—"

"This is no citizen of Whitechapel!" hissed the Earl. "Where did she come from!"

"F…From the streets…" said the manservant, definite fear now evident in his voice. "She is just like all the others."

"She is *not* like the others!" roared the Earl.

There was a loud crashing as something was knocked to the floor, a clattering and clanging of something across cold stone.

"I know the faces of everyone here!" yelled the Earl. "I know the faces of every citizen of Whitechapel! Every one of them!...Now, I will only ask this one…more…time…Who is this woman!"

"I do not know, sir!" cried the manservant in a vocal panic.

James took that opportunity to enter this chamber of horrors, Kit following right behind him. He stepped around some standing wooden shelves filled with numerous female body parts to view a surgical table with the prone, unconscious form of Lenore laid across it, both the Earl and his manservant standing over her, a tossed white cloth sheet on the floor just off the far side of the table. There was a large grate beneath the table, that grate designed to slough off blood and offal, a terrible and distinct indication of what had happened to the Earl's previous victims.

Every time one of these women died, their trapped souls were released back into the city with no memory of their own murder…This sick sucker had been killing them over and over again, and they had no idea…

Oh, yeah. The Earl was going down once and for all.

James stepped into view and leveled his pistol. He could have said, "Stop right there!," or "Halt!," but he had something better in mind.

"Raijin's Thunder," said James in a firm, clear voice.

A rune lit up on James' piece, that rune lighting up with a vivid yellow light, a bright glow in the dim oil lighting of the chamber of horrors they were all currently in.

"Raijin's Thunder," repeated Kit.

The Earl gazed upon the both of them with nothing but sheer hatred in his menacing blue eyes.

"You two!" hissed the man.

He turned his vitriol upon his own manservant, his tone murderous and unforgiving.

"You led them here, you fool!" he cried.

"B…But I did nothing of the—" began the servant, but he was destined to never finish what he was going to say.

The Earl waved his right hand and drew a blade from nowhere, a long and shadowy rapier that appeared out of thin air, and then the old manservant's head flew from his shoulders in a fountain of blood, the neck stump spraying that crimson liquid everywhere as the body fell to the floor and the head rolled across cold grey stone.

"Riddle him!" yelled James as he pulled the trigger of his Rune Maker.

He and Kit unloaded upon the Earl, their Rune Makers stamping each bullet with the Raijin's Thunder rune as the metal slugs left their respective barrels. The evil nobleman danced as twelve magic rounds entered his unprotected body; the wispy shadow blade in his right hand faded out in a black mist as both James and Kit emptied their enchanted ammo into the terrible murderer.

The Earl went down to one knee behind the surgical table as his body crackled with bright-yellow electricity, but he stood up a second later, the electric sparks surrounding him waning to nothing while spent bullets dropped to the floor out of the very holes they had just made. He fluffed out his suit jacket after that and then gave them both a grim smile.

Much to James' chagrin, the Earl looked untouched, though the man's clothes bore some small streams of smoke from where the bullets had entered.

"Oh, it is most definitely my turn now, good sirs," he spat.

The undying man raised his right hand, the deathly shadow blade he had wielded before reformed in all its deadly glory, and then he pointed that unholy weapon directly at James.

"Aww, crap," breathed James.

There was no time to reload…but this did not mean he was defenseless.

James holstered his Rune Maker, drew his cavalry saber, and intoned the only command he could think of that could protect him.

"Seraph's Light," he said firmly.

A white rune on his blade lit up in a brilliant white light, and that holy light meant he was ready to go…If the Earl was going to throw down with him, then the man was going to have to deal with James' own arsenal.

Kit drew his own blade, his enchanted rapier, and made the same invocation as James had, lighting his own blade with the same holy light as James had just done. This was good, because James figured that particular enchantment was the only thing that was going to be able to parry the Earl's own unholy, necromantic shadow blade.

The Earl was on them in a heartbeat, and he was fast with his blade, fast to the point where both James and

Kit were on the defensive, the evil nobleman unafraid of any kind of attack in return.

James parried three shots to his own center mass as Kit deflected some fierce and fast slashing attacks to the boy's own throat. Thankfully, both James and Kit had their helmets up. Their heads and necks were protected by enchanted steel, so the shadow blade deflected off of the top of James' helmet at least once and across Kit's neck guard twice.

James deflected a shot aimed at his groin and countered with a quick slash across the Earl's right knee. The man stumbled as Kit stabbed him through the chest, and then James sliced through the Earl's throat, the man's head coming clean off in much the same manner as his manservant's had.

The terrible murderer had come at them full force, unafraid of receiving attacks in return, and with good reason…

He simply wouldn't die.

There was no blood this time. No, the Earl's head came off in a liquid string of inky black, and then it was sucked right back down onto the stump of his neck, merging flesh with flesh as if he had never been cut at all.

Kit backed away and spat out a low curse.

"He's not going down, señor!" yelled the boy. "What do we do!"

"You die, fool!" hissed the Earl. "I tire of this game already! It is time to end you!"

The murderous nobleman vanished in a blink of shadowy black, sucked into a pinpoint of darkness that appeared like a miniature black hole behind him, and then Kit cried out in pain as the Earl's shadowy blade pushed its dark tip through the young man's back and out the right side of Kit's chest, straight through the boy's right lung.

The murderous nobleman had suddenly appeared behind James' well-meaning sidekick, stepping into existence from a portal of darkness that had coalesced from nowhere.

"Kit!" yelled James.

The young man staggered forwards, then backwards, and then he slumped down next to a desk laden with the jars of preserved female organs.

"Damn you, sucker!" yelled James.

The Earl winked out of existence, but James was not Kit. For one thing, James had dealt with teleporters before. He was not green in the gills, so the first thing he did was turn and slash behind himself.

The Earl's right hand flew from his body, his shadowy blade dissolving because of the attack, but once again, the man's severed limb was sucked back onto himself by a liquid string of pure, inky black.

James took that opportunity to cut off the Earl's head yet again, but the murderer's head simply reattached as it had before.

"You cannot…kill me…fool!" gasped the Earl, but he was momentarily staggered by the holy magics surging through him.

The man could not be killed, even by the Seraph's Light enchantment, but that holy enchantment was temporarily slowing down the vile serial killer, giving James enough time to think things through.

What the Earl had said about James not being able to kill him was true. Something was protecting the man from Death, and whatever was protecting the Earl from Death had to be destroyed, or nothing James did to him was going to matter. James had to fatally injure the Earl in order for Death to take the infamous serial-killer's soul, and that wasn't going to happen until the Earl's protection was destroyed.

It occurred to James that whatever was protecting the Earl had to be laced with powerful runes that could ward off Death, and he seriously doubted that this was due to the ruins below, or the original inhabitants of Poe would have also been Undying, which they were most certainly not.

The Earl's protection had to be something the man had personally constructed and enchanted, something that was heavily laced with runes, something that could survive punishment from both physical and magical damage, because the Earl would want such a thing protected above all else, but there was nothing James had seen in here that fit that bill…

James mentally smacked himself on the head…The Earl had indeed built something just like that, and it was lying on a table in the next room.

There had to be a way to get to the minotaur golem, though, and because it was immune to magic, even if James did get to it, there was no way to destroy it. Normal bullets and sword swings weren't going to cut it, both physically and idiomatically.

As he was turning his head to look for something that could destroy the Earl's protection, James gave a brief glance toward Kit, and he breathed out a sigh of relief that the boy was not dead, just grievously injured. If Kit could hold out a little longer, James could use his artifact med-kit and heal the young man in an instant. The boy just had to hold on.

It was then that James spied the golden tube that Kit had strapped to his back, the golden tube that looked like a scroll or map case, the golden tube that held a very different purpose than that of holding scrolls or maps…

If Kit's claims about that tube were true, then there was indeed a way to destroy the minotaur construct that was protecting the Earl, but the problem was getting to the minotaur itself. James could grab the portable cannon from Kit, but the Earl would be on him before he could do anything about it. Furthermore, the Earl could teleport, and he could cut off any route James could take, and that meant cutting off any route to getting back into "the lab."

Of course, James figured he could always bring the damned thing to him, or rather, bring it to Kit, and that was probably what he was going to have to do…That, of course, meant a little fishing was in order. All he had to do was get the Earl to bite.

"I'm better than you!" yelled James. "In fact, I can do this all day, punk! I can kick your butt till the end of time if I need to!…No, you ain't Jack, Jack!…Or should I call you, 'The Ripper!'"

The Earl staggered backwards as he shook off the Seraph's Light enchantment, and then he held his silvered head for a second as if to gather his wits, reforming his shadowy blade in his reattached right hand.

The look on the man's face was priceless upon the reception of his true identity.

"Where did you hear that name!" demanded the infamous serial killer.

"Oh, you're infamous where I come from," said James grimly. "Jack the Ripper…A big, big man killing prostitutes on the street…Oh, it takes a real man to do that…I noticed how you never hunted soldiers or brawlers or anyone else that could actually fold you in half…

"You're nothing but a coward…You haven't changed one bit! You were a coward back then, and you're a coward now! In fact, I think I'll just stick around and kick your butt until I get bored, and then I'll kick your butt some more out of habit!"

The Earl roared in pure rage as he charged and then beat upon James' saber with his own shadowy blade, but James really was better than the murderous nobleman, so he returned the favor by countering with quick but powerful slices that severed limbs at the joints, cutting off the Earl's right hand, then the murderer's left arm at the elbow, and then even beheading the man one more time.

Of course, the Earl reformed each time, automatically reattaching his limbs and head after each attack.

"You can't beat me!" goaded James. "That's because I'm a real fighter and a real man, not a pathetic castrato like you!"

James parried an enraged swing and then sliced off the Earl's head yet again, but as the head flew through the air, James quickly stabbed the tip of his saber through the Earl's unprotected crotch, that saber punching all the way through to the other side.

"*Ooooh*, that had to hurt!" laughed James as he planted one big leather boot into the Earl's stomach, only to knock the body down while the Earl's head was still in the air. "Oh, I can do this forever, punk! I frickin' love this! In fact, you got nothing on me!"

The notorious serial killer reformed, his head reattaching, the pale cheeks of that sallow face reddened with rage, and then he bellowed once more, but this time his shout was for backup, which was exactly what James had been fishing for.

"Taurus!" cried the Earl. "TAURUS, TO ME!"

James backed away from the Earl's prone form as the menace that was the mechanical minotaur flung wide the huge door that led from the lab to the Earl's private chamber of horrors.

James turned and saw Kit struggling to stand, but in the boy's current condition, that wasn't going to happen. Nevertheless, Kit could still do what needed to be done from a sitting position.

"Remember that tube on your back, Kit!" spouted off James. "It's time to use it! Get rid of that clockwork beast, and I'll finish the Earl once and for all!"

"Sí…señor," wheezed Kit through bloody lips.

The young man quickly and painfully unstrapped his portable cannon as James stared down the nine-foot-tall beast.

But the infamous serial killer of London ignored James' side conversation with Kit, the evil nobleman intent only on revenge.

"Taurus!" yelled the Earl. "Kill them! Kill these foreign fools!"

The great mechanical beast's glowing eyes leveled themselves upon Kit's downed figure.

James just needed time for Kit to line up a shot, or everything was going to go south fast…True, James was definitely a better fighter than the Earl, but there was no way he could actually fight forever, so the decision to attract the mechanical beast's attention right frickin' now was both a swift and logical one…He did not want that thing taking out Kit before Kit could take it out instead.

"Yeah!" yelled James at the fake minotaur. "Over here, you fat cow!...Right here! I'm right here! Come get me, sucker!"

The big automaton swiveled its massive head towards James, snorting hot steam from both of its huge nostrils, and then it kicked back both its hooves, scraping the stone with them, readying its charge.

Kit quickly removed the caps of his portable railgun, and through great pain and even greater willpower, the boy rose to one knee and placed the cannon on his right shoulder. A large, circular, crosshairs sight of alchemical gold popped up at the front of the cannon, Kit lined up that sight, and then he gave the command word to fire just as the mechanical beast was about to charge.

"Destruere!" coughed out the boy.

The cannon roared hot blue flames out its back end as the front end fired the ensorcelled titanium shaft. The huge missile shot forward and speared right through the fake minotaur's chest, piercing the automaton's formerly invulnerable armor, right where its "heart" would have been.

Kit dropped the cannon and then slumped back down after that, and unfortunately, James did not know if the boy was dead or just unconscious.

The mechanical beast, however, the notorious "Minotaur of Whitechapel," fizzled and sparked from various joints, and then its head lit aflame as the whole of it, from its head to its hooves, toppled backwards through the doorway and into the Earl's lab.

The Earl popped up from his prone position, a look of pure panic etched upon his pale face.

"N…No!" he choked out.

The infamous murderer reformed his shadowy blade and backed away as James leveled his own enchanted blade back at him, but this poor example of a standoff did not last long, because it appeared James would not have to fatally injure the Earl after all.

No, a new development had occurred…Death had finally and personally come for the Earl…James was not needed for this part.

"Well done, James," came a deep and sonorous voice.

He turned to see Lenore sit up on the medical table she had been laid out upon. She slid off the table to plant her laced boots firmly upon the bloodstained floor, and then she transformed, growing and darkening until all of her had been replaced by the ominous and imposing form of the Grim Reaper.

James turned his head so as to not stare directly at Death. He was not stupid.

"No!" cried the Earl. "No, I won't go! NO!...NOOOOOO!"

The Earl collapsed in on himself as Death approached him, the infamous serial killer collapsing inwards into an inky black sphere that flew into Death's skeletal right hand. The angel of death then took that ebony sphere into his tattered black robes, and as soon as that dark and twisted soul was pocketed, everything began to fall apart.

With its creator gone, the city of Whitechapel crumbled around the three of them, white spheres of light erupting skywards as the souls of the former city of Poe were finally and fully released.

James stumbled and fell as the earth shook beneath his feet. He landed on his butt as the walls and desks and shelves and all the horrors of the Earl's chamber were sucked upwards within a funnel of blue light along with the freed souls of Whitechapel, the huge mechanical minotaur floating upwards to disappear as well within that brightly-lit, sapphire tunnel.

James watched in strange wonder as all of the buildings, goods, and sundries of Whitechapel disappeared forever, leaving behind nothing but the stone floor beneath him and a grim and stark blanket of choking grey fields around him, fields of pall ash dotted only by blackened, fossilized trees and the occasional lonesome boulder.

The funnel of blue light died down to nothing after that, the last remnants of Whitechapel gone for good.

The angel of death then looked skyward, and two ragged and spanned wings of pure pitch erupted from the skeletal frame of his back and through his tattered cloak. He was gone after that, rocketing skyward until he was nothing but a black dot, a dot blacker than the pitch sky above them, and even that sable dot vanished into the darkness of the starlit sky after a few seconds.

"Hey!" yelled James in a flash of fury. "You owe us, you son of a—!"

"S…señor…" choked out Kit.

James clipped his ranting before it could begin.

"Damn!" he said as he hopped to his feet and frantically removed his brown leather jacket. "Hang on, kid!"

Sewn within the interior back of his jacket was his wide pocket, a pocket wide enough to hold his larger equipment, so he reached within that extradimensional space to pull forth his artifact medical kit. James popped open the med-kit, fished around for a tiny packet containing two aspirin, palmed that packet, closed the kit, and then shoved his med-kit back into his wide pocket before slipping his jacket back on as quickly as he could.

"Hang tight, bud," grunted James as he ripped open the packet and spilled the two pills into his gloved right hand.

With his empty left hand, James reached into one of his right interior jacket pockets and pulled forth a steel bottle of purified water.

"It's too late…for me…James," wheezed Kit. "I'm not…going to…make it…Tell…the Moncada family…I died well…"

"Don't be such a drama queen, kid," grunted James. "You're not gonna die. If you were gonna bite the bullet, Death would have taken you with him. Now shut up and swallow these…Come on, kid, retract your helmet."

James removed Kit's Gaucho hat as the young man reached up and pressed the button on his steel neck collar to retract his own helm. The boy slowly and painfully took James' pills into his own right hand, swallowed those pills, and then drank deeply from James' water bottle that James held up to the boy's bloody lips.

And it did not take long for those pills to take effect. It took mere seconds for a bright-white light to shine through Kit's grievous and mortal wound after Kit was done drinking. That holy glow then died down and out, the fatal wound closing shut with no sign of a scar to show for it.

Kit breathed out a long sigh of relief, and then James offered his own hand to help the boy up.

The young man stood, grinned, and then shook his head once.

"What did you give me, señor!" he asked in unbridled amazement. "I'm healed! In fact, I feel a million times better!"

"Dug out my med-kit," shrugged James. "Found it at a breach site. Everything in it is an artifact with an extreme-healing enchantment, but the supplies in it are limited…Doubt I'll find another one anytime soon…Oh, well…That's what it's for…You're welcome."

"That's just like the one *Marcos*—" began the young man, but James waved him off.

"Yeah, yeah," said James. "I know. I think ol' Marcos has the things you need to have in order to keep breathing if you're gonna live the life of a merc, Kit, so there's that. Probably a smart idea to follow his blueprint to the letter."

"Oh, I have," grinned the young man. "There are some things I still have to find, like your watch and that med-kit, but I am on the right track, I think."

"That you are," replied James. "Anyway…we'd better get a move on and get out of the Mourning Field. I think it's probably safe to travel through here now, but…I'd rather not stick around."

"Sí, señor," nodded Kit. "Let's go back to Hollowstone. We can celebrate there…I have means, you know."

James reached into his own right jacket pocket with his left hand and pulled forth a small rune-lamp, a golden tube he carried around for emergencies. Normally, he relied on his helmet for night vision, but for now, he switched on the small lamp for one very important reason…

He reached up and pressed the steel button on his neck collar and retracted his own helmet. He wanted to make sure Kit could see the amused expression on his face within the glow of the lamp.

"Good, because you owe me," snorted James.

"That I do, mi amigo," grinned Kit. "If you ever want to team up again, just call me. My family will hear of your name and what you did for me. The Moncadas will always consider you a friend…There is one thing I would like to know, though…because I find this thing very strange."

"What's that?" asked James.

"If you've never read the *Marcos the Riftwalker* books," asked Kit, "then why do you have almost the same gear as Marcos? Your gear is nearly identical to his…Is this gear something all experienced mercenaries know to have?"

James shook his head once and gave a short chuckle.

"I'll tell you when you're older," he grinned.

#9…BUTTONS

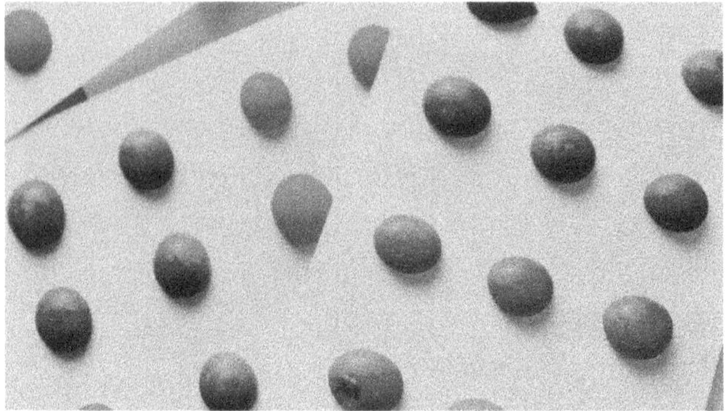

Some buttons are hard to swallow.

Asher walked directly behind Mrs. Edgerton as they were led to the testing area.

The only one that wasn't in their pod right now was Georgina, because she had been bad. She had thrown a tantrum because she had not gotten the doll she had wanted during quiet play, so two big men in white coats had come and taken her away. That was bad, because the big men in the white coats were scary, and no one had wanted to go with them. Asher certainly didn't want to go with them.

Today was a test day. They were all going to the testing area, so Georgina was going to have to make up that test somehow, and that probably meant she'd have to go during quiet play, so maybe the big men in the white coats had already taken her to the testing area, but Asher really didn't know. All he knew was that he didn't want to miss quiet play. Quiet play was the only time any of them got to actually play.

His days were pretty simple. He woke up with the other children at 06:00 hours, and they were all led to the showers after that. All of them took their showers, and that took twenty minutes, and then they were led to their homeroom to be given their morning snacks, and morning snack time was thirty minutes. They ate, and then they started their learning. They had quiet play four times a day for thirty minutes each, lunch and dinner were forty-five minutes each, and they had naptime once a day for one hour. They all used the restroom periodically throughout the day, but every other part of the day was for learning, and that was the life Asher led, the life they all led.

Mrs. Edgerton was their pod mother. The whole class loved Mrs. Edgerton, even though she was very strict. She was in charge of all twenty children, ten boys and ten girls, and she made sure all of them stayed good and didn't throw tantrums or fight or anything else like that. None of the kids wanted to get in trouble with her, because then Mrs. Edgerton would put them in the alone room, and you didn't want that. The alone room had no sound, no sound at all, so no one could hear your screaming and crying. Even you couldn't hear your screaming and crying.

That's why Asher had been afraid when the big men in white coats had come and taken Georgina away. That had never happened before. He could tell that the other kids had been scared too, because they had gotten really quiet when the big men had come to get Georgina.

But that wasn't important right now, because now they were all walking down the white hallway to the testing area.

But it wasn't just the testing area that was white. Everything here was white. Their clothes were all white; everybody wore a sleeveless white shirt with white scrubs and soft, padded, white shoes with no socks. The rooms and everything in the rooms were all white too; all of the walls were white, the floors and ceilings were white, the desks were white, and their sleeping pods were white…Even their food blocks were white, served on white food trays…Everything here was white.

Well, not everything. Their toys during quiet play were bright with different colors, and that's why Georgina had gotten in trouble. She had wanted the doll with the red dress and the black hair, but that toy had been assigned to Bracey, and Georgina had gotten the doll with the yellow dress and the yellow hair instead, and that's why Georgina had thrown a tantrum, and that's why the big men in the white coats had taken her away.

Asher didn't like Bracey. Bracey was mean. She was the meanest kid in their pod, Pod Eight. The little girl would often get the other kids in their pod in trouble, and then she would gloat about it with a mean smile on her face. She liked doing mean and bad things, but she was smart, really smart, so she never got caught by Mrs. Edgerton.

No, Asher didn't like her at all. He was certain that Bracey had been taunting Georgina before Georgina had gotten in trouble. That's why Georgina had thrown her tantrum. That's why Georgina had gotten in trouble.

Asher didn't want to think about it anymore. No, he just dutifully followed Mrs. Edgerton to the testing area, the rest of the pod in tow.

Mrs. Edgerton led them to the testing area, a big white room filled with white desks and white chairs, but they were not ordered to their desks like they had been every other time they'd come here. In fact, their pod mother stepped aside to reveal another lady and two big men, the two big men that had taken Georgina away. The new lady and the two big men wore the white coats, and that made them different from Mrs. Edgerton. That made them scary.

All of the kids of Pod Eight were in a line according to their names in alphabetical order. Asher knew his letters, so he knew he was always first in line, with Bracey being second. He had a number after his name, 0801, and that was his full name, Asher-0801. He knew his full name by heart. This is why it did not surprise him when he was called first.

"Asher-0801," called out the lady in the white coat.

She had a learning tablet in her hand; Asher could see the glowing orange letters on the black screen. Asher had used learning tablets since he had first started coming to the testing areas, but the tablets he had used were embedded in the desks, not something you carried by hand. The tablets were all black with glowing orange writing on them, so they were different colors, like their quiet-play toys, and that made learning fun…Well, not really fun. The colored tablets made learning a little less boring.

Mrs. Edgerton pushed Asher forward, but he looked up at her in fear.

"Go on, Asher," said the woman in a calm tone. "You'll go with them to a new testing area. Everyone's going to go in one at a time."

Asher nodded his head in understanding. He was scared to go with anyone other than Mrs. Edgerton, but he did not want to get in trouble, so he stepped forward without further delay.

He was led to the door in the east wall. Asher did not know what was behind that door, because that door had always been closed in the past, and no one had ever gone in or out of it, not ever.

The lady in the white coat opened the east wall door. She opened the door with a keycard that was attached to her coat by an extendable metal line. Only important people had keycards…That's what Mrs. Edgerton had told them all a long time ago.

The lady in the white coat opened the door with a keycard swipe, and then Asher was led through that door and down another long white hallway with more white doors lining the north and south walls. He was led down this hallway to the next-to-the-last door on the north wall. The lady in the white coat opened that door too, and Asher was ushered through it by the two big men behind him.

The room was empty save for a single desk in its center, but this desk was different from a learning desk. The white desk in this room didn't have a learning tablet embedded in it. No, it had a sloped surface with a single large red button in the middle of it instead.

Asher was ushered to the small white chair in front of the desk and was ordered to sit. The two big men in white coats then left the room to go somewhere else, but the lady in the white coat stayed behind.

"You will sit here for the test," said the lady in the white coat. "You will not push the button until I say so. Do you understand?"

"Yes, marm," replied Asher.

He would push the button when she said so. He wanted to do well on this test. This test had to be an important one, because he was not at his own desk in the normal testing area this time.

"First, you will eat what I give you," said the lady in the white coat.

The lady reached into one of her coat pockets and pulled forth a small square of paper. She put the paper on the desk in front of the large red button, and on that paper were four smaller buttons, each one a different color. The four bright little buttons on the paper were red, green, blue, and yellow.

"These are candy buttons," said the lady. "You peel them off the paper and eat them."

Asher picked up the small square of paper and looked at the colorful buttons in strange wonder. He had never heard of buttons you could eat.

"Peel them off the paper and eat them," ordered the lady in the white coat.

"Yes, marm," replied Asher.

The small square of paper had a strange feel to it, not like the regular paper he had sometimes had to work with. This strange feel made the little bright buttons on it easy to peel off.

He peeled off the little red "candy" button with ease and then popped it in his mouth.

It was beyond delicious…He had never tasted anything like it before. This "candy" was nothing like the white food blocks everyone ate. This "candy" button tasted so good that Asher couldn't wait to eat the rest of them. In fact, he could not even describe the taste that melted across his tongue. All he knew was that it was wonderful.

He chewed and swallowed the first button, and then he quickly devoured the rest. In fact, he wanted more. Maybe the lady in the white coat would give him more.

He looked up at her in expectation, but she simply smiled down upon him.

"Good," she said matter-of-factly. "Now it's time for the test."

Asher was disappointed. He had really wanted more of those "candy" buttons. Nevertheless, it was time for the test, and if he did well, perhaps he would get more candy buttons to eat.

"Look toward the next room," said the lady in the white coat.

Asher stared ahead at the plain white wall in front of him. That wall was actually made of glass, and the white of that glass faded until he could see into the room beyond it.

In the next room was heavy white machinery surrounding a small white chair. In that chair was Georgina, but something wasn't right. Pasted to her little body were many small white electrodes, and Asher knew what electrodes were; he'd had them attached to him for "biometric" tests in the past.

In Georgina's mouth was a white leather strap of some sort, so she couldn't talk, and her arms and legs were strapped down to the small white chair to where she could not move. She even had straps across her chest and stomach to keep her from pushing forward. She had tears streaming down her face, and this sight made Asher feel uncomfortable…He did not know what was going on, but whatever was going on, it was not good.

He looked up toward the lady in the white coat with no small amount of fear coursing through him.

"Look ahead," ordered the woman. "The test is about to begin."

Asher stared back into the room ahead of them, and he could see Georgina, and Georgina could see him, but he did not like the look on her pale face.

"Georgina has been bad," stated the lady in the white coat. "You will punish Georgina for being bad. You will push the big red button and punish Georgina. Once you punish Georgina, you will be rewarded with more candy buttons. Now push the button and punish Georgina."

Asher reached for the button in the center of the desk and pushed it. After all, Georgina had been bad, so she was going to be punished anyway, but more importantly, Asher was going to be rewarded with more "candy" buttons.

This test was the easiest test he'd ever taken.

But it really wasn't. For one thing, he could hear every sound that occurred in the next room, the white room beyond the glass in front of him. He couldn't hear the sound when the glass had been white, but now that it was clear, he could hear everything.

He pushed down the button, and the moment he did so, the white machinery in the next room lit up with various lights. There was a loud buzzing sound, the lights in the next room faded in and out as Georgina shook for a couple of seconds, and then she started wailing, although that crying out was muffled due to the white leather strap in her mouth.

Asher stared at Georgina's pained, horrified expression. He did not know what had just happened, but by the way she had shook and shimmied and by the terrible expression etched upon her small face, whatever had just happened had not been good.

"Good," said the lady in the white coat. "Here is your reward."

She reached into her coat pocket and pulled forth another small square of white paper. She handed the little square to Asher, and he quickly ate the delicious little buttons off of it.

"That's good," nodded the lady in the white coat. "Now, it's time to continue with the test."

Asher stared up at her in confusion. He had thought the test was over.

"Georgina must be punished," said the lady in the white coat. "You will push the button again. This time the punishment will be longer. Once Georgina has been punished, you will be rewarded with more candy buttons."

"Yes, marm," said Asher.

He stared back at Georgina.

Her sobbing face was twisted with fear, and she shook her head no, the little blonde curls on her head swaying back and forth from that vigorous motion.

Asher was unsure. Georgina had already been punished, and it seemed unfair to punish her again, but he was not going to disobey the lady in the white coat. Georgina was going to be mad at him for this, but on the bright side, he did get to eat more candy buttons.

He reached forward and pushed the big red button. The machinery in the other room lit up, the loud buzzing noise sounded out, and the lights in the other room flickered, but this time, the effect lasted for a full ten seconds.

During that horrifying ten seconds, Georgina spasmed and pushed against the straps in her chair, her muscles tightening, straining. Her eyes squeezed shut in tremendous visible pain, and her body shook and twitched with involuntary motion.

She continued to wail and scream into the leather strap in her mouth.

Asher did not like this at all. Something was really wrong. It looked like Georgina was being hurt really bad, and he did not want to do this again.

He stared up at the lady in the white coat and asked a question out of turn. He normally did not talk to adults unprompted, but he was scared, so he asked anyway.

"Is the test over?" he asked.

"No," said the lady in the white coat. "You will continue the test until I say it's over."

"Y…Yes, marm," stammered Asher.

Tears came to his eyes as he accepted the next square of paper with four candy buttons. He ate them one at a time, but he had tears rolling down his cheeks by the time he was finished.

He was scared, and he did not want to do this anymore.

"Georgina has been bad," said the lady in the white coat. "You will push the button and punish Georgina. This time she will be punished for a longer length of time. You will be rewarded with more candy buttons after you punish Georgina."

Asher clumsily wiped at his tears as he reached one shaking hand toward the big red button. He did not want to push it and hurt Georgina again. She was being hurt really bad, but he was scared, so he would do as he was told.

Georgina shook her head no and struggled frantically against her bonds as Asher's little right hand hovered over the big red button.

"Push the button and punish Georgina," ordered the lady in the white coat. "Commence with the punishment, and you will receive your reward."

Asher felt really, really bad this time as he pushed down on the big red button.

The machines sparked to life in the next room, the loud buzzing went off again, the lights in the other room flickered and flickered, and then Georgina spasmed and shook yet again, but the punishment went on for what seemed like forever. She thrashed uncontrollably against the straps holding her down as her blue eyes rolled up in the whites. Her little chest strained and strained against the straps as the lights went off and on, off and on…

And then it was suddenly over. She slumped over in her chair, her eyes squeezed shut, and her muffled, weak, and whining cries pierced right through Asher's heart. It got to him this time, and it got to him in a bad, bad way.

He didn't want to do this anymore…He didn't want to take this test anymore.

Tears rolled down his hot face as he shook in place.

"Excellent," said the lady in the white coat. "Here is your reward."

She pulled forth another small, square piece of paper from her coat pocket.

Asher took his "reward" and tried to calm down as he peeled the candy buttons from the paper with shaking fingers. He ate the candy buttons one by one, but the incredible taste of those buttons soured in his mind due to what was happening in the next room, what he was making happen in the next room.

At the very least, the test was over; it had to be.

But he was wrong.

"The test will continue," said the lady in the white coat. "Georgina has been bad and must be punished. You will punish Georgina by pushing the button. This time, the punishment will be for a longer length of time. Once you have punished Georgina, you will receive more candy buttons as your reward."

Asher felt nothing beat in his heart but pure, unmitigated horror, and that horror overwhelmed him to the point where he could barely think.

He was not doing this again. He *could* not do this again.

Something snapped. Something snapped in his very young mind, because he could not do this again, and because he could not do this again, he was going to have to disobey. He was going to have to disobey an adult.

"N…No…" said Asher quietly.

"What was that?" asked the lady in the white coat.

He would have never disobeyed an adult in the past, but now was different. It was wrong what they were doing to Georgina. She was hurting really, *really* bad…It was wrong…It was wrong!

He could see Georgina's pained and tear-strewn face, and he could hear her weak sobbing, and then something snapped…something *really* snapped.

"I said NO!" screeched Asher.

He hopped out of the test chair, his little body trembling from the horror of it all.

"I don't want any more candy buttons!" he shrieked. "I don't want to do this anymore! I want to go back to the pod! I want Mrs. Edgerton!...This is bad! You're bad! You're hurting Georgina, and you're bad!"

"The test for this subject is over!" called out the lady in the white coat. "Process Asher-0801 for punishment and release Georgina-0806! We will proceed to the next test subject."

The wall of glass in front of Asher clouded over into white once more.

The two big men in white coats entered the room and advanced upon Asher. They gripped him by his little arms and forced him out into the hallway, and then he was led to the very last door on the north wall at the end of the hallway, the room where Georgina was.

One of the big men in the white coats opened the last door, and then they forced Asher inside.

The other big man removed the electrodes on Georgina and then unstrapped her from the chair. He then shuffled her past Asher, and Asher's and Georgina's eyes met for a split second, but the horror, terror, and pain in the little girl's ocean-blue eyes sank into Asher like a fog of impending doom...

He knew what was coming.

Asher took her place in the chair as the sobbing little girl was given back her freedom.

Asher was summarily bound in place by his arms, legs, chest, and stomach, and the white leather strap was forced into his mouth as well. He could feel the residual heat from the chair's previous occupant, and he could smell electricity in the air as electrodes were pasted all over him in strategic places.

He let his tears flow as he shook in place. He was terrified, and that terror only grew as he waited for the inevitable, and he did not have to wait for long.

The wall of glass in front of him became clear again as he stared at the bright and happy face of Bracey. The mean little girl was sitting in the test-taker's chair, the big red button right in front of her.

She spied Asher and then grinned, and he shook in place as the wicked glint in her dark eyes gleamed over his captive form, but Asher could only concentrate on one thing, and that one thing filled him with a terrible, terrible fear, something that made his previous terror seem inconsequential...

There was a small, white, crumpled, square piece of paper pinched between the slender fingers of Bracey's little left hand.

#9a…BONUS STORY: THE DEVIL AND THE DOUG

Let me tell you a tale of fear and woe, of maidens and a fearsome foe, of a third-grade class known for trouble, and of the boy who saved them twice-over-double. This is the tale of a cursed mug and of the coolest kid in class, that kid known only as…"The Doug."

The Doug held all the girls' fancy, held all the guys' respect, with slicked back hair and shades like black decks, and he wore his leather jacket well, so smooth it could keep out the burning-hot fires of Hell. He was a trooper, a keeper, a brownstone sweeper, and he could tame a wild dog with nothing but a smirk and a pointed finger. He was The Doug, and we all most certainly miss him.

It all started in the small town of Devlin; it started with Miss Bevlin, or her absence really, 'cause she got called to the office, and this left the classroom empty. It was Jimmy Bees who knocked over the cursed mug; it fell from the top shelf and shattered, and that was what started the trouble, burst the bubble, the safety of the class crumbled, and that was all at the moment mattered.

"That was Missy Missus' mug!" cried Betty Lens. "She's the girl who sold her soul and went to Hell…all for a dollar-forty-five and a big brass bell!"

The students held their collective breaths as a black smoke arose from the shards, everyone but one…The Doug. Yes, the Devil appeared and showed his ugly mug, but only one kid stepped up to face him…and that kid was…The Doug.

"At last, I'm free!" cried the Devil with glee. "Now I'll reward you all for this travesty! You can either die right now in a horrible way, or sign over your souls and die another day!"

"I don't think so," said The Doug. "I may not be a preacher…Heck, I'm not even in the choir, but I do know one thing for sure…the Devil is a liar."

"You're a smart one, little boy," grinned the Devil, "but all of you are set for me to kill. You see, you set me free, and that's a sin. There's a toll to pay, and that's a no win…not for you, little boy, not without a deal, not without a soul to steal."

"I'll sign over," said The Doug, "and we'll make a deal, but the rest of the class is free from your grip, but only if you and I take a trip, the place of my choosing, and that's the deal if it's my soul I'm losing. Take it or leave it, Old Scratch; that's the deal, 'cause The Doug's for real, and my classmates' souls ain't yours to steal."

"It's a deal, little heel, but I guarantee you'll squeal," said the Devil. "Name your place of choosing, and think hard, little guard, 'cause it's your soul you're losing."

"The Devil lies and confuses, but that's the reason he loses," said The Doug to the class. "He chose three sixes 'stead of seven, so the place I choose to go is…Heaven!"

#10...X MARKS THE SPOT

Finding what you're looking for isn't always fun.

Pamela stared down at the map in her hands.

It looked like something out of an elementary-school book, maybe something conceived by a bored fourth grader, and it had clearly been made on an art program, but poorly; the houses and trees were of different models, as were the roads, and the road lines didn't even match up, but...it was good enough.

The landmarks upon the map were clear enough to follow, even for someone as unenterprising and unimaginative as Damian. There wouldn't be any trouble getting to the secret treasure buried beneath the clichéd red X, a treasure so profound, so lifechanging, it was mind-blowing.

"We just have to follow the map," smiled Pamela. "This is my great-uncle's legacy we're talking about here."

"That 'map' looks like it took two minutes to make," grunted Damian. "The neighbor's five-year-old could have drawn something better. It honestly reminds me of one of those paper coloring sheets you get for kids at any sit-down restaurant…Let me tell you, your great-uncle was a nut-bag."

"It'll work," stated Pamela. "Even a child could follow it."

"That's because it looks like a child made it," frowned Damian. "And how come I've never heard of this 'Great Uncle Samuel' of yours anyway? You've never mentioned him before…You must have been close with him if he left you a fortune."

"Something like that," smiled Pamela. "He's a real character…Hard to believe, actually. It's like he's imaginary."

"Was," said Damian. "It *was* like he's imaginary. He's dead now."

"Passed on," she corrected.

"A nut-bag who's passed on," recorrected Damian.

She ran a finger along the muscles of Damian's bare chest, that finger tracing around the finely-detailed dagger tattoo on his left pectoral, the scent of roses hanging about her. That scent was the fragrance of her perfume wafting about as the fan blew in the cool night air from the bedroom window, the curtains gently flapping, the pale light of the moon their only source of illumination…

"Yeah, but he was a rich nut bag," replied Pamela. "He left me quite a haul, something that's going to set everything right."

"It better," frowned Damian. "I don't want to go out on some crazy woodlands trek with nothing to show for it…The forest is dangerous…I'm not an outdoorsman, and last time I checked, you're not a woodsy type, either."

"It'll be fine," smiled Pamela. "It'll be our little adventure together."

She stared in frowning disapproval at the big black truck. It was a gas guzzler, and she had told Damian to get something cheaper when he had first floated the idea, but he was stubborn, so he hadn't listened. It wasn't like they needed to haul anything, but it was something he felt he needed, not out of any practical reason, mind you, but simply out of pride, just ridiculous pride, and that was and always had been his greatest sin...

She stared out the window of Damian's big black truck. There were the usual Midwestern houses of the middleclass in this small town, but Main Street had its charm with its small shops and restaurants.

"This looks like a nice neighborhood," said Pamela. "Oh, look at those hills in the distance!...There's the water tower...I wouldn't mind moving here...*Ooo*! They have a little antique shop here! I should visit that sometime."

"Engles is out in the middle of nowhere," frowned Damian. "You really want to come out here for an antique shop?"

"Why not?" asked Pamela. "I'm sure they have some things I want...Besides, I'm coming into money very soon."

"We don't even know what your great-uncle, Nut-Bag, buried out there in the woods," grunted Damian. "Plus, we don't want to waste it if it is a lot of money."

"Oh, I'll make sure it doesn't go to waste," replied Pamela with a sly smirk.

It was the arguing that cut into her, not so much what was said, but how it was said, with such open disdain for her reasoning. They needed to save money, not waste it. There was no reason to redo the basement, but Damian had not been satisfied with the little things, with the little pleasures in life.

He had not been content to wait until they were in a better financial position, so he had made his little man cave, had fashioned the bar himself, had ordered the pool table and had moved it in on their dime, and he had even brought in the two arcade machines. That had cost them, and they had suffered for it, or rather, she had suffered for it, had suffered in sacrifice by going without her own mercies for what had seemed like an eternity...

They exited Engles rather quickly, and now they were on the highway, just like on the map.

"Have you seen Janey lately?" asked Damian.

"I just talked to her on Monday," shrugged Pamela. "Why?"

"Huh…I tried calling her yesterday, but she never picked up," said Damian. "It's Thursday…I texted her, but I never got a reply. I wonder what's going on with her?"

"Why?" asked Pamela. "You know my sister. She's probably off with some man. That's her M.O."

"She better not be," said Damian unhappily.

"Why?" asked Pamela. "You know my sister. If she's not man-hopping, she's off spending someone else's money."

"Nah, your sister's better than that," said Damian.

"How would you know?" asked Pamela. "Why do you want to talk to her anyway? Are you not telling me something?"

"Don't be jealous," scowled Damian. "We just like to talk. Besides, she's into Paul."

"What is that supposed to mean?" asked Pamela. "Are you saying that if she wasn't into Paul—"

"I'd still be with you," said Damian. "I'm stuck with you one way or another."

"Stuck with me?" asked Pamela. "What is *that* supposed to mean?"

"It doesn't mean anything," frowned Damian. "I was just wondering where your sister is. Stop being jealous."

"I'm not jealous…I'm sure Janey is around somewhere," shrugged Pamela. "You know her…Oh, look, there's the graveyard! It's the next landmark on the map!"

"It's pretty big," grunted Damian.

"Yeah," she said whimsically. "It's the largest graveyard in the county."

Janey had not supported her in her argument. No, Janey had enjoyed the bar and the arcade machines and the pool table and the mingling with Damian's friends down below. First, it had been Bob, then Jeremy, and then Paul, but all the while Pamela's errant husband had been in the background, amused at Janey's little game.

It was insufferable to think that her younger sister was such a tease, a wanton little pass-along that hopped from one lap to the next, but that was the way Janey had always been, so there had been no surprise there, but Damian had always been in the background, and he and Janey had talked, sometimes deep into the evening hours, and sometimes…sometimes it felt like Janey spent more time with him than she did…

The highway was behind them, and they had made the appropriate left at the intersection on the map.

"Now we just follow to the end of this road…and…there!" said Pamela excitedly.

"I see it," grunted Damian.

They drove up to the little camping/rest site and pulled into a large paved lot. Damian parked the truck, and they both exited the big black vehicle.

Pamela grabbed the little brown travel bag from out of her seat, shut the passenger's-side door, and grinned.

"Isn't this exciting!" she said happily. "I am so stoked!"

"Grab a shovel out of the back," said Damian. "I brought two."

"I can't dig," said Pamela. "You'll have to do it…Do I look like a man?"

"I guess you've got a point there," smirked Damian. "You'd probably bruise those big knockers on your chest trying to dig. Those honkers are the reason I started dating you in the first place. Can't damage those."

"Hey, I'm more than just my breasts," frowned Pamela. "I've got a lot more going for me than that. Come on…"

Damian grimaced and shook his head. He took one look at her after that and nodded toward her little brown travel bag.

"Leave that bag behind," he grunted. "You don't need it."

She slung the bag's leather strap around her left shoulder so that the bag was balanced on her right hip. It was a blatant act of defiance, true, but a necessary one.

"I do need it," argued Pamela. "It has emergency stuff…Ugh…Never mind…Just get a shovel…Don't argue with me on this…Besides, I want to get the second part of this trip started. It's time for an adventure in the woods!"

"Oh, boy," said Damian dryly. "Sheer fun. Can't wait."

She touched Damian on the shoulder and ran her palms down his bare chest, but he turned away. He was not interested, making some poor excuse that he was "tired" and that he had "some things to do tomorrow." In truth, there was no excuse. It was the weekend, and it had been three-and-a-half months since she had felt his touch, three-and-a-half months since she had enjoyed her husband's passionate embrace...

Pamela stepped around a number of prickly bushes before continuing along a weathered dirt trail that led through this woodland hell. The prize was worth the trek, however, and she simply couldn't wait to find the buried treasure waiting for them both at the end of this portentous journey.

"Are you sure you haven't heard from Janey?" asked Damian.

"I told you, I spoke to her on Monday," said Pamela nonchalantly. "Is there something I should know? Are you in love with my sister or something?"

"Don't be jealous," grunted Damian. "Grow up."

She turned and gave him the staredown. Damian stopped and stared back at her in return.

"What?" he asked, but that asking was more of a demand, not friendly, not compassionate or caring like he used to be.

Still, maybe she could get a rise out of him. Maybe there was some redemption here.

"You know, we could just strip down right here and be like animals," said Pamela with a wicked smile. "I'll just bend over by that tree, rest my hands on it…you know."

"Are you nuts?" asked Damian. "We're not banging out here in the woods!"

"Okay," she shrugged. "I gave you one last chance."

"One last chance for what?" he asked in audible frustration. "Is that a threat, because it better not be…Hey, don't turn away! I'm talking to you! Are you threatening me!"

"Never mind," she replied in a huff. "I just wanted some love from *my* husband…You know what? Let's just go. I'm done with…with uhhhh…N…Never mind. Let's just go."

"Whatever," grunted Damian.

She stared in disbelief at the texts, that phone a mocking symbol of injustice, of dreams crushed beneath the heavy weight of broken vows and meaningless platitudes. Her husband's spoken words held reassurance without form, fidelity without substance, but only to her, not to Janey, not to that soul-sucking parasite who absorbed all love like a vampiric sponge, a sponge that had continuously absorbed every man Pamela had ever known. No, Damian was different with Janey, honest, and even in text, she could tell that…

"There it is!" said Pamela with more excitement than ever. "That's the tree!"

She wasn't even tired from the trek they had just taken. Hopefully, Damian wasn't tired either, because he was going to have to dig.

She'd led the way, of course, because she knew where they were going, even if Damian did not.

"How do you know that's the one?" asked Damian in audible doubt.

"It looks just like the one on the map," said Pamela.

"That map looks like it was made by a five-year-old," argued Damian. "I thought I told you that before."

"You did," shrugged Pamela.

"Your great uncle, Nut-Bag, is probably pulling your leg from beyond the grave," grunted Damian.

"I don't have a leg to pull," smirked Pamela. "A bean to flick, maybe."

"Whatever," said Damian dryly. "It doesn't matter, because you've overlooked one very important detail…We don't even know where to dig, Pam."

"Sure, we do!" said Pamela in renewed excitement. "There are two branches on the ground right there! They form an X!...Plus, they're spraypainted red."

There were indeed two small branches that formed a rather large "X" before the tree, both branches coated with a thin layer of red paint.

"What the…?" started Damian. "You've got to be kidding me, right! How in the hell did your deathbed nut-bag great uncle get anyone out here to do this?...And how come no one else has messed with it by now?"

She ignored him and quickly tossed the spraypainted branches aside.

"*Ooo*, look, Damian!" breathed Pamela. "The earth's been freshly dug here under these branches! This is where we dig!"

"Okay," shrugged Damian. "Guess I'll get to work…but this is the strangest thing I've ever done. Your great-uncle, Nut-bag, was definitely a space case."

He slung the shovel off of his right shoulder and planted the blade in the freshly turned-over earth that had been resting beneath the reddened branches.

It was time to dig.

It was the confrontation of the ages, the older sister betrayed, the younger sister the betrayer, but there was no denial of the transgression, not with Janey. Pamela's sister had simply laughed at her pain and had told her to "get over it." That little Jezebel had then rubbed it in her face, calling her a "boring loser," telling her that she had "deserved" what she had gotten, that she deserved this hell, that it was SHE who had failed, not Damian, and certainly not Janey.

Of course, there was only one thing left to do, and thankfully, she had that solution right here in her purse...

Damian wiped his brow with a handkerchief. He stared up at Pamela with no small amount of wrathful vehemence in his gaze.

"You lazy cow!" he said angrily. "Five feet! I've dug at least five feet, and the sun is going down! There's nothing here!...Not to mention that all you've done is play on your phone while I've had to dig!"

"It's fine," said Pamela calmly. "One more foot, love. I remember Great-Uncle Samuel telling me six feet."

"What!" cried Damian angrily. "Why didn't you tell me that to begin with!...I should've made you dig, you dumb...Oh, you are in deep once we get back to the truck. I'm going to spank you so hard your butt will look like a stoplight."

"Oh, I love it when you talk dirty, baby," grinned Pamela. "One more foot, love. Just one more."

"One more," said Damian as he held up his right index finger. "One more, and then I'm pulling down your pants and bending you over my knee...What I should do is spank the hell out of you right in front of my friends, show them I'm the boss here...Yeah, that sounds like an idea..."

"If that's your kink, hon," shrugged Pamela. "I don't mind. That kind of turns me on."

"You crazy..." muttered Damian. "You are just as nuts as your dead great uncle...You know what? You really are getting a whoopin'. I'm not joking, Pam. You're not going to like it when I take my right hand to your big bare butt...It's not going to be fun...It's not going to be a turn on...I'm talking cherry red, like glowing hot. You won't be able to sit down for a month."

"I've tried to be exciting for you, hon," sighed Pamela. "I've tried, I really have, but you…you just never seem interested anymore."

He ignored her honest confession about their love life. No, he went right back to berating her, just like he always did.

"You're going to look like one of those baboons at the zoo when I'm done with you," muttered Damian. "I'm not kidding. I'm going to pull down those pants right frickin' here and give you a whoopin'. It's lava-hot time as soon as I'm done here…Just wait."

Pamela opened up her little travel bag and removed a small but powerful flashlight from it. She turned on the small light and shone the beam down at Damian's feet.

"One more foot, love," repeated Pamela. "Just one more."

Damian scowled as he pushed the blade in one more time. The shovel's blade thunked into solid wood at that fateful moment, Damian whispered something inaudible in surprise, and then he brushed loose dirt aside to reveal something large beneath the shallow earth.

"It's…It's a crate," he breathed.

The sun was quickly falling behind the trees, and those trees were already blocking out most of that fading light. Nevertheless, the prize they had been seeking was right at their feet.

"Shine that light down here," ordered Damian. "I'm going to open this sucker as soon as I dig it out a little."

"I told you everything would work out," grinned Pamela. "Now it's time to see what's in there…It's a surprise."

"It had better be," growled Damian.

She pulled the trigger again. Janey choked out a high-pitched squeal as the bullet impacted the little harlot right between the legs this time, right where the source of the torment had begun, that second bullet for lust, the cause of all of this madness in the first place.

The first bullet had been in the stomach, and that bullet had been for gluttony, because Janey never had known when to stop...She just consumed and consumed and consumed, though this gluttony had never been for a want of food, no, but for the pleasures of the flesh, for the consummate touch that belonged to other women and other women alone.

Yes, that first bullet had inflicted pain, real pain, but that pain was nothing compared to the pain of the second bullet, because shooting Janey's cave of wonders had left the vile succubus with no weapons whatsoever, and thus the world was right again.

She let Janey squirm in her own blood, the little whore's mouth wide open in a silent scream, blue eyes wide, and then the third bullet ended it all, because that bullet was for pride, something that was laced like a poison all throughout Janey's plotting mind...

Damian grunted as he wedged the blade of the shovel into the crack of the lid of the crate.

"Keep that light on my shovel!" he said unhappily. "Dammit, Pam! Don't move it!...Don't move it...And here...we...go..."

He pulled up hard, but the lid of the large, once-buried crate opened with ease without need of such concentrated effort. He pushed up on that lid and propped it up against loose dirt, but his tired figure froze as he stared down at the contents of said once-buried crate.

The smell that came out of the open crate was nearly unbearable, a choking cloud that threatened to overwhelm them both. Thankfully, the cool night air helped relieve some of that horrific odor.

Damian held his hand to his mouth and nose as he backed away a bit. Even with that powerful and noxious odor, however, he removed his hand as his mouth dropped open in a shuddering gasp.

The bright circle of Pamela's flashlight revealed it all.

"What the…!" said Damian in audible shock, a tremor in his voice, but that tremulous voice trailed off in what could only be pure horror.

They both stared down at the crumpled and folded body of Pamela's younger sister, Janey. The woman's white dress shirt was soaked with blood, there was a large bloody hole in her brown business slacks, right between her legs, but it was the very visible bloodstained bullet hole between her open and sightless blue eyes that really stood out.

"I told you it was something valuable," said Pamela quickly. "Of course, I never said it was valuable to me. Only to you, love, only to you…I guess you should have kept your hands to yourself…It doesn't matter anymore, I suppose, but hey, I told you it would be a surprise!"

Damian stared up at Pamela in visible horror as comprehension slowly set in.

"You…You…You crazy…!" babbled Damian. "You set this up! There was no great uncle, was there!...It was just you! It was all you! You killed Janey! You killed Janey, you stupid, jealous cow!"

"Oh, it was me, but that doesn't matter," said Pamela matter-of-factly. "The only thing that matters is the answer to one simple question…Do you know what that question is, love?"

"No, you crazy—" began Damian.

"Now, now," said Pamela. "There's no need for name calling. Don't you want to know what the question is?"

"What is it?" asked Damian, his voice breaking, cracking. "And what could that question possibly be, Pam? Why don't you ask me that question before I call the police…You killed Janey, you jealous idiot! You've murdered your own sister!"

"She stole you from me," shrugged Pamela. "She stole my husband just like she's stolen every other man I've ever had, and this time…this time I just couldn't take it. I couldn't take it anymore. Boyfriends are one thing, but a husband?...A husband is unforgivable."

Pamela switched her flashlight to her left hand and then withdrew the second "emergency" item from her little brown travel bag with her right hand. She was ready now, ready to put an end to this irredeemable, soiled relationship.

Damian shook his head in choked disgust.

"I already know what the question is," he grimaced. "You want to know if I was having an affair, right?...The answer is 'yes,' Pam, I was cheating on you, and I know that's wrong, but what you've done is…this is…She was just a better person than you, Pam…That's all there is to it. She was a better person, she was better looking, she made more money than you, and she was flat out better in bed…We were in love…

"I was going to get a divorce, do this the civil way, but that's not happening now…No, I'm going to have to call the police. I should kill you…I should, I really should, but I'll be merciful…You've got to go to prison…I'm calling the police."

"Mercy would have been being something called 'faithful,'" scowled Pamela.

He ignored her and reached into his back pocket in order to pull out his smartphone, but the cold hard truth begged to differ, because this action was meaningless.

She knew he could not see the barrel of her gun from his position in the pit, the gun that had been resting in her little brown travel bag this entire time, the gun that had been eagerly awaiting the right moment to make itself known. No, he could not see that instrument of justice in her right hand, not with the complete darkness of a forest night surrounding them, not with the glare of the flashlight shining down upon his enraged face, that handsome face full of pure, unadulterated, emotional agony.

She felt a twinge of regret, something almost alien to her at this point, but she had come too far to turn back now. No, it was time for the million-dollar question, and that question was her form of 'mercy.'...Of course, there was only one answer to that question.

He started to dial 911 on his phone before she interrupted him.

"Don't you want to know what the question is?" she asked again.

That got to him. That shut down his currently unwanted action and focused his attention back on her, though his naked hostility was more than evident.

"I answered your question!" spat Damian. "What other question could there possibly be!"

"You only said what I already knew," shrugged Pamela. "That wasn't what I wanted to ask."

He cast an even more pained expression as he shook his head no.

"You've killed your own sister, you jealous moron!" he said in a choked voice. "What question could you possibly have to ask!"

"This one," said Pamela in a cold voice. "What was the last thing that went through Janey's mind?"

"What?" asked Damian in clear confusion.

"Here's a hint," said Pamela.

She aimed and pulled the trigger.

#10a...BONUS STORY: TWO PEAS

Rachie was ecstatic. She was finally on a date with her dream guy, Lonnie, and he was everything she'd imagined he'd be.

She'd taken pictures of him while he'd been on his way to class on campus, she'd followed him to his apartment and had taken pictures of him while he'd been unlocking his door, and she'd even made a key to his apartment, snuck in, and taken pictures of him while he'd slept. She wanted to get one of him while he was in the shower, but that was a little too much to ask for as of yet.

As it stood, they'd gone out to eat, and she'd found out he liked all the same foods that she did, and he even had the same type of backpack she carried around. He liked all the same bands she did, which was weird, because she liked New Age girl bands, but he knew them all anyway, and that was just odd, but she'd gone along with it just the same.

Now she'd found herself back in his apartment, but there was a slight problem. Actually, it was a major problem, and she wasn't sure how she was going to fix it.

She'd gone to the bathroom for a few minutes, and when she had come out, he was looking through her backpack. More importantly, however, he was looking through the pictures she'd taken of him, and he had her stun gun laid out on the coffee table…and her rope, and her handkerchief, and her bottle of chloroform, too.

It wasn't looking good right now. More than likely, he'd already called the police, and she wasn't sure what she was going to do…Not…at…all. She nearly panicked at the sight of it.

"You planned all of this for me?" he said as he turned toward her.

"Uhhhh…" was all Rachie could say. "Well…uhhhh…"

He smiled and shook his head as he waved her off.

"Silly!" he said happily. "Come here! I want to show you something…"

He picked up her stun gun and took her by the arm, so it wasn't like she had much of a choice. She wasn't really scared of him so much as she was scared of the police, but he hadn't done anything *untoward* yet, so she just went along with it.

He led her into his bedroom and to his locked closet door. That was the one place she had *not* investigated when she had been sneaking around his apartment.

He unlocked his closet and opened it to reveal a huge shrine dedicated only to her. There were pictures of her going to class, going into stores, a couple where she was sleeping in bed…

Rachie was astounded. She had not even considered the possibility that he was just like her.

"You really do understand!" she cried out in utter joy.

Lonnie leaned forward and kissed her, and Rachie knew right then that he was the one…and there had been *many* before him…and they had *never* ended well.

About the Author

Mr. Marlott has a background in psychology and classic literature, and he enjoys literature of all types and genres. Mr. Marlott lives somewhere within the United States, has two Gen-Z children, and enjoys telling stories to anyone who will listen.

Books and Sites

You can read new stories of mine for free at bloodytwine.com. This site is my workshop where I work on new stories and perfect them for publication.

For more twisted tales with twisted endings, you can purchase *Bloody Twine #1-5* wherever they are sold.

If you want the basic building blocks to writing genre fiction, you can explore my two cents on the subject in *The Quick and Easy Guide to Writing Genre Fiction*.

For great cosmic horror, you can read some awesome eldritch-horror tales by Bert S. Lechner. You can purchase Mr. Lechner's collection of cosmic horror, *The Roots Grow into the Earth*, wherever it is sold. You can also check out Mr. Lechner's personal website at bertwriteshorror.com.

For a mix of traditional horror and cosmic horror, check out some incredible short stories by James Dermond. You can purchase Mr. Dermond's Doorways to the Unseen series wherever it is sold. You can also visit Mr. Dermond's website at jamesdermond.com.

If you like this book, give it a good review and tell me what your favorite story was in this bundle.

THE BLOODY TWINE SERIES

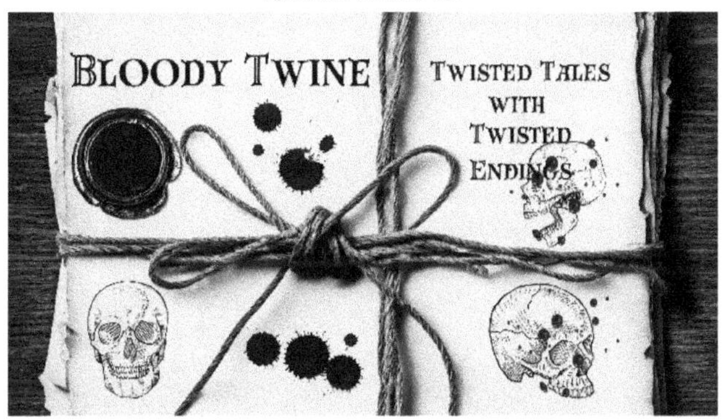

𝔚𝔢𝔩𝔠𝔬𝔪𝔢 to the Bloody Twine Series, a collection of short horror stories written specifically for horror fans everywhere. These books contain a minimum of 10 traditional short horror stories for the collections, a minimum of 5 traditional short horror stories for the selections, and one traditional short horror novelette or novella for the presentations, all for your terrifying entertainment, so go someplace quiet, dim the lights, sit back, and enjoy some twisted tales with twisted endings.

Imagine walking into an abandoned storage room filled with old newspapers and magazines, all articles stacked in bundles neatly tied with twine, but then you discover other bundles, bundles not so neatly tied, ragged bundles of yellowed and partially-charred paper tied in bloodstained twine.

You see, some stories are meant to educate, and some stories are meant to entertain, but some stories…some stories are simply looking for a victim.

Enjoy.

Matthew L. Marlott

THE QUICK AND EASY GUIDE TO WRITING GENRE FICTION

Thinking of writing your own tale of love, redemption, and heroics? Writing genre fiction is an art, and *The Quick and Easy Guide to Writing Genre Fiction* provides the building blocks for being successful in this art. Learn all of the necessary techniques to get yourself started with writing in your chosen genre. Whether you're writing a mystery, a romance, a thriller, science-fiction, horror, fantasy, or any other genre, you'll have the foundation for writing great stories right here at your fingertips in this guide.

Included in this guide is a step-by-step instruction of what it takes to put together your creation in any genre. Also included in this guide is the complete creation process of an original short story by author Matthew L. Marlott, so you, too, can have an easy example of how to create your own stories, whether those stories are short stories, novels, or novellas. You'll be able to create your own worlds and your own universes, so learn the basics of writing genre fiction for the purpose of selling, for publication on a site, for fanfiction, or just for your own personal satisfaction.

Remember, if you want real life, you can just walk out the front door. Why not write down your own story on paper or screen instead? Get started with your journey into genre fiction by learning from this invaluable guide. Don't wait until you're on your deathbed. Get started today.

Matthew L. Marlott

THE ROOTS GROW INTO THE EARTH

"In the dark we found them…"

In this collection of nine short stories and novelettes, you will find tales of unfathomable predators, cosmic gods, dark magic, and the people who cross their path: from archaeologists, long on the search for the find of the century, ensnared by a being beyond their understanding, to a man who notices a detail on a wall in his house for the first time, unwittingly inviting the attention of a malefic force from beyond the stars.

The Roots Grow Into the Earth consists of nine of Bert S. Lechner's previously published works, including three stories available as standalone eBooks: Interstate, the Wall, and Joanne's Vault.

Bert S. Lechner

DOORWAYS TO THE UNSEEN

"The Doorways to the Unseen series is a collection of short story books from author James Dermond. The stories take the reader around the world and through time, with each tale offering a glimpse into a supernatural episode. Every volume in the series contains six short horror stories meant to chill the blood and inspire unimaginable terror in their readers.

"So, step inside and find that which has been hidden from you all along. Where the unknown and the unimaginable meet."

James Dermond

Bloody Twine #6
Twisted Tales with Twisted Endings
Copyright 1st ed. © 2025 Matthew L. Marlott